The Electrical Affairs
of Dr. Victor Franklin

Mad Scientists Society

Book 2

ISBN: 978-1-949862-45-4

Book cover and interior design by E. McAuley: www.emcauley.com

To all past women who pushed the boundaries
and to those who continue to do so today.
You make the future.

The Electrical Affairs of Dr. Victor Franklin

*"Mrs. Clay! I was under the impression
you never wanted to see me again."*

Chapter 1

The Consequences of Not Thinking

Detroit, Michigan
January, 1892

Victor dodged just in time to avoid being clobbered in the head by the weighty A-D volume of the *Encyclopædia Mechanica*. Unfortunately, he did not fare so well with volume E-I.

"Ow! Goddammit!"

Volume J-M struck him a glancing blow in the shoulder.

"You selfish lout!" N-Q slammed into the wall beside him. "How could you?"

Victor threw up his arms to shield himself as R-T and U-Z came flying at him together. "What did I do?"

"What did you *do*?" his occasional scientific collaborator shrieked. "*What* did you *do*?" She reached up to the next shelf for something new to hurl at him.

Victor sprinted across the laboratory. "Wait. Please. Don't throw anything else." He stopped a few feet from her and held up his hands in surrender. "Whatever it is, I'm sorry, but I truly don't know what you're talking about."

Mrs. Mary Clay, ordinarily a quiet and good-natured scientist, looked down at the Electro-magnetic Actuator in her hands. Fragile and expensive, it wasn't the sort of device that ought to be thrown at any man, much less one who didn't even know his own crime. Victor held out a hand, giving her an imploring look.

She scowled. The looks that worked on most people never seemed to work on her. In the two years he'd known her, Victor had yet to discover why that was.

"Please," he said again. "Let's talk first. At least give me the chance to understand what's happened."

Mary returned the Actuator to the shelf, but none of the fury receded from her pale-blue eyes. Her short blond curls were always a bit unruly, but now they fell over her ears and into her face. She drew herself up to her full height—which still only reached his chin—and took a menacing step toward him. Victor shifted to his left, putting the large, rectangular worktable behind him. That way, if she shoved him, he wouldn't have far to go.

"You betrayed me." The words held a note of anguish beneath the snarl. Whatever she thought he had done, it had hurt.

"Betrayed you?" Victor examined her closely, looking for any signs she wasn't in her right state of mind. These days it was all too easy to accidentally ingest a drink or a drug with unexpected side-effects. His friend Hal Finch— formerly Jekyll—could attest to that.

Mary's cheeks were rosy, but that could easily have been from the anger. Her pupils were a normal size, and her eyes clear. She was neither breathing hard nor perspiring overmuch. Nothing about her appeared in any way altered except her temper.

"Are you certain you have the right man?" Victor asked. "I'm Dr. Victor Franklin."

If she was under the influence of some strange substance, she could have confused him with her philandering lout of a husband. From what Victor knew of the situation, the man had married her for her money, then dropped her like week-old porridge. Augustus Clay lived outside of town these days, but periodically wandered in to attend some show or event with another woman on his arm. *He* deserved an encyclopædia to the head.

Mary did try to shove Victor this time, though not especially hard. Braced against the worktable, he barely moved.

"I know who you are, you oaf!" she exclaimed. "You cheated me out of my rightful place! You stole all the credit!"

Victor raised both eyebrows. "Stole the credit for what?"

She threw her hands in the air. "The hydroconductor, of course!"

"What are you talking about? Your name is on the patent, right next to mine. In front of mine, in fact, because we're listed in alphabetical order."

Mary made a noise of extreme frustration and turned away. Her fists clenched at her sides. "I'm talking about the article in the paper."

"I haven't read the paper," Victor admitted. "I haven't even had breakfast. I only got up half an hour ago."

She turned back, some of her anger now replaced with disbelief. "It's three o'clock in the afternoon!"

"I went to bed at eight a.m."

"Oh, never mind that." Mary jabbed an accusing finger at him. "You did an interview with the newspaper."

"Yes. I did. But I never claimed the hydroconductor was all mine. In fact, I'm certain I mentioned that it took a collaborative effort both to build and to test."

"Did you even bother to mention my name?"

"Um." Victor tried to think back to the interview. It had been weeks ago. And at the uncivilized hour of ten a.m. "I think so."

"Oh, you think so." Mary folded her arms across her chest. "Well, isn't that just peachy. Do you know how many times the article mentioned me?"

"I told you I haven't read the paper."

"Zero. Zero times. Nothing. Nil."

"I understand the term." Victor rubbed a spot in the center of his forehead where a headache was beginning to form.

"Not even a hint. Not even an implication of anyone but you." Mary's voice cut like a knife. The slight waver at the end of every sentence only shoved the blade in further.

"I never intended to cut you out."

"But you did. You didn't push for me. You didn't talk about my contributions. You didn't even ask me to join you for the interview!"

All true. He'd hurt her without thinking. He'd hurt her *because* he hadn't been thinking.

"I'm sorry." He didn't bother with excuses. They would only waste breath.

"We were partners." Her voice was rife with sorrow now. "I thought you respected me. I thought you cared about me and my career."

He did care. More than she knew. He'd woken up at nine a.m. every damn day for three months straight to work on that hydroconductor with her. It had not only upset his sleep schedule, but it had delayed much of his work on his mechanical man. And he hadn't even regretted it.

But science was a man's world. He'd been invited to chat with the boys. Hanging about, smoking cigars in a room that had probably never seen a woman except perhaps when it was cleaned. Of course they hadn't mentioned Mary's name. She was irrelevant, no matter how much she'd contributed.

Victor should have known better. He, of all people, really should have known better.

Instead, like a fool, he'd done what he always did, as if he hadn't even had a partner. She'd be doing interviews of her own, right? Wrong. No one would ask her. No one would care.

Victor cared. But caring wasn't enough when it didn't go along with doing. She was right. He'd betrayed her.

"I'm sorry," he said again. "I'll write to the paper. Ask them to issue a correction. What else can I do to make it up to you?"

Mary shook her head. "It's too late. *You're* too late. Consider our next project canceled." She spun away and walked out, not sparing him so much as a parting glance.

Victor crumpled onto the nearest stool and put his head in his hands. For two years he'd lived in agony, pining for the love of a woman who could never be his. He'd had her friendship, though, and he'd treasured every second of it.

Now, he had nothing. He looked across the room at the man-shaped metal shell propped in the corner. Hollow. Empty.

"I guess it's just you and me now, buddy."

Chapter 2

Good Morning to Bad Rubbish

An unusual buzz hummed in the air around Amesbury Copper Works this morning. Not quite a sound, not quite a feeling. Almost like an electrical charge, primed to spark. Mary's breath crystalized into fog in the frosty morning air as she scurried the few yards between the autocab and the factory. The wind off the river was bitter today. To match her mood, apparently.

She slipped inside and pulled the door securely shut behind her. Yes, something was most definitely odd today. All the men were at work, performing their usual tasks, but idly, as if something else vied for their attention.

Had something happened? Mary hoped there hadn't been any accidents. Her father had established rigorous safety protocols, but her husband wasn't nearly so conscientious. If the company needed to cut costs, he'd choose money over safety without a second thought. And Mary had no notion of the current financial state of the company. She'd been cut out of her family's legacy the instant the minister had declared, "man and wife."

The *bang, bang* of a hammer snagged her attention. Her head swiveled. Above the main entrance, a man dressed in rough laborer's garb pounded nails into a wooden sign.

A sign that had replaced the beautiful scrollwork placard bearing the Amesbury Copper Works name.

Clay Copper Ltd. the new sign read.

"That bastard," Mary hissed. Yes, Augustus was the owner, ever since her father had foolishly handed over the company as part of her marriage settlement. But the only mark Clay had ever left on the business was that of negligence. He spent the bulk of his time out of town, overseeing his marginally profitable agricultural shipping business, leaving the copper works to fend for itself. Making him money he hadn't earned.

Mary stomped through the factory on her way to the old office space she'd set up as her laboratory. It was dark and cramped, but having access to extra tools from the factory whenever she needed them was convenient. Maybe she'd try to fix up the space a bit, now that she no longer had the option of visiting Victor's lab.

Dr. Franklin, she corrected herself, scowling at mere thought of him. He didn't deserve such intimacy of address. Not after he'd shown his true indifference to her.

Thank God I'm married.

The thought brought a bitter little laugh. At least her undeserving, company-stealing husband was good for something. Without him, she might not have kept her romantic fantasies hidden safely away. How much worse would things have been, if Victor had been both partner and lover?

Mary shivered. She'd avoided that scenario. A tiny relief to her aching heart.

She dug in her pocket for the key to the office, only to stumble to a halt the moment her fingers touched metal. The door ahead of her stood open.

"My projects!" she gasped, breaking into a run. Her

laboratory door was never unlocked. The room held too many fragile, valuable, or outright dangerous things. And if someone had left the door standing open, even if they didn't mean to touch what was inside, the dust and grime from the factory could have damaged equipment or contaminated an experiment.

"Well, well," came an icy baritone voice.

Mary's already battered heart lurched. Her husband stepped out of the office, a sneer on his handsome face.

"If it isn't my wayward wife."

Mary drew herself up straight. As if *she* were the one who had walked out? She'd been here the whole time. He was the deserter.

"Augustus," she greeted him impassively. "What a surprise to see you."

"I assume you are to blame for this… disturbance in my factory?" He waved a hand at the room behind him.

"I have made use of an unoccupied space, yes."

"I see. And who authorized this use?"

Oh, no. She wasn't going to let him play that game. If she named even a single worker who'd known about her laboratory—and everyone here knew—Augustus would dismiss the man on the spot. A lesson to everyone: if you side with her over me, I'll hurt you.

"*I* authorized it. This was one of my father's rooms. It was empty, so I put it to good use. I didn't realize you had a key."

"This is no lady's playplace." His sneer had turned condescending, his voice honeyed. "I can't have you putting yourself in danger with all these machines and rough men about. You should be at home, doing needlepoint."

Mary gave him a frosty smile. "For what purpose?

There's never a husband there to lay his head on my embroidered pillows."

Augustus dropped the pretense in favor of an all-out scowl. "I am returning to supervise this factory, with no intention of leaving. You have no claim on this space and no right to use it without my permission. As of right now, your little toys are just so much rubbish to be disposed of."

Panic clawed at Mary's throat, but she clenched her fists and tried not to let it show. "If you provide me with the funds to rent a new studio, I would be happy to remove everything."

He sniffed. "You can't honestly think I would contribute to such a revoltingly unfeminine pursuit? You have two days to clear this space. Don't say I never give you anything."

"Two days?" Mary blurted. "Impossible. I could never secure another location so quickly."

"Two days," Augustus repeated. "Then I begin removing it all myself."

Her cool facade cracked. "Why do you hate me? What have I ever done to you? You got the company. You got everything you wanted. Why can't you let me be? You don't want me. Why not agree to a divorce?"

It would be a scandal, of course, but she preferred scandal to remaining forever trapped. She already lived outside the bounds of society's rules for women, and certainly none of her friends would ever shame her for it. But whenever she'd pressed him, he'd always insisted that if she went to the courts he would contest her case.

"And lose the company of my charming wife?" he mocked. "Don't be silly. Two days, Mary. After that, I am taking control of this room and the entire factory with it." He strode past her into the heart of the factory, not even giving her the courtesy of a nod of farewell.

 CATHERINE STEIN

Tears gathered in the corners of Mary's eyes, but she refused to let them fall. He would not win. She would never let him destroy the life she'd built. With the help of a few friends, she could get her equipment moved in two days. All she needed was a place to put everything.

Unfortunately, only one viable option sprang to mind.

So be it. Emergency situations called for emergency solutions.

Chapter 3
Late to Bed, Early to Rise

What was that knocking? Something had gone wrong with the machine, hadn't it? Victor had thought the joint prototype had been sound. But now it seemed to be moving when it wasn't supposed to and making an awful racket.

"Dr. Franklin," a youthful male voice begged from somewhere in the vicinity of the knocking. "*Please*, can you wake up? I don't have a key, and if you don't come and get these ladies and their things off the porch soon your father is going to find out and cause a ruckus."

"What?" Victor blinked, his head clearing as he sat up. He wasn't in the laboratory. And judging by the sliver of sunlight peeking between his heavy bedroom curtains, he hadn't been asleep long.

The knock sounded again. "Please wake up, Dr. Franklin."

Victor stumbled out of bed and crossed the room, trying to make sense of what he thought he'd heard. Ladies on the porch? Was that right? God, he was so groggy. What time was it, anyway?

He opened the door, and the young man sighed in relief. Victor didn't recognize him. The youth was dressed in a neat blue uniform with a matching cap. A new footman or driver, perhaps. Victor's unusual schedule meant he rarely interacted with the staff at Franklin Castle.

"Dr. Franklin, you must come with me," the boy insisted. "The lady says they won't move until she's spoken with you."

"Me?" Victor scrubbed a hand across his face. "What time is it?"

"Quarter past nine, sir."

"Damnation."

The footman grimaced at the cursing. "If you'd follow me, sir?"

"Absolutely not," Victor replied. "Bad enough I've been dragged out of the bed I barely crawled into. I won't go meeting people at the door in my nightshirt. Tell whoever it is they can damn well wait."

The boy winced again. "Do you need help dressing, sir?"

"No." Dr. Franklin the elder kept a valet, of course, but Victor shunned every attempt his father made to hire him a manservant. He found the idea of needing an assistant for dressing and grooming ridiculously out-dated. "I'll only be a moment."

Victor threw on a clean shirt and trousers and ran a comb quickly through his hair. He added a vest to his outfit, in case the ladies causing the trouble were from that bothersome Detroit Ladies' Committee Against Vice, but didn't put on a tie or a coat for the same reason. Undressed enough to shock, but not enough to make anyone faint.

He tromped downstairs after the anxious servant to the large foyer, where Sakai, a native of Japan and the family's long-time butler, stood waiting. Sakai's aging face was twisted into an unusually stern frown. He gestured at the front door.

"If you could please take care of this problem, Master Victor?" the butler said, his tone all but an order.

Victor sighed. How old did he have to be before Sakai

began addressing him as anything but a child? Though some of that might be his own fault. Even as a teenager, he'd regularly begged the butler to regale him with stories of Japan and Russia and several other places he'd lived before making his way to Detroit. And Victor did spend most of his time playing with toys, in a way. A large part of him would never grow up.

"What's the trouble?" Victor asked.

"A pair of ladies," Sakai explained. "Unloading a cartful of things onto the porch and the walkway. Acquaintances of yours. Mrs. Finch and Mrs. Clay."

Victor jumped, and his heart began to race. Mary? Here? What reason could she possibly have to come here, after declaring she never wanted to speak to him again? And what the hell could he possibly say to her? He'd yet to crawl out from beneath the mountain of shame his behavior had brought down upon him. The urge to march right back upstairs and return to bed shuddered through him.

Sakai opened the door, rendering retreat an impossibility. Victor screwed up his courage, put on his best charming smile, and sauntered out to assess the trouble for himself.

Boxes of books and scientific equipment littered the long porch that ran between the mansion's two front turrets. Victor stepped carefully, finding an open spot where he could prop himself against the wall and take in the scene in his customary nonchalant manner. Too bad he couldn't make his inside match his outside. His heart had begun hammering wildly the moment he'd spied Mary. She lifted another box from the cart parked in the road and started for the house.

What the everloving hell was going on?

"Hi, Victor." Mrs. Calliope Finch, wife of one of Victor's dearest friends, plopped something on the ground at Victor's feet. When she straightened up, she made a show of rubbing her back, thrusting out the already noticeable swell of her belly. "Going to lend a hand?"

"Callie, what is all this?" Did Hal know she was here, hauling boxes? Then again, Callie carried around books for her library every day, so this probably wasn't much different.

"You'll have to ask Mrs. Clay," Callie replied, turning and heading back to the cart.

Victor abandoned his slouch and strode to the steps, waiting as Callie and Mary shuffled around one another.

"Mrs. Clay," he said stiffly. "I was under the impression you never wanted to see me again."

"Sometimes unexpected situations arise," she replied, not making eye contact. "Go help unload the cart. The driver has other things to do today. And you really aren't going to make Mrs. Finch do all the work in her condition, are you?"

Victor wandered over to the cart, his sleepy brain trying to make sense of everything. Maybe this was some kind of strange punishment. He was pretty sure he actually *was* awake.

The cart was almost empty. He grabbed a toolbox that looked heavy and hefted it over the side. "Is this your laboratory equipment?" he asked Mary as they crossed paths again.

She didn't reply. She wasn't getting rid of all this, was she? Giving up her career? Fuck.

No. Never. He couldn't imagine her doing that, no matter how much he'd hurt her. Unless she was trying to make him *think* he'd driven her to that.

Victor set the toolbox down on the porch and scratched his head. No. It wasn't like her to be manipulative. She was quiet—usually—and private, but honest. Her anger had been one hundred percent genuine emotion.

He walked back to the cart, where Callie shoved a box into his hands.

"That's the last of it," she declared. She clambered up into the cart. "I'm going to hitch a ride home. You'll let me know if you need anything else, won't you, Mary?"

"Definitely." Mary raised a hand and waved, and a moment later the cart trundled off, puffing steam as it went.

Victor carried the final box to the porch. "Care to explain all this?"

Mary looked him in the eye for the first time that morning. "I need a temporary place to store my things. And you owe me."

Yes. He certainly did. What he didn't understand was why she was trusting him with anything at all. And what had happened to her laboratory? A fire? A flood?

Victor didn't ask. It wasn't his place to pry, no matter how much he wanted to, and he didn't dare do anything that might lead to another massive mistake.

"Of course," he said. "You may keep your things here as long as you wish." He had plenty of room. His laboratory was an enormous two-story space, twenty-five feet wide in either direction. And even that was only a fraction of Franklin Castle's twenty-one thousand square feet. One porch-worth of books and tools would hardly make a difference. "I'll ask the staff to transport everything to my laboratory. No need to carry anything else yourself."

Mary stubbornly hefted a box. "Many of these things are fragile."

"I know. I promise the staff here will be extremely careful. I'll help you move anything especially delicate, if you like."

She hesitated, then sighed. "Fine. Those two."

Victor picked up the boxes she pointed at, one in each arm. "Follow me."

He kicked at the door, since he couldn't knock, and Sakai answered promptly.

"I will have the lady's things brought inside," the butler said. "Where would you like them?"

"My laboratory, please," Victor replied. "This way, Mrs. Clay."

Mary had never been through the house before, always entering through the side door that led directly to his lab. Convenient for a person, but not for deliveries. His own equipment usually came through the rear entrance, by the carriage house.

Victor noticed the way her eyes darted back and forth, taking in the opulent surroundings. He didn't dare ask what she thought. It was none of his business. This was about doing her a favor as part of his penance. It wasn't a social call. If she wanted to say anything at all to him, she could, but he wasn't going to go harassing her with questions.

By the time they reached his lab, his arms were beginning to ache from the awkward way he'd been carrying the boxes. He set them down atop his worktable, nudging several unattached pieces of his mechanical man aside. He could clean it all up later.

"There should be plenty of room for your things," Victor said. "Especially on that side of the room." He gestured to his left. Most of his own tools and equipment were on the opposite side of the room. Mary could leave whatever she wanted here without worrying that she'd interfere with his projects or vice versa. "How long do you think you'll need the space? Should I expect to move your things again in a few days?"

Blast. Already he'd failed his attempt to not ask questions.

It didn't matter how long. If she wanted to leave everything here for years, he'd let her.

"I don't know yet," she admitted. "Not long. But it won't cause any trouble. You only work at night. I'll make certain I'm only here during the day, and we will never need to see each other."

Ouch. The blunt words brought a stabbing reminder of his folly. He'd best be out of here. No sense lingering and prolonging the torture.

"That sounds reasonable," Victor said as calmly as he could manage. "Feel free to take your time getting situated. I won't be back until evening. And I'll ask Sakai to get you a key to the side door so you can come and go as you like."

Mary nodded. "Thank you. I'm sure neither of us will even notice the other is here."

"Right." Victor gave her a curt nod. "Good day, Mrs. Clay."

He hurried away, taking the stairs up to his bedroom two at a time. Peeling off his clothing as quickly as possible, he threw himself down on the bedsheets.

Mary Clay. In his laboratory. All day, every day, for some indefinite period of time. He might never sleep again for nerves.

Although now that he was back in bed, with his eyes closed, exhaustion began to take its toll. Maybe she would merely haunt his dreams.

And maybe, just maybe, she would be nearby long enough that he could begin to show her how very sorry he was.

Chapter 4
On Thursdays We Make Plans

Mary visited the Ladies' Lending Library run by her friend Mrs. Finch every Thursday without fail. Today was no exception. It didn't matter that her life had been upended in the last two days or that she struggled to concentrate on any book she picked up. The library was a special refuge, and Mary never failed to leave in better spirits than when she'd arrived.

It was here that she'd met her dearest friends—like-minded women who'd welcomed her with open arms. Here, no one had ever doubted her or condescended. Here, her ideas and projects were met with interest and enthusiasm. The library was the exact opposite of the male-dominated scientific societies she'd visited in years past, where only Victor took her seriously. It was friendly, accepting, and em-powering—all the things Mary hoped to be for the women of science who came after her.

Today, she sat with her friends in one of the upstairs reading rooms, a cozy space with plush armchairs, a warm fireplace, and ample electric light. A temporary solution to her laboratory problem had been implemented. Now, with the assistance of the other ladies, she would find a permanent one.

"I'm afraid I can't be of any help." Nisha Majhi leaned back in her chair and crossed her trouser-clad legs. "I do almost all of my engineering outdoors. My tools are stored in a shed. No room for additional equipment, especially not in the middle of winter."

Mary muttered a mild oath. Nisha had been her best hope for an alternative to Victor's laboratory. It would have been so nice to work beside another woman scientist.

"January is when I concentrate primarily on design and small-scale experimentation," Nisha continued. "My family loves it when I do hydrodynamic tests in the bathtub." Her dark eyebrows arched as she gave an impish grin, her warm brown skin crinkling at the corners of her eyes.

"Do you know of any other spaces I might utilize?" Mary asked.

Nisha pursed her lips. "None come to mind."

"I suppose I'll have to look into renting a room somewhere." If she could find a place that was both suitable and affordable. Her monthly allowance—supplied through earnings from the copper works—wasn't intended to cover large expenses. Her husband was supposed to do that, but Augustus wouldn't give her a penny toward this sort of venture. In fact, if he discovered what she was doing, he might try to cut off her funds altogether.

"Or you could keep everything at Victor's and make the best of it," Callie suggested.

Mary's gaze jerked toward her. "Make the best of it? After he cheated me out of my rightful recognition for the hydroconductor?"

"I'm sure he's anxious to apologize for that," Callie replied. "I can't imagine he would have done it on purpose."

"No," Nisha agreed. "Victor's not cruel. But he can be dense."

"Thoughtless and careless," Mary affirmed. "And he did tell me he was sorry. But words can't undo the damage. He didn't think enough of me to, well, think of me, and I can't trust that it won't happen again."

She would keep repeating those words to herself until enough time had passed that she stopped thinking of him altogether. Already, her rage had vanished, replaced by a slight embarrassment at the extent of her fury. She needed to cling to the lingering irritation, or she'd fall right back into her old habits. Unacceptable.

"You don't have to work with him," Callie pointed out. "You said you were going to be there only when he wasn't."

Mary nodded. "I get the daytime, he gets the night."

"That settles it." Callie began to tick off items on her fingers. "You have the space for your equipment and your work. You have the timing arranged so you don't need to actually interact with Victor. You don't have to spend any money to stay there. He knows how fragile and delicate some of your things are and will take care not to damage them. If you find yourself needing additional tools, he will have plenty to choose from. We can help hold him accountable for treating you right. And no one will have to move all your boxes *again*."

"You make it sound so sensible."

Callie grinned. "It's a talent of mine. And good thing, too. Hal can be given to flights of fancy. Someone has to keep the family grounded."

At the mention of her husband, Callie smiled fondly and rested a hand against the swell of her belly. Mary felt a stab of jealousy. Not for the baby—she was grateful to not have any children—but for the clear adoration between Callie and Dr. Finch. Mary had hoped for that, once upon a time. Back when she'd believed Augustus Clay the kind, charming man he'd pretended to be.

She pushed the unpleasant thought aside. She had a

different man to worry about. One who wouldn't intentionally destroy all her work, at least.

"I suppose I can stay for a week or two and see how it goes," Mary conceded. "But I'll still be looking for other options."

"Sounds good to me," Nisha replied. She popped up from her seat. "I should be going. I've got evening plans."

Mary stood as well. "And I need to look for some books while I'm here."

"What are you in the mood for?" Callie asked, rising to her feet to join the other ladies.

"Something lighthearted." She needed an escape, and a happy ending.

Callie grinned. "I know just the thing. Follow me."

The women descended the stairs to the library stacks, row after row of knowledge and joy. Whatever else happened, this place would always feel like home.

* * *

Victor downed the glass of whiskey and poured himself another one. He propped himself against the mantelpiece in his usual half-slouch. The small alcove on the second floor of the building had once been part of a bedroom suite, before the entire townhouse had been transformed into a gentlemen's (and a few daring ladies') club. Over the years, it had come to feel like an extension of home. A place for a nice drink by a cracking fire with his favorite people. With only enough room for a few chairs, the space exuded intimacy and comfort. There was no better meeting spot for the Mad Scientists Society.

"Thought of a good way to apologize yet?" Nemo asked. As always, the "Captain" lounged in the armchair to the left of the fireplace, sipping a drink.

"I hadn't even recovered from her furious departure when she showed up at my doorstep, insisting I take all her things into my laboratory," Victor protested. "I haven't had time to think up an apology." He gulped more whiskey. "Why? Do you have a suggestion?"

"Do you think I would tell you if I did?"

Victor rubbed his temple. "No."

Hal poured himself a cup of tea from the porcelain teapot he'd brought from home so he could avoid using the club's autokettles. He gave Victor a mischievous grin. "Well, you'd better figure something out. Callie thinks you and Mrs. Clay would make an adorable couple."

Victor flinched so forcefully his drink sloshed. "Don't be daft," he snarled, trying to hide the mix of excitement and panic the comment had caused. "She's married."

Hal shrugged. "I don't think Callie considers the negligent Mr. Clay any impediment. Besides, clear adultery would be helpful when arguing for a divorce."

Victor finished the whiskey and seriously considered pouring a third glass. "Didn't you used to be a prude?" he accused Hal. "Then you marry a demimondaine and look what happens to you."

"To be fair, it happened *before* he married her," Nemo pointed out. "While they were wildly fornicating."

Hal's lopsided grin managed to be both sheepish and proud. "I can be myself with Callie."

Victor nodded. "We should all be so lucky."

He was always himself, and yet never himself. His social side, flirtatious and cynical, was one hundred percent real. But it masked the serious part of him that came out when he worked. The part that believed he could make a difference in the world.

It also hid the part that was lonely and celibate. Some

men could find satisfaction in the purely physical, even when their affections lay elsewhere. Victor had discovered he was not one of them.

His gaze lingered on Hal's adorable, bespectacled visage. Once, nineteen-year-old Victor had been utterly besotted with his new friend. They'd shared one extremely brief, extremely awkward kiss that had left Hal saying, "Nope, sorry, definitely not interested that way." Heartsick Victor had attempted to ease the ache by bedding another friend, only to end the night sobbing on her floor.

Lesson learned. He'd recovered, eventually, and returned to his roguish ways until Mary Clay had walked into his life. Now his flirtations, enjoyable as they were, never went beyond the room where they started. Not even his friends knew how long it had been.

"Dammit, we've just made him worse," Hal muttered, frowning up at Victor.

"You should apologize to her," Nemo insisted. "I think it will help her *and* you, as long as you do it sincerely."

He would. He'd make it up to her in whatever way he could, and he'd do his damnedest to be better in the future. But it wouldn't change the situation.

"Enough," he insisted. "I don't want to talk about this anymore. We are supposed to be a scientific society. Let's talk about science. I have the joint prototype for my mechanical man working now. It moves when triggered by an electrical signal. Now I need to make them in all the right shapes and sizes and he'll be able to move."

Hal cocked his head to one side. "How will you control his movements? You can't mean to have wires coming out everywhere and a switchboard for operating him." He chuckled. "You'd look ridiculous, tromping behind your creation with your arms full of equipment, flicking things on and off."

"I mean for him to move on his own," Victor insisted. "He'll have sensors to respond to stimuli, which will trigger the electrical signals. I'm working on those, too. The sound sensors are all but finished."

The light sensors were another matter. Much trickier, and they needed to be highly sensitive if the mecha-man's eyes were to be able to distinguish real-world objects. Extensive testing both indoors and outdoors would be necessary.

Which meant working during sunlight hours. When Mary was in the lab.

His heart thumped wildly and his guts turned inside out. He could see her, talk to her, make things right.

You could make things even worse.

Well, shit.

Victor poured himself another drink.

Chapter 5
Trade of the Tools

Mary shut the laboratory door behind her and shook the snow from her cloak before hanging it on the convenient peg she'd installed. She stepped out of her rubber overshoes, then unhooked the clips hiking up her skirt and smoothed it down. On a day like this, she could see why women like Nisha preferred the convenience of trousers.

That sort of fashion was too edgy for Mary. She liked simplicity and comfort, but straying too far from the norm made her anxious. She kept to her plain skirts, unadorned shirtwaists, and an occasional pair of bloomers in private when necessary. Perhaps this made her dreadfully boring, but she'd always preferred being overlooked to drawing too much attention.

Except in her career. This new project would be the one that made her a name in the scientific community. When her home cooling device was perfected, everyone would have to acknowledge her contributions.

Donning her leather apron to protect her clothes, she walked toward the large worktable where she'd left her small prototype. She'd grown more comfortable with her situation over the last four days, settling into a routine. The laboratory space was clean, well-lit, and plenty large enough to house both her work and Victor's. The solid walls and steam heating kept the cold and snow at bay, and when she needed a break from work, the windows in the south wall offered a pleasant view of Windsor, Canada, barely more than a half-mile away across the Detroit River.

As she'd requested, Victor stayed away from the laboratory during daylight hours. It didn't erase his presence entirely, of course. The mechanical man lay on the opposite half of the massive table, patiently awaiting whatever modification Dr. Franklin had in mind tonight. Even the organization of the lab itself was a reflection of its owner. Every tool had an exact location, all neatly labeled, and Victor returned each one to its place at the end of every night. Not once had Mary seen even a screw or bolt left behind.

Until today.

There, sitting beside her partially complete cooling coil, was the adjustable tube bender she'd been using to curve the straight copper piping she'd brought from the copper works. She'd had to borrow it from Victor, because in the past she'd always used the tools from the factory or had one of the workers bend pipes to her specifications.

Mary reached for the tool and froze. No. This wasn't Victor's pipe bender. This was a newer model, more highly adjustable, both for sizes of pipe and angle of bend. It was shiny, sturdy, gorgeous.

She picked it up, running her fingers over the sleek metal and the rubber grips. It was just what she needed to create smooth, uniform curves in her air cooler.

The tool clattered on the table as she jerked her hand away. Was this some kind of bribe? An effort to coax her into forgetting what he'd done to her? Maybe it was his way of telling her not to touch his tools. At the very least, it meant he'd been spying on her.

Mary lowered herself onto a stool. No. Not spying. Or if it was, then she'd been spying on him as well. She'd wasted an imprudent amount of time examining his work over the last few days. She'd been especially entranced by the delicate joints in the hands: exquisitely crafted miniature versions of the larger joints elsewhere. Multiple times she'd had to stop herself from touching the man, to feel how effortlessly the parts moved.

She couldn't know Victor's intentions, but she also couldn't fault him for his curiosity about her work. Scientists were knowledge seekers. Therefore, she would treat the pipe bender as though it were a gift. An indication that he took enough interest in her project to ensure she had the proper tools to continue it to the best of her ability. And she would return the favor in kind.

When her work for the day was completed, and the sun was sinking low in the sky, she dug through her belongings for the perfect response, then headed out into the snow with a spring in her step.

* * *

Victor picked up the spool of wire and turned it over in his hands. The copper gleamed under the electric lights. Gorgeous. He could find no note or markings on the spool, but the placement beside the mecha-man's hand was enough. Mary meant this for his use.

It was perfect, of course. Wire thin enough to run electricity to all the delicate moving parts in the hands, but sturdy enough to last. Victor's heart beat a wild dance of hope in his chest. She had to have studied his work carefully to determine exactly what he needed. Her work was thriving here in his laboratory and his own project had caught her interest. Maybe she wouldn't leave. Maybe she didn't hate him. Maybe, someday, he could earn her forgiveness.

He set to work.

* * *

Mary picked through the assortment of switches and dials Victor had left beside her machine. Quality parts. And he hadn't assumed to know what sizes and types she preferred. He *could* be thoughtful, when he was trying. But why was he trying at all? What did he want from her?

She sat down on the stool and paused to take a dose of her migraine tonic. Stress could exacerbate the headaches, and this morning had tried her nerves. She'd stopped by the copper works to gather more supplies, only to find that her husband hadn't exaggerated about his intent to oversee the business. He'd taken over her old laboratory and, according to the workers, was there every day.

Why? She couldn't fathom his reasoning. He knew nothing about the copper business.

At least she'd managed to gather the parts she'd wanted without him discovering she was there. She had enough piping and wire for several projects now.

And enough bits to repay Victor for his latest offering.

Mary picked up one of the dials from the pile on the table. Yes, it would do nicely.

* * *

Victor was running out of ideas. After several days of swapping items back and forth, he had no more tools or parts to offer. Mary's project looked more spectacular every day. He wished it were August instead of January so they could thoroughly test it out. He'd love a way to cool the lab in summer.

He walked around the table, admiring her work from every angle. Lord, how he wished she were here to tell him all about it. He knew exactly how she would look, blue eyes shining, red lips bent in a wide smile. He could hear her voice, growing higher and faster as she talked. This was how he'd fallen in love with her, watching excitement burst from her usually quiet body whenever something sparked her scientific curiosity. The charming rake, laid low by the wallflower. He could never resist the secretly passionate, scholarly types.

Victor spun away from the worktable and began to pace the laboratory, desperate to think of something he could give her. Some way he could show he cared. That he valued both her and her work.

But what? She needed no more tools or parts. Her prototype was all but complete. The next phase would be testing, and she didn't need anything for that but space. Next would come refinement. Tweaks and changes. Redesigns of some areas, perhaps.

He jogged to his desk. Of course. A new notebook. Perfect, untouched pens. Perhaps a nice, clean straightedge for precise lines and measurements. Digging through his drawers, he gathered up the best of all the design tools he'd never used and laid them on the worktable beside Mary's machine. He topped off the pile with a stamped envelope addressed to the patent office.

There. The last of his gifts. He hoped they had provided a bit of help and a few smiles as she worked on her air cooler. Now, though, it was time for his atonement to move into phase two. It would take a bit of work. Research. Possibly phone calls. A certain amount of activity during daylight hours.

Being up and about while knowing she was in his laboratory working would be a special kind of torture. One he deserved, he supposed. It wouldn't be so different than before. His sleep was restless anyway. What mattered was that Mary was still here. And as long as that held true, he'd keep saying he was sorry, in any way he could.

Chapter 6
Read All Over

A gust of wind sprayed snow across Mary's boots as she paused to look at the river. She squinted in the early morning light and shielded her eyes with her hand. Had that been a vehicle of some sort, moving across the frozen surface? Difficult to tell, with the sunlight reflecting off the ice.

Maybe it was only her imagination, acting up after reading an article in yesterday's newspaper, reminding people of the dangers of going out onto the ice. A number of recent reports of cars driving on the river at night had prompted the notice, the paper had said.

She wasn't sure what to make of the article. The river froze at least partially every year, and she couldn't recall this situation having been remarked on in the past. Perhaps it had something to do with the proliferation of steam cars in the last several years. More people with vehicles meant more people attempting silly stunts with them.

She turned her gaze back to the street in front of her. What was she looking for, anyway?

Just because driving a car on the ice sounds exactly the sort of thing Victor would do...

Her sigh created a small cloud of fog. It didn't matter that she was still angry at what he'd done. She still cared, and right now she was worried about him.

The gifts of parts and tools had stopped several days ago, and the progress on his mechanical man had slowed to a crawl. He wasn't working, or at least not working much. She hoped his project hadn't hit some snag he couldn't puzzle out. More likely he'd grown tired of sharing the laboratory and taken himself off elsewhere. Whatever the reason, something had drawn his attention away from his work, and now her concern was distracting her from her own work.

And that wouldn't do. Their arrangement had turned out better than she'd ever hoped. She loved the laboratory for its comfort, good lighting, and efficient use of space. It was by far the nicest place she'd worked, and now that she'd been using it full-time, she didn't want to go anywhere else. Not unless and until she could find a space equally good. She sincerely hoped Victor wasn't regretting her presence.

You could always ask him.

Mary shivered, telling herself it was from the cold and not from the anticipation of speaking to him again. Why not ask? She'd created the rules for their situation. If need be, she could change them. And she didn't need to speak to him directly. A simple note would suffice. She could frame her question as an inquiry into the suitability of their arrangement.

The remainder of her walk provided ample time to plan out an appropriate missive, and she arrived confident the idea was a sound one: check on Victor, make certain their compromise continued to be effective, not have to see him in person.

Mary stepped into the warmth of the laboratory and began to tug off her cloak. She'd dash off the note first, then get to work with a clear head. Her gaze drifted across the room and she froze.

Papers covered the worktable.

Another gift? She quickly finished shedding her outerwear and hurried over to examine the stack. Lists. Magazines with pages marked. Newspaper clippings. Victor had left her a comprehensive guide to publications covering scientific news. Some she was familiar with, but many were new to her. Victor had circled or marked contacts who handled submissions and those who conducted interviews. The papers were even sorted by which publications were most likely to be interested in her invention. He'd saved her days of research. Well. That explained what he'd been doing on his own time.

Mary picked up one of the magazines and thumbed through it. This particular periodical had rejected her in the past, but she would keep trying. Someone in these lists would be interested in her air cooler. And even if they weren't, Victor was.

She abandoned the papers to examine his mechanical man. It was unchanged from yesterday, as far as she could tell. A sense of relief flooded through her, the knowledge of what he had been doing these past few days washing away all her earlier worries. He wasn't in trouble, and he didn't want her gone. Best of all, Mary no longer had to fear that her feelings toward him were unnecessarily lenient.

Because he was sorry. Truly sorry.

He'd been apologizing to her from the moment he'd welcomed her into his home, in whatever ways he could. This latest offering made it abundantly clear. He valued her work, and wanted to see her succeed. He wanted her to have recognition for her work. It didn't absolve him of wrongdoing or mean she could trust he wouldn't make the same sort of mistakes in the future, but he did care.

"So much for my carefully crafted note," she laughed. She would write him a different one. At the very least she would thank him for saving her time she'd much rather spend with a tool in her hand. The first steps, perhaps, to removing a few stones from the wall she'd erected between them.

* * *

Whoever had decided to install the wall clock in the dining room was pure evil. Victor could see it perfectly from his seat, its hands ticking along with all the alacrity of a laudanum-addled slug. Six forty-one. Six forty-two. Six forty-two and thirty seconds.

"I trust you're not involved this time?" Dr. Edward Franklin frowned across the table at his son.

"Involved in what?" Victor asked. Apparently he'd missed part of the conversation. He was dying to escape this interminable dinner. The streets outside were completely dark. Mary would be back home after another day's work, and Victor could think of nothing but the papers he'd left for her. Was she pleased? Angry? Indifferent? Had she responded in any way?

His father coughed and Victor snapped back to attention.

"The incidents in the paper," the older man explained, his tone suggesting his patience was wearing thin. Well, so was Victor's, which made them even.

"I believe the most recent time I was mentioned in the papers was the interview I did regarding the hydroconductor project I undertook with Mrs. Clay. I have yet to be contacted regarding my mechanical man," Victor said calmly.

Surprisingly calmly, given his current antipathy for that particular publication. He'd contacted them a few days ago about the possibility of arranging another interview for Mary to explain her own contributions to the hydroconductor. They'd laughed at him. Literally laughed, the scornful, tinny sound echoing over the telephone receiver.

"I'm talking about this rash of strange activity," Victor's father snapped, no longer hiding his displeasure. "The last time the papers had this many reports of youngsters behaving badly, your friend Jekyll was neck-deep in all of it."

"Finch," Victor corrected.

"What sort of man uses his wife's name? You better not be drinking any of his potions, Victor. I wouldn't trust them not to addle your brain."

Victor considered replying that the entire point of Hal's medicines was to treat ailments effectively *without* addling the brain, but another glance at the clock kept him silent. He really didn't want to start yet another argument about how his unconventional friends might sully the Franklin family's good name.

"Are you certain you don't know anything about the men who made a ruckus in a restaurant after drinking some tainted whiskey?" his father pressed. "Sounds like your friends again."

Victor's jaw clenched. It did sound like what had happened with Hal and the tonic water. Too much. But whatever this was, it had nothing to do with anyone Victor knew.

"The temperance folks will be crowing again, mark my words," the elder Dr. Franklin continued. "The 'demon liquor' from Windsor. I don't want to hear that you're involved."

Victor held his father's mistrustful gaze. "I'm not."

"And the people driving cars on the frozen river?"

Well, now. That *did* sound fun. And Victor had been tinkering with an all-electric automobile out in the carriage house on the days he was up before sunset. No fires. No hot boilers. Perfect for a jaunt out on the ice.

"Uh, not me either." *Yet.* He could take Mary for a midnight spin before warming up inside, drinking cocoa while they snuggled together in front of a fire.

Victor scrubbed a hand across his face. He damn well needed to get to the laboratory and see how she'd responded before his fantasies got even more out of control.

"Let's keep it that way." Victor's father brandished a fork, even though he'd finished his food ages ago. "This family has a long and proud tradition of serious scientific study and contributions to the welfare of the nation. I expect you to live up to your name." A robotic servant wheeled over and he relinquished his cutlery to a grasping pincer. Dinner was over. Thank God.

"Yes, sir," Victor replied, nudging his own dishes in the direction of the automaton. Why couldn't his father accept that he *was* serious about his projects? So what if they tended toward the outlandish? It was what he loved. He wanted to push boundaries and see what happened. Try things people called impossible. The Mad Scientists Society had been his idea, and he was proud of it. Where most people viewed mad scientists in novels as cautionary tales, Victor considered them inspiration.

At ten seconds shy of six forty-nine, Victor finally escaped his place at the table. He walked casually from the room, then sprinted for the laboratory.

All the papers he'd left for Mary had been cleared away. Her side of the table, in fact, was completely empty, her air cooler set carefully aside in a corner with a thin cloth draped over it.

"Please let her be moving on to something new or

working on design issues and not planning to leave," Victor murmured.

He'd never insist on her remaining here indefinitely, but he needed more time. He'd yet to find a publication that wanted to hear her speak about the hydroconductor. The best possibility so far was a science magazine aimed specifically at women, but they wouldn't talk to *him*. And he couldn't forgive himself until he'd given her back the recognition she deserved. Maybe not even then.

Victor took a seat beside his mecha-man. He'd neglected the creature the last few days, and it was time to get back to work.

His rear end had barely touched the stool when he shot back to his feet in surprise. Clenched in the automaton's steel fingers was a folded piece of paper. Victor eased it out and opened it.

I've been admiring your metal man. The joints are exquisite and you've made excellent use of the wire I provided. How are the sensors coming? I admit that I played a bit with the hearing sensor, and I have some small suggestions (see diagram below). How is the sight sensor? Do you need to test it during daytime hours? Is there anything else you'd like me to test? Thank you for saving me research time with the papers. I appreciate it. Let me know if I can help you in any way. I look forward to collaborating.

-M

"Fucking hell." Victor sank down onto the stool. He'd never expected this. He eyed the diagram she'd sketched at the bottom of the note. Excellent. He'd make those tweaks today. As for the rest...

He couldn't even think how he might respond, only that he had to do so. He couldn't lose the opportunity to bring her into this project. How amazing would the mecha-man be with both of them working together on him? They could make him pass as human. He knew it in his gut. Together, they could do the unimaginable. The possibilities made his head spin.

Victor gripped the table, forcing himself to focus on the real rather than the fantastical. Whatever happened, he'd keep working. Keep trying to be a better man, in the hopes that someday they'd collaborate in person again. Be friends again.

And as for his father's insistence on "serious" study? Hah! Victor was a Mad Scientist through and through, and even if the whole world thought his work was ridiculous, he didn't care.

He patted the mechanical man. "Mary likes you, buddy. Let's make you worthy of her."

Chapter 7
The Courage to Change

And done. Mary set down her tools and paused to stretch out her neck and shoulders. The last of the delicate wires was in place and tomorrow she could take the reworked sight sensor out in full sunlight for a test. She glanced out the window. The reddish glow of the setting sun suggested fair skies tomorrow. Perfect.

She turned back to her work. She had just enough time to jot off a note to Victor about the sensor and make a few minor adjustments before she headed home for the day. The mecha-man, as he called it, would be fully built within the week. She couldn't wait to see him walking around. Even in this initial stage, he was so much more sophisticated than she'd expected.

Victor was truly a visionary. When he had an idea, he sat down and implemented it, without any consideration for what was supposed to be possible. He wasn't afraid to try things, and he wasn't afraid to fail and try again. The mark of a great scientist.

Her pen had hardly scratched the paper when a knock at the internal door interrupted. Mary jumped. In all the days she'd been working here, not once had anyone come to the laboratory.

A chill washed over her skin. Something was wrong.

Maybe Victor's father had decided to throw her out. Maybe a fire had broken out in the kitchen and the house needed to be evacuated. Maybe Victor was hurt and someone in the household had decided she needed to know.

The knock sounded again. "Mrs. Clay?" called a deep voice with a bit of a Japanese accent. Mr. Sakai, the butler. "Are you still here?"

Mary hurried over to open the door. "I'm here. Is something wrong?" Dire possibilities began to play in her head again.

"There is a telephone call for you, madam."

"Oh!" A phone call? Here? Mary had never in her life received a phone call. She'd made a few, using the telephone at the copper works, but that was the extent of her experience with the device. Augustus had never spent the money to install a phone in her house, naturally.

Where was Mr. Clay keeping himself these days, anyhow? He certainly hadn't moved in with her. Thank the Lord.

"If you would follow me, I will show you to the telephone," Sakai said.

Mary nodded and trailed after him into the mansion. He led her to an elegant study, where a telephone rested on the massive carved-oak desk.

"Take as long as you need," the butler told her. He gave her a brief bow and left the room, closing the door behind him.

Mary slid into the large, leather chair and picked up the telephone receiver. "Hello?"

"Mrs. Clay?" a man's voice inquired. "It's Mr. Gage."

"Mr. Gage," she responded in surprise. The factory foreman, who had known her since childhood, had always been friendly and willing to help if she wanted a tool or had a question. "Can I help you?"

"I'm not sure. To be honest, we're not even certain whether there's a problem, but we thought you might be able to offer at least a small clarification on the matter."

Mary wracked her brain for anything she might know that could be helpful to the men at the copper works. Nothing came to mind. She'd never had any part in the running of the company. All her knowledge came from simply being there, first with her father, and more recently in her mini laboratory.

"What seems to be the trouble?" she asked.

"Mr. Clay has been coming to the factory every day. He blusters about, tells us to work harder and faster. He knows nothing about our operation, and as far as we can tell, he hasn't done any real work. I'm sorry to have to put him down so, Mrs. Clay."

Mary sniffed. "Don't hold back on my account. I know what the man is like."

"We thought you did. To be frank, we all liked it better when he kept himself elsewhere. The men are restless. They don't know what to do and they're worried he'll have them fired if they don't meet his nonsensical demands. We're trying to keep things running smoothly, but his presence makes everyone nervous."

"I can imagine. I'm so sorry. I truly don't know what he means to do. He's never shown interest in the copper works before."

"I'm not sure he's interested now." Gage sighed. "He's keeping odd hours. Arriving before dawn or staying after dark. He's also got a handful of outsiders who sometimes come with him. They've been inspecting the shipments going out, but I can't figure why. They haven't changed anything or kept any records. Do you have any notion at all what Mr. Clay might be up to?"

"I wish I did. The only thing I can think is that he might be preparing to funnel our products through his shipping company. They've always dealt in agricultural products, but I could understand if he wanted to expand. But then why not just say so? He gains nothing from sneaking around being mysterious."

"I agree. You have no ideas, then? Nothing you've heard that might even give us a hint?"

"I haven't even spoken to Clay since the day he arrived," Mary admitted. "He's not living at the house and he's made no attempt to contact me."

"I'm sorry." Gage sounded genuinely sympathetic. "You deserve so much better, Miss Mary."

"Thank you, Mr. Gage. I get along fine. And I have the benefit of friends I can rely upon."

"Well, if it comes to a fight, I can tell you the men here will back you over your husband any day." She could hear the smile in his voice.

"Thank you. Oh, before I go—how did you find me at this number?"

Gage chuckled. "Mrs. Clay, everyone knows you've been working at the castle."

She blinked. "They do?"

"Of course. The men have been taking guesses at what you might be working on. Someone said they heard a rumor of a mechanical man, if you can believe that. Word is, the young doctor is full of wild ideas. Bit of a mad genius, they say."

"Dr. Franklin is a visionary," Mary replied, voicing her

earlier thoughts. "He has a vivid imagination and isn't afraid to try things."

A soft laugh came through the receiver. "He sounds like exactly your sort, Miss Mary. You always were something of a dreamer yourself."

Mary stiffened, refusing to let those words spark fantasies of a future that could not be. She wasn't a girl anymore. Life was hard, and she made the best of it. And even if she weren't shackled to Clay, men weren't to be trusted. Victor had demonstrated that clearly. Even the nice ones were trained to disregard women.

"I'm sorry I can't be of more help to you," Mary said, shifting the topic back to something safe. "If I learn anything or hear from Clay, I'll let you know."

"Thank you kindly, Mrs. Clay," Gage replied. "You have a good evening."

"And you."

Mary hung up the phone and rose from her seat. She still had a bit of work to finish before she departed. The matter of her feckless husband's strange behavior would have to wait.

A peek out the door revealed no one waiting for her, so she made her way back to the laboratory on her own, only taking a single wrong turn. This house was ridiculous. Why would anyone need dozens of rooms for a family of three? Did they ever use more than a quarter of them? She'd have to ask Victor for details.

No, no, she corrected herself. That was too friendly. Her communications with him were to be professional and concentrated on their work. She plonked herself down on the stool by the worktable and reached for the note she'd barely started. Drat. What had she meant to write? Something about the sight sensor, but the specifics escaped her.

She scrawled one line, then paused. Her brain refused to

focus. What strange scheme was Clay concocting? Because surely he had one. He didn't do anything without some plan of how to profit from it. And the way Gage had chuckled about her working at Franklin Castle! If it was common knowledge, surely people were making assumptions about her and Victor. Lord, how mortifying.

Or maybe it was only her mind thinking of him in inappropriate ways. Which was even more mortifying. Of course women had urges like that, but they didn't admit to them. Not unless they were confident and daring, like Callie. Which Mary was not. Absolutely, definitely not.

She managed another line of her note. It was difficult not to think of Victor and write to him at the same time. Still, she couldn't leave for the day until she'd given him an update. Bit by bit, she forced out a reasonably coherent note. Her mind was still in a muddle, but soon she'd be home, where a hot bath and a night's rest would calm her.

The interior door opened.

"Mar— Mrs. Clay," Victor blurted, stumbling to a halt one step into the laboratory. His dark eyes had gone wide with surprise, and he raked a hand through his sandy hair in an agitated fashion. Had he always been so pale? When was the last time he'd been outside in the sunlight?

Mary made a quick check of the time. This was her fault. She'd dithered too long over her note and overstayed her allotted time.

"Please excuse me," she murmured. "I lost track of the hour."

"No, no," Victor replied hurriedly. "You're welcome to stay as long as you like. I just, uh, wasn't expecting to see you." He shoved his hands in his pockets and shifted his weight from one foot to the other.

Mary had never seen this side of him. Ordinarily, Victor

exuded supreme confidence, walking into any room as if certain he could charm every person within. Which he could, from everything she'd seen. He made ladies sigh, and some men too. Important people listened to him. He could slip effortlessly into any group of any size.

Mary herself had been utterly charmed the moment they'd met, seduced by his impish smile and easy manners. Not letting it affect her behavior or decisions had been a daily struggle.

This face-to-face meeting had been inevitable, she had to admit. Ever since she'd begun to help with the mecha-man she'd been staying later each day. Some part of her had wanted this. And despite the uncertainty churning in her belly, she didn't regret that it had happened.

"I was just writing you a note about my changes to the sight sensor," she told him, waving a hand at the paper. "But I've been distracted by some outside issues, so it took me longer than I expected to finish."

Victor walked toward the worktable, his expression changing from surprise to concern. "Outside issues? Is there some trouble? It's not my father is it? He promised this laboratory was for my exclusive use, so he shouldn't have any say in who I invite—"

Mary held up a hand. "No, nothing like that. It's my husband."

A scowl flashed across Victor's features, but he quickly schooled it, slipping back into his usual facade of calm. A facade which appeared to hide deeper emotions than Mary would have guessed. Fascinating, how a change in circumstances could reveal things about a person that might otherwise have remained hidden.

She took an involuntary step back. If she was noticing new things about him, he might be noticing similar things about her. Sharing herself and her secrets was not on the agenda. Tonight or ever.

Her movement caused Victor to freeze. Blast. How could she explain it wasn't his presence she feared, but his insight?

She called up her own mask and turned to her best and favorite distraction: science. "Never mind Clay. He's nosing about at the copper works, is all. Let me show you what I did with the sensor. It will make far more sense than whatever rubbish I put on that paper."

Victor stepped closer, his hesitation so slight Mary wouldn't have noticed if she hadn't been attuned to his current state of discomposure.

"You've curved it!" he exclaimed, bending down for a better look.

"Yes. Because the sensors will be his eyes, I thought we could get greater coverage if we made them round instead of flat. Then we can press them directly up against the lenses and expose all parts equally."

"He'll probably have better peripheral vision than we do," Victor laughed. "Excellent thinking. He'll still be colorblind, but he should be able to see light and shadow and distinguish objects, if we get him all wired up correctly."

"Perhaps someday we can develop sensors that can better mimic the human eye. That can go on the future to-do list."

"Yes, that would be brilliant. Let's see—"

"Let me show you—"

Their hands collided as they both reached for the sensor at the same time. A spark of awareness shot up Mary's arm and she sprang back.

"Sorry," Victor mumbled, staring down at his hand as if her touch had branded him. Then his gaze lifted and their eyes locked.

Good heavens, he had beautiful eyes. Deep, mahogany brown and seemingly endless. He could hold secrets in those eyes. Or depths of passion usually reserved for characters in a gothic novel.

Several seconds passed before Mary realized she was staring, but even then, she didn't look away. He held her with that hypnotic gaze, keeping her in place not because she couldn't move, but because she didn't want to. And that was infinitely more dangerous.

"I'm so sorry," Victor said softly. He was speaking not of bumping her, but of his part in the hydroconductor debacle. The same words he'd said before, but with a vastly greater impact, now that Mary had seen his attempts to atone.

"I know." Her fingers itched to reach out and touch him, but that would be too intimate. Too far. Forgiveness was one thing. Opening herself to a deeper wound was an entirely different matter. "I should be going. It's dark and I ought to be home."

He nodded and stepped away from her. "Of course. I'll call for the car. You shouldn't be walking alone at night."

Mary moved to the exit and took her cloak down from the peg. "Thank you. That's very kind of you." A warm, quick ride sounded far better than a walk in the winter wind.

"Common courtesy." Victor pressed a button on the wall near the inner door, and a distant bell sounded. Mary's nose wrinkled. What else did this laboratory hide that she'd never known about?

She fastened her cloak around her shoulders, her gaze still on Victor, still slightly mesmerized by the memory of his ardent stare.

"Victor?"

He flinched at the familiar address, but once again rapidly composed himself. "Yes?"

Mary took a deep breath. The words came in a rush, tumbling out before she could think better of it. "I'd like to change the terms of our arrangement."

Chapter 8

Nary a Cloud

Victor allowed himself a few hours of sleep and several cups of coffee before setting out for the laboratory at the respectable hour of quarter to noon. It wouldn't do to look too eager. Correction: it wouldn't do to *be* too eager. Whatever this reconciliation was, it still didn't change the fact that she had never shown even the slightest susceptibility to his usual charms and was married to someone else. Working with her every day would be a constant reminder of what he could never have.

He rolled his shoulders and straightened his spine. "Bring on the torture," he declared. He'd managed to shift his feelings for Hal into a platonic friendship. Surely as a fully grown man, he could do the same with Mary. Taking a final fortifying breath, he strode off down the hall with a carefully cultivated confidence even his father couldn't object to.

"Victor. A word."

Speak of the devil.

Victor turned toward the sound of his father's voice. The older man waved a newspaper. "Poisoned apples," he said.

Victor's brow furrowed. "Pardon?"

"Poisoned apples. Caused over two hundred people to

fall ill and experience strange hallucinations at a wedding over the weekend. Would you know anything about that?"

Victor gaped at his father. "You think I would *poison* people? For God's sake, I'm your son! How can you think so ill of me?"

"I don't think you would do it intentionally, Victor." Edward Franklin tapped the newspaper against his opposite hand. "But you've had more than one project go awry in the past. And the groom in this case was Martin Pilz. You know him from school."

"I… Yes, I suppose." Pilz. Damn. Victor hadn't thought of him in years. The family was among Detroit's elite—his parents' social circle. The social circle Victor had promptly abandoned the moment he was away at college. He vastly preferred his less wealthy, more scientific friends.

"So?" his father prompted.

"So, I know nothing about it," Victor replied. "Pilz and I aren't friends, and as far as I know he's not even interested in science. Probably a kitchen worker didn't wash their hands. If people would pay more heed to the study of microbes—"

"You don't need to preach to me, son." Victor's father gave a nod and began to walk away. "I'm glad you had no knowledge of this. But if anything untoward *does* occur with you, I want to know about it *before* it appears in the papers. Understood?"

"Yes, sir."

Victor spent most of the rest of the way to the laboratory shaking his head. Where was this all coming from? One of his father's friends must have said something, because this level of suspicion was unusual, even for the esteemed Dr. Edward Franklin.

The door to the laboratory stood open, and Victor slipped inside without disturbing Mary, who sat with her head bent over the second of Mecha-Man's eyes. He allowed himself a moment to study her. People spoke of frowns as negative things, but clearly they'd never observed the little frown of concentration Mary wore when hard at work. It was bewitching, that frown. It pouted out her lower lip in a way that provoked a dozen fantasies of kissing. Her pale blue eyes focused on the project in her hands, gleaming with an intensity that made his heart stutter in his chest. If she ever looked at him that way, he'd surely melt.

Victor pulled the door closed behind him and leaned against the wall. He adopted his calm, casual persona, dampening the flames of his desires beneath his armor of cool indifference. Mary looked up.

"Mind if I complain a bit?" he asked.

Nice, Franklin, he scolded himself. *Very suave. Couldn't even begin with a "good morning"?*

"Not about me, I hope," Mary replied.

"My father. He's taken it into his head that I'm bent on causing trouble. He's bringing me every strange thing he reads in the papers, asking if it's my fault."

"Yikes." She gave him a sympathetic smile. "I'm sorry."

"He's a little obsessed with the family reputation, I'm afraid. I think he really wanted me to be a theoretical scientist and sit around all day in a plush armchair pondering the mysteries of the universe."

Mary patted Mecha-Man. "Soon you'll have a wonderful demonstration of your talents, and I'm sure he'll be proud of your achievements."

Victor shrugged. "Or he'll call it a big toy."

"Nonsense. Just think of all the benefits of an automaton of this nature! A mechanical man could do any number of jobs that are dangerous for people."

"Thanks." He let his mouth quirk upward into a half-smile. "At least someone appreciates my ideas."

"I think many people will appreciate your ideas, once you put them out in the world. The hydroconductor got positive press, after all, and it can be put to more uses than powering a mechanical fish."

Victor winced internally at the mention of the hydroconductor. Mary referenced it so casually, as if it had never caused the intense pain he'd witnessed in her that day. She was so damned resilient. Did anyone ever take her in their arms and comfort her? If only he were allowed to do so.

"Nemo loves my mechanical fish," he answered breezily.

"Really. An engineer building a giant submersible loves your fish? How surprising. I'm sure Dr. Finch likes it too. You'll have plenty of support, even if you can't meet your father's approval."

"Yeah." Victor tried to push off the melancholy. Some people had parents who were truly awful. And some had none at all. In the grand scheme of things, his problems were minor.

Mary bent back over the sensor. "Give me a few minutes to get these last wires in place. Then we can take it outside for a proper test."

"I'll go grab my overcoat."

By the time Victor had dashed to the front hall and back, Mary had finished up her wiring. She stood by the table with a fuzzy black hat pulled down over her blond curls and her cloak slung over her arm. The two completed sight sensors rested on the table, along with the control box that acted as Mecha-Man's brain. Victor buttoned his coat, pulled on a pair of leather gloves, and picked up the brain and attached eyeballs.

"Ready to go?"

Mary's cloak swirled and settled over her shoulders. She clasped it snuggly at her throat and nodded. "Ready."

Outside, the sun streamed down from a cloudless sky, bringing a touch of warmth to the late January weather. The temperature hovered close to the freezing point, Victor guessed. The cold didn't sting his cheeks much, and the thin layer of snow beneath his boots didn't squeak, which made it a gorgeous day, in his opinion.

"Beautiful weather," Mary echoed his thoughts. "We couldn't have asked for a more perfect day."

Victor grinned at her. He liked a person who could appreciate Michigan winters. One more log to heap on the pyre of his hopeless love. At least he'd stay warm.

They walked together past the grand carriage house to the equally large boathouse on the river. Most people with boats kept them at the marina, or at the Yacht Club over on Belle Isle. Not Victor's father. He'd built his house right on the water so he could sail in and out like a pirate captain with a smuggler's lair.

"Maybe my father is secretly a smuggler. That would explain a lot."

"Like how he could afford all this?" Mary waved a hand at the boat house.

"I meant like why he's so worried I'm going to get into trouble in some public fashion." Victor raised a hand to shield his eyes from the glare off the ice. "Is that a truck out on the river? Over there, on the Canadian bank."

"Could be. I saw something near that same spot the other day, as well."

Victor walked all the way to the water's edge, squinting at the icy river. "Well, if I were them, I'd get it off the ice. It's been too warm this week. You can see the water moving out there."

"Maybe they got stuck on the other side and are waiting for another cold spell so they can get back."

Victor gave her his best mischievous smile. "If we get another cold spell, I'm taking my electric car out on the river."

Mary cocked her head and raised one eyebrow. "I'm sure that will please your father," she said dryly.

Victor laughed so hard he almost choked. "Oh, Lord. This in-person business is so much better than before. Absolutely worth the lack of sleep. Whatever were we thinking to do it any other way?"

Mary stiffened. Dammit. He'd made things awkward. Now she'd be remembering why she hadn't wanted him around in the first place.

"Sorry," he added hurriedly.

She lifted one shoulder in a half-shrug. "Never mind that. You're right that it's nice to have someone to talk to. Let's get to work on those sensors. I think right here will do." She tucked her cloak carefully beneath her as she took a seat on the snow-dusted grass.

Victor lowered himself down beside her, adjusting his overcoat to ensure he didn't soak his clothing. Despite the sunshine, a cold breeze blew over them. He fought the urge to scoot closer to Mary for warmth.

Holding Mecha-Man's brain in his lap, Victor positioned the eyes toward the sun and then flipped the switch that connected the temporary battery. Mecha-Man had a bigger, far more efficient battery built directly into his chest, but for testing individual parts this was sufficient.

Lights on the brain began to flicker.

"Oh, it's working!" Mary passed a hand in front of one of the eyes, causing the array of lights to change as the sensor picked up different signals. "Fabulous!"

"You sound surprised," Victor teased. "Did you really think your project wouldn't work?"

A slight blush tinged her cheeks. "Well…"

"I'm always surprised," he admitted. "No matter what I do or how many things I've built, I never actually expect them to function."

Her airy laughter caused a hot flush across his skin, despite the cold. When she shifted closer he blew out a cloud of moist air, willing his body to relax.

Mary picked up one of the eyes and rotated it, beaming down at the machine as she moved it in and out of the shadows cast by their bodies. "I want to watch each of the indicator lights one at a time so we can be certain he'll be moving correctly in response to what he sees."

"Absolutely," Victor replied. "Have at it."

She slid even closer, her shoulder and thigh pressing against his as she worked. He wanted to put an arm around her. Could easily have done so. She deserved a hug, and he suspected she didn't receive one often. But he had no right.

Victor bent his head close to hers, joining in the testing and basking in her delighted enthusiasm. It was enough. His heart might always ache a bit, but he couldn't argue the truth of her earlier words. He couldn't have asked for a more perfect day.

Chapter 9

Quietly Into the Night

Mary stifled a yawn. Nine p.m. Goodness. She'd been working for nearly twelve hours, with few breaks.

The result was worth it, though. Mecha-Man was complete. Tomorrow they would start him up and take him outside for his first full test.

"And done." Victor snapped the last piece of the shell into place and straightened up, wearing his schoolboy grin. "Done! Can you believe it?" He bounced in place. "A full month ahead of what I'd expected. And all because of your help. Damn, what a team we make!"

Warmth crept over Mary's cheeks, turning them pink, no doubt. "I think our skill sets complement one another."

"A drastic understatement, my dear." Victor bounced again. "God, I just want to dance you all around the laboratory."

He spun in a circle to demonstrate. Good heavens, where did he get all his energy? He'd been working as long as she had, and had risen far earlier than was his custom.

"We should celebrate, at the very least," Victor went on. "Champagne? I can run and fetch a bottle from the wine cellar."

"No, thank you. I—" Another yawn rose, and this time she was unable to stop it. "Excuse me."

"Oh." Victor grew still. He checked his watch. "Oh. I'm sorry. It must be very late for you. I shouldn't have kept you so long."

"I wanted to stay. I'm glad we finished. But I *am* growing tired."

"Let me drive you home. The electric car could use a good outing." His grin returned. "And I promise I won't drive us out onto the ice."

Victor added a flirtatious lift of his eyebrows, causing an immediate fluttering in Mary's belly. He was too darned handsome. Too darned charming. She looked away.

"A ride would be welcome, thank you. I'll gather up my things."

Mary began to question her prompt acceptance the moment she saw Victor's electric automobile. Considerably less bulky than its steam-powered counterparts, the high seat and open construction reminded her of a horse-drawn phaeton. This was a car built for sport and speed rather than easy and safe transportation. Modify the tires, and it could zip around on the frozen river as easily as a boat on the water.

She took Victor's hand and stepped carefully into the passenger seat. "Why do I feel like an innocent debutante being whisked away to danger and seduction by a villain-ous rake?"

His lips quirked as he hopped up into his own seat. "No seduction, minimal danger. There's not even a steam engine to potentially blow up. Worst that will happen is we hit an icy patch on the street. I'll go slow, since it's dark."

"I appreciate that." She tugged her furry hat down to fully cover her ears as the car rolled out of the carriage house. A moment later, they were gliding down the street, smooth and soundless. "This is much nicer than an autocab," she had to admit.

"She's a beauty, isn't she? Light and quiet, without any of that steam or rumbling from a standard car. The downside is that she does have to be plugged in to an electrical power source to recharge the battery. So I can't go too far or I won't be able to get back home. But if you want a stealthy midnight jaunt…"

He turned that devilish smile on her again. Mary ran her hand over the dashboard, admiring the car to distract herself.

They drove on in silence, past docks and boats and into a more industrial area near the railroad depots. The copper works lay just ahead, her own modest house a few blocks beyond. Here, where the businesses and factories had closed for the day, the streets were quiet. Occasional streetlamps cast small pools of light into the moonless darkness.

Mary's gaze turned automatically to the copper works as they passed. As much as she liked Victor's laboratory, she still missed seeing the people at the factory on a regular basis and feeling she had some sense of how the business was faring. Lights winked at her from somewhere near the back of the building.

She seized Victor's arm. "Slow down."

The automobile slowed to a crawl. "What's wrong?"

"Something's going on at the copper works. It should all be shut down by this time of night."

Victor steered the car to the side of the road. "Do you want to stop and take a look?"

Mary hesitated. Technically, it was none of her business. But Mr. Gage and the other workers were concerned, and she couldn't bear the idea of seeing her grandfather's legacy fall apart because Clay did something foolish. She needed to know.

"Yes, please. If you can park the car in an unobtrusive location?"

The streetlamp gave off just enough light for Mary to see Victor's eyebrows lift. "So you mean to sneak up and spy on whomever is working?"

"Well… yes."

"Sounds intriguing." He drove around the next corner, then brought the vehicle to a stop. "This spot should do." He shut down the car, then popped open a small compartment in the dashboard. "And I'll bring my glow rod, in case we need to light our way."

"Your what?"

"Something Hal and I discovered in our college days. Mix a certain two chemicals together and they start to glow. We made little glass tubes with the chemicals in separate sections. If I push the button on the end, it pops the seal and the chemicals mix, giving me a glowing tube."

Mary eyed the small device. It would be interesting to see it in action, but she also would have liked to see it during the day when she could examine the mechanism in good lighting.

She climbed down from the car, putting aside thoughts of science to focus on the problems at the copper works. Everything else could wait until tomorrow.

"Let's go."

Mary led the way to the copper works, taking the longer way around the building to keep away from the entrance and the lights. As they neared the back of the building, she caught the faint sound of voices. She pressed up against the wall, peeking around the corner before ducking back under cover.

Victor stepped up behind her, leaning in to whisper. "What did you see?"

She shook her head. She couldn't be sure without a better, longer look. Once again she dared to stick her head out. The usual stacks of pallets and shipping crates lined the back wall of the factory. Beyond, shrouded in shadow, sat a dark-colored, steam-powered box truck with no obvious logo. Two men hefted a thirty-six inch cube crate into the truck while a third held a lantern. That task accomplished, they turned and headed into the factory through the rear door.

Mary tugged on Victor's sleeve, urging him to follow her. She slipped around the corner, moving as noiselessly as possible. Soft voices came from inside the building, but she couldn't make out any words, even after tugging up her hat to uncover her ears. Finding a shadowy gap between piles of empty crates, she hid herself once more. Victor squeezed in beside her.

"I gather they're not supposed to be transporting anything at night," he murmured in her ear.

She shook her head. "That's not the sort of truck we use."

Time crawled by, but the men did not return. Mary studied the truck. Even up close she could see no writing or distinguishing markings. Without the lantern shining on it, it nearly disappeared in the darkness. Finally, after what seemed an eternity, the men reappeared, carrying another crate. They loaded it onto the truck, then returned again to the building.

Victor gave her a nudge. "Let's see what they're putting in that truck, shall we?" He rose from his crouch and crept toward the vehicle. For a moment, Mary stood frozen in place, staring after him. She hadn't even had time to contemplate her next step and he was already charging ahead. Grabbing her skirts, she rushed after him.

When they reached the back of the truck, Victor bent and laced his hands together to make a step for her. This time, Mary didn't hesitate, letting him boost her up and into the vehicle. He followed right behind. A small *pop* broke the silence. An instant later, a dim greenish glow emanated from the small tube in Victor's hand.

Four unmarked crates sat in the center of the cargo box. Instead of the usual nailed-down lids, these crates were hinged and latched for easy opening and reuse. Victor moved behind them, knelt down, and undid the latch on the rearmost box. Mary crouched beside him, taking the glow rod from him so he could use both hands.

Victor lifted the lid to reveal nothing more than straw and wood shavings. He plunged a hand into the packing material and rummaged around, eventually producing a small glass bottle filled with a clear liquid. The bottle bore no label or tag.

"Curious," he murmured, and tucked the bottle away somewhere inside his coat. He reached into the box once more.

Outside, a shuffling of footsteps announced the return of the men. Mary shoved the glow rod beneath her coat to hide the light, and Victor lowered the lid of the crate. Together, they huddled as low as possible.

The next crate landed inside the truck with a *thump*. Wood scraped over metal as someone pushed it against the others. Mary clenched her muscles and held her breath. Who knew who these men were, or what they might do if they found her snooping?

Slowly, she let the air out of her lungs. She could wait this out. The men would leave to fetch the next crate, and she and Victor could sneak back to his car. They'd gotten a peek inside the crate, and Victor had a bottle. That would provide enough information for tonight.

One of the heavy metal doors on the back of the truck slammed closed, sending a vibration through the floor and up into Mary's body. A second later, the other door slammed, plunging the interior of the truck into darkness.

Oh, no.

"Fuck," Victor swore softly.

Metal clanged again as the bar lock fell into place, trapping them inside. So much for her plan.

Chapter 10
Going Where

The truck rumbled and shifted beneath them. Victor swore again. And again. Why did he have to be such a goddamned fool, flinging himself into action before giving even the slightest thought to the consequences? No wonder his father expected him to be in constant trouble.

"Sorry for the language," he mumbled, shifting to sit on the floor of the truck. "Sorry for all of this." He waved a hand at the interior of the truck, lit by the faint greenish light of the glow rod Mary held.

"I'm sure it seemed a good idea at the time," she replied, surprisingly calm for someone who'd just been trapped inside what was likely a smuggler's vehicle. "It's not as though I tried to stop you."

"I don't imagine you have any idea where they might be taking us?"

"None."

Silence descended. The truck bounced along, its steam engine huffing faintly outside the metal walls. Mary picked at a loose thread on her cloak, her face eerily pale in the green light. Victor's arms twitched with the desire to hug and comfort her. Not that she needed it. She didn't cry, didn't tremble, didn't even complain. Her stoic acceptance was almost as terrifying as the situation.

Victor turned to the back wall of the truck, running his hand over the metal. Unlike some trucks, this model had no door or window to open into the driver's cab. Whoever was on the other side might still be able to hear if he knocked, though.

"Don't," Mary warned.

Victor swung around to face her. "Don't what?"

"If you're thinking of making noise to alert them, don't. We have better options."

"Wait until we stop, then jump out at them when they open the door?" he suggested. "With the element of surprise, we'll easily knock them down and have time to get away before they can even think to guess who we are."

She glanced up at the ceiling. "Or we can hide behind the crates and sneak out the way we snuck in."

"Not as fun, but sensible."

"I like sensible," Mary said stiffly.

"Yes, I know."

A long pause ensued before she asked, "Are you cold?"

Victor frowned. "No. Why?" All the excitement had his blood pumping. At the moment, the overcoat seemed almost unnecessary.

"This truck isn't much warmer than outside," she pointed out. "We might want to sit closer together to conserve heat."

Right. There was that sensibleness again. Mary was a small woman. She probably got cold easily. She slid towards him.

"Or we could keep moving," Victor blurted, before she could touch him. "Do more digging through the crates. See what else we can find."

Mary pushed up on her knees, then stood, bracing herself against the crates to compensate for the sway of the truck. "Good idea. But one crate at a time. We don't want to be caught with them all open when we stop."

Victor refrained from pointing out that they might not stop for hours. He popped a crate open and they both reached inside.

Within a quarter of an hour, they had inspected each of the five crates. All of them held unlabeled bottles of various shapes and sizes, liberally padded with straw and wood shavings. Nothing that could tell them more. All the activity did was keep them occupied and warm. Very warm, in Victor's case. Every time he accidentally grasped Mary's hand instead of a bottle, another burst of heat flashed through him. If her touch had affected anything else the way it did him, the entire truck would have burst into flames by now.

He sat down atop one of the crates. Mary hopped up beside him, her feet dangling above the floor. She scooted up against him, and this time he did put an arm around her, tucking her close to his side.

"Warm enough?" he asked.

"For now. Thank you."

Victor checked his watch again. Time was all but meaningless when the journey had no definite end in sight, but for some reason he felt the need to know how long they'd been here.

"At least the ride is still smooth," he remarked. "That means we're still on well-kept roads." The truck bounced as it turned a corner. "Unfortunately, I lost track of our turns ages ago, so I couldn't say what direction—"

The crates shifted beneath them as the truck slowed abruptly. It bumped around another corner, then came to a stop. Moments later, the engine shut down, letting off a hiss of steam.

Victor and Mary slid down to hide behind the crates once again, and Mary tucked the glow rod out of sight.

"Let them offload the first crate, then sneak out?" he whispered.

"Wait until after the second crate," she replied. "Then we'll know better how much time we have."

Outside, the cab doors opened and closed as the men exited the vehicle. Victor strained to make sense of the muffled noises, trying to determine how many men might be there. The same three who had loaded the truck? The murmur of voices suggested at least two.

The sounds quickly faded. Victor held as still as possible, barely breathing. Mary had pressed against him, but for once the sensation brought only comfort. They were still together. Still safe.

Silence fell. Victor prayed the men didn't return with too much additional help. If more than one crate was unloaded at a time, it would upset their escape plan. Damnation. If everything went to hell, he'd fling himself at whomever was out there and give Mary a chance to run to safety.

Minutes crawled by.

"They're not coming back," Mary whispered.

No. No, this couldn't happen. They had to come back. There had to be a way out of this truck. Victor clambered up and over the crates, shoving at the double doors that locked him in. They didn't budge. He pushed again, harder, but all that caused was a faint rattle.

"Victor." Mary's voice was sharp, but the hand that touched his shoulder a moment later was soothing. "We're trapped until someone opens the door. We'll have to make the best of it."

He spun around. She looked so pale in the light of the glow rod. Pale and small and fragile.

"We'll freeze," he blurted. Without the engine giving off heat, the temperature of the truck would drop steadily.

No. No! She would not die here because of his folly. He would not allow it.

Victor raised his fist and hammered on the door. "Let us out!" he shouted. He pounded again, ignoring the pain shuddering through his fist with every furious blow. "Let us out, goddammit!"

Before he could strike the door again, Mary grabbed the back of his coat and hauled him backward. He flailed, grasping at air, then toppled to the ground, sending one of the crates skittering.

"They're gone, Victor." Mary knelt at his side. "We're trapped here until they return. But we're dressed in warm layers and we can huddle together."

Victor scrubbed both hands across his face, fighting the panic. She was right. He had to think about this logically. Sitting up, he pushed the crate he'd moved back into place. It slid easily.

He bolted to his feet. "We have insulation!" He grabbed the crate, opened the lid, and tipped it on its side, spilling the contents onto the floor.

Understanding immediately, Mary jumped in to help, digging out all the straw and shoving the bottles to the side. Together, they emptied all five crates, building a nest of packing material in the back of the truck. Mary loaded all the bottles back into the empty crates, positioning the boxes as close to their original locations as possible.

"There," she declared. "We can huddle in the nest for warmth, and we'll remain hidden for whenever they return." She let out a long breath and her shoulders slumped. For the first time that evening her supreme composure had cracked.

Victor unbuttoned his overcoat and tugged his arms

free, leaving it dangling from his shoulders like a cape. "Here." He took hold of her arm and drew her toward his chest. "I'll lie down and wrap my overcoat around us both. Then we'll put your cloak over the top for another layer and burrow down into the straw."

Mary nodded and let him guide her into the nest. A bit of adjusting, and they were wrapped together in their impromptu bed.

"It's not so bad," Victor murmured, mostly to himself. In fact, it was wonderful. Incandescently glorious. Mary lay fully atop him, her head pillowed on his chest, her whole body crushed to his. Even through the layers of clothing, he could feel the shape of her curves. He kept his arms wrapped snugly around her, holding them together while trying not to be confining or presumptuous.

He had apparently succeeded, because she gave an exhausted sigh and wriggled a little, trying to snuggle even closer.

"Are you warm enough?" Victor asked. He snaked one hand out from beneath their garments and heaped more packing straw atop them.

"Yes, thank you. I think we will be safe." She yawned. "But I'm sleepy."

Again she wriggled, rubbing her whole body against his as she made herself comfortable. Desire coursed through him. His cock stirred.

Oh, God.

Wonderful was now also horrifying. He could not, would not, be a lecherous oaf on top of all his other sins this evening.

"I'm so sorry," he mumbled. For everything.

"You couldn't have known," Mary replied, her voice

thick and weary. Her fingers brushed the hairs at the nape of his neck. "We'll be fine. You're nice and warm."

Cold, Victor thought. *Ice. Snow.*

He needed something boring to focus on. Something that would never in a million years excite either his mind or his body. Like those boring speeches he'd had to read in Latin years ago. Cicero.

Ovid.

Dammit. That's what he got for sneaking looks at the *Ars Amatoria* instead of memorizing dull political oratory. He stared up at the ceiling and willed his body to relax and behave.

Within minutes, Mary's breathing had slowed to the soft rhythm of slumber. Now and then she would give a little sigh and snuggle against him. Beautiful torture.

Victor remained wide awake, not having yet adjusted to the daytime schedule. Perhaps it was for the best. He could watch out for her and make certain she stayed warm as the night grew colder. It was his duty, as the instigator of their troubles. And it didn't matter how painful or difficult it was for him.

All those times I wished to hold her in my arms... Clearly, I should have been more specific.

It was going to be a long night.

Chapter 11

There's Only One Truck Bed

Mary twisted, trying to ease the discomfort of her corset boning digging into her side. Why had she allowed herself to fall asleep fully dressed again? The air above her was chilly, but the bed beneath was warm and smelled of machine oil and cedarwood soap. She wanted to burrow into it.

No. Not the bed. The man.

Memories of the night before came back in a rush. The copper works. The smuggling. The truck.

For a long moment, Mary lay motionless, grappling with everything that had happened. The long day and the peculiar ordeal had left her exhausted. Now she lay in a nest of straw, wrapped in Victor's arms, feeling the slow rise and fall of his chest as he breathed. She turned her head to the side, pressing her ear to his chest, and listened to the steady beat of his heart. Despite the chill in the air and the uncertainty of their situation, she felt safe here. Protected.

She needed to get up. Now.

Carefully, she slipped from his grasp and climbed off him, readjusting his overcoat so he was completely covered and wrapping her cloak around her. She shivered at the loss of his warmth, but it wouldn't do to let herself go all mushy over a man, no matter how comforting his body and his scent.

She checked her watch. The light of the glow rod was fading, but still provided enough illumination to move about the truck, and when she held it close to the watch she could read the numbers. Twenty past six. The sky would be lightening. Would someone be coming to fetch the crates, now that day was approaching?

She couldn't let them catch her unprepared.

While Victor slept on, Mary began repacking one of the crates, piling straw into it and stuffing the bottles down into the center where they wouldn't rattle or break. When the crate was sufficiently filled, she pushed it around the others, positioning it closest to the door. She moved on to a second crate. She was dismantling their warm nest, and Victor would grow cold, but he needed to wake up soon anyway. The more crates they could restore to their original condition, the better their chance for escape. They could never entirely hide the evidence of their overnight stay, but the more they could delay discovery, the more opportunity they would have to sneak out.

Less than halfway through packing the second crate, her ears pricked up at the sound of crunching gravel outside. Footsteps. Approaching.

Muttering a not-very-nice word, she rushed to close up the crate and scurried around to the back to wake Victor. She knelt in the straw beside him and shook him gently, her other hand poised to cover his mouth if he tried to speak. He shifted and stretched, his lashes fluttering as his eyes opened slowly. Long, pretty lashes, framing gorgeous, dark eyes.

"Don't make a sound," she whispered, determined to focus on the things that mattered and not the way the sight of him made her long to rub her body all up and down his. She caught another whiff of his scent and her skin tingled in response.

Victor blinked at her, his expression one of groggy confusion.

Mary lay down beside him, checking that they would be hidden behind the crates. She put her mouth nearly up to Victor's ear to keep her voice as low as possible. "They're coming. I repacked one crate. After they unload it, we sneak out."

He continued to frown, but eventually nodded. He shifted enough to stick his arms through the sleeves of his overcoat, then settled himself back into the pile of straw, holding completely still.

Outside, the men had begun talking. Mary couldn't distinguish words, but the tone sounded casual. They weren't expecting anything unusual.

The bar lock clanged open and she jumped. This was it. If her preparations worked, they would have a brief time in which to exit the vehicle and run for cover. If not… Mary had no contingency plan. She wasn't and never had been a fighter, and all she had were the clothes on her back. Her heart began to pound, and she clenched her fingers on the wool of her cloak.

The truck doors opened, one at a time. The first crate was within easy reach of the back of the truck, and Mary prayed they'd grab it without climbing up into the vehicle.

Wood scraped over metal. They were sliding the crate out. She sent up another prayer, this time of thanks.

"Help me out with this," a man said. "It ain't heavy, but it's damned awkward."

"I got it," a second voice replied.

They started off with the crate, the crunch of their footsteps growing quieter as they walked away from the truck. When she couldn't hear the sound any longer, Mary dared to poke her head out. She could see nothing in the pre-dawn light but an empty lot and the building beyond.

She nudged Victor. "Now."

He still looked sleepy, but he responded to her command, getting to his feet and climbing around the crates to hop down from the back of the truck. Mary scampered down beside him. Her eyes darted back and forth, taking in their surroundings, looking for any place to hide. The building in front of them was a plain brick factory, not unlike the copper works. A faded sign reading, "Simpson Fine Soaps and Lotions," hung over the door.

Beyond the building was the road and a grassy field. Not ideal for hiding, with the grasses dormant and packed down with snow.

Before she could consider any other option, Victor darted around the side of the truck. Mary raced after him. Wherever they hid, they needed to stick together. She didn't want either of them becoming lost all alone in the cold in an unknown location.

Instead of running toward any possible hiding place, Victor stopped at the front of the truck, threw up the hood, and bent down to fiddle with something. Was he warming up the engine?

"Why are you starting the truck?" she hissed.

He didn't look up. "We need a quick escape. Thank God the pilot was left burning. Hop up into the cab, check the gauges, and flush the cylinders if it hasn't been done already."

Mary climbed up into the cab of the truck. If nothing else, it was a temporary place to hide, and the boiler was quiet enough that no one was likely to notice until the engine started chugging. She checked the gauges. The water level was sufficiently high. Already, the temperature was rising steadily and pressure was building. The system was flushed and ready. She turned a few knobs to prepare for departure. Nice of Victor to assume she understood the machinery.

"You can't really mean to steal this truck," she insisted, when he joined her a moment later.

"We need to get away. Do you have a better idea?"

She didn't. Unfortunately. He was absolutely right about the need to escape, and trying to walk back to the city sounded worse than borrowing the truck.

The problem was, even a modern truck like this one would take time to heat up, and she had no idea how much time they had to spare. As the needles crept up the dials, she waited, listening for the sounds that would mark the return of the smugglers.

"What in hell's the point of all this anyway?"

The distant grumble of voices jarred Mary from her fixation on the dashboard controls. She straightened up, then quickly ducked down below the level of the windows. Victor remained where he was, sitting calmly behind the wheel, eyes on the gauges.

"Hide the bottles, send the boxes back," the approaching man went on. "What's the point? Isn't it all just perfumes and things for the soaps?"

"I don't know what the point is, and I don't care," a second voice growled. "It's none of our business. We do the job, we get paid. That's all I care about."

The men tromped closer. Mary glanced at the pressure gauge. Not high enough to drive away. And when the smugglers pulled out another crate, they'd know something was wrong. She wiped sweaty hands on her cloak and willed herself to breathe.

"Come on." Victor's whisper was nearly inaudible. He ran a hand gently over the dashboard. "You can do it."

So they'd reached the talking-to-inanimate-objects stage of desperation. Mary closed her eyes, mentally cataloging anything in and around the cab of the truck they might employ as a weapon. Her list was uncomfortably short.

The truck bounced suddenly. One of the smugglers had climbed in the back to retrieve the next crate. The scrape of the box along the floor was accompanied by the faint tinkle of glass.

"What the devil?" the smuggler exclaimed. "This one's packed wrong."

The truck shifted again as man and box exited the truck. Mary's eyes flew open, checking the pressure again before looking to Victor. He shook his head.

She placed a finger on the dial, a few ticks higher than the needle's current location.

Victor shrugged.

"It's not even half packed," complained one of the smugglers.

"Stupid oafs couldn't do it right," the other man agreed. "Check the next crate."

Again, the man's weight sent a slight vibration through the truck. Another crate rattled. Silence fell. Victor gripped the steering wheel with one hand, the throttle with the other.

"It's a goddamned mess in here!" the smuggler cried. "Like somebody dumped out all the crates on purpose."

"What? Let me see?"

Mary winced. Now both men were in the back of the truck. Any second and they'd put the pieces together.

"Looks like someone was sleeping here," one smuggler remarked.

"Sleeping? Well, then, where is he now?"

A long silence fell, followed by thumping and swearing. The instant the sound of rubber boots grinding into gravel hit Mary's ears, the truck lurched into motion, throwing her back against the seat.

"Hang on," Victor instructed, swinging the vehicle into a hairpin turn. Mary clung to the seat as the truck slewed precariously. In the cargo hold behind them, crates and bottles tumbled and smashed.

Through the window, she caught a glimpse of the smugglers, waving their arms and shouting. They were too late. The truck flew away from the factory and down the road, its bulk no challenge for the massive amounts of torque the engine produced.

"Atta girl," Victor said, patting the wheel. A triumphant grin spread across his face. "At this speed we'll be home in no time."

"At this speed we'll blow through the fuel and water before we're inside the city," Mary argued, her gaze once more on the controls.

Victor leaned out the window and glanced behind them. "I want to make sure we're far enough ahead they can't follow us. Then we can ease off a bit. Any guess where we might be?"

"West of the city," Mary replied. "By several miles, I'd say. Head south until we see the river, then follow that."

"All roads lead to Detroit?"

"Right now I certainly hope so." She shifted over to the window and stuck her head out to check behind them. Already the soap factory was fading into the distance. Any car starting after them now would lose them after a turn or two. She slipped back down into her seat. "We should make a plan."

Victor's mouth twitched. "Plan away, my dear Mrs. Clay."

"We drive into the city only far enough that we can hail a cab or ride the trolley and leave the truck there," Mary declared, thinking aloud. "Fetch your car from where we left it and drive back to your house. Put everything away, and shut ourselves in the laboratory. If anyone asks, we were there all night, and we should instruct your staff to say the same if anyone inquires. Once we're settled, we write a few messages to people who can be trusted and find someone who can analyze the substance in that bottle you stole."

"The apothecary Hal uses," Victor suggested. "Robert, I believe his name is. He'll have everything we need and he's discreet. But there's a flaw in your plan."

Mary blinked, then gave him a puzzled look. "There is?"

"If we tell people we were together all night, they *will* get ideas. Salacious and potentially harmful ideas. Perhaps we should revise our story to say I drove you home, I returned promptly, and you rejoined me very early this morning. We can leave out the part about your remarkably similar outfit and the bits of straw clinging to it."

Reflexively, Mary brushed a hand over her skirts. "Yes. Good thinking. We'll tell everyone exactly that. See, this is why planning is an effective strategy. It allows us to find and correct errors before they are implemented."

Victor stared straight out the window. "Mmm-hmm."

Her gaze drifted back and forth between him and the pressure gauge, now holding steady. "Sometimes your quick thinking is a good strategy, too. It allowed us to escape the mess we were in."

He didn't look at her. "I put us in it. Least I could do was get us out of it. And I'm sure there's some massive flaw in this idea of mine."

Massive flaw. Like the one that remained in her plan. No matter what they intended to tell people, they *had* spent the entire night together. In a shockingly intimate fashion.

And she'd liked it.

Chapter 12
Partial Truths

Smoke billowed from Mecha-Man's joints as he seized up once again. Mary grabbed one arm and Victor the other, guiding the automaton to the ground before it toppled. A few stray snowflakes floated down to land on the metal man, melting the instant they touched warm brass.

"Even out here in the cold he overheats," Victor lamented. "It's hopeless."

Mary wasn't ready to be quite so fatalistic, but she, too, had had enough for one day. "Let's take him back inside. We'll regroup tomorrow and determine our next steps."

Testing Mecha-Man hadn't provided the happy distraction she'd hoped for after last night's wild adventure. Since the moment they'd started him up that morning, he'd been overheating, no matter what adjustments they made.

Victor gripped the automaton under the arms, and Mary took hold of his legs. Together they carried him back into the laboratory and placed him on the table.

"Flawed. A completely flawed design." Victor fell heavily onto the stool. He looked close to tears. "Even with all the space for air circulation. He'll never work. I'm going to have to start all over."

Mary's heart lurched at Victor's stricken expression.

The urge to turn away and give him privacy warred with the urge to hug him.

Turning away won. She would have to be a fool to stray even further into inappropriate territory.

"You don't need to start over," she declared with more confidence than she felt. "We'll think of something. But not today." She fetched her cloak and wrapped it around herself. "I need to return some books to the library, and you need some rest. When was the last night you slept for more than a few hours?"

"I'm not sure," he admitted.

"Get some sleep and your brain will be all recharged for tomorrow. You'll think up some brilliant solution, I'm sure."

"Maybe." He ran a hand through his hair. "Do you need a ride?"

"No. I'll walk and then hop on the trolley. But thank you."

Their gazes locked and held for several seconds. Something had shifted between them overnight. They were a team now, in a way they'd never been before. They'd shared an adventure. Shared a bed—of a sort. Shared the oddly soothing experience of picking straw from one another's hair and clothing to hide the evidence. Mary wasn't sure what this new connection meant for the future, but she knew it couldn't be undone.

So far no one had questioned her whereabouts last night, but the servants at Franklin Castle would know she and Victor had been out together. Word could spread. Her reputation could be in jeopardy.

Mary looked away from Victor and reached for the door. She'd deal with problems of that sort if and when they arose.

"I'll be back in the morning. Hopefully you'll dream up something brilliant tonight."

He let out a little huff. "Right."

Mary opened the door, but before she could step out, he called her name. "Yes?" she asked, looking over her shoulder.

"Thank you. For all your help."

"My pleasure." She offered him a comforting smile, then departed, hoping he'd take her advice and get some rest. She intended to turn in early tonight as well. A proper night's sleep in a proper bed—alone—was a necessity if she wanted the mental and emotional capacity to consider all the strange happenings of the last twenty-four hours.

Mary missed catching a trolley by seconds, but chose to wait for the next to come along rather than walking. She needed to ride all the way home to fetch her books before going to the library, and walking would slow her even more than waiting. Either way, she was late for her usual Thursday visit for the first time since Mrs. Finch's Ladies' Lending Library had opened.

"Mary! Hello," Callie called out when Mary at last walked through the library door and plunked her returns down on the counter. "I'd begun to wonder if you weren't coming."

"I got a bit of a late start, is all."

Callie's eyebrows twitched. "Got caught up with Victor in the laboratory, did you?"

Mary ignored the innuendo. As a former courtesan, Callie was relaxed and open about her sexuality and happy to discuss such topics with anyone. Mary could never be so free and easy with her own private life. She tended toward the awkward and embarrassed, and preferred that no one ever discover her intimate secrets.

"Our project was having some technical difficulties," she explained. "But we'll find a solution soon enough."

"With both of you working on it, I'm sure you will."

Was that another innuendo? Mary couldn't tell. The librarian always had an impish smile, and the one she wore now wasn't any different.

"Is there anything I can help you find today?" Callie asked. "We've gotten a few new novels in this week."

"Actually, I had a non-library question for you. We need to have something analyzed, and Dr. Franklin said your husband knew an apothecary who might be able to help us?"

"Oh, yes. Mr. Robert. He's a good friend and extremely competent. What is it you need analyzed?"

"An unlabeled substance we found at the copper works," Mary replied, keeping her words truthful without revealing too much.

Callie glanced around the library, then leaned closer. "A suspicious substance?" Her eyes gleamed with excitement. "You must tell me more. What happened? How did you come across it? Is there anything I can do to help?"

"I stumbled on it by chance." Close enough to the truth. And this time Mary had remembered to say "I" and not "we." She didn't need anyone, even her friends, knowing what had happened last night. It was between her and Victor and no one else. "I'm afraid my husband may be involved in a smuggling operation."

Callie straightened up, her lips parting in a surprised gasp. "Oh, dear."

"Yes."

"I'm so sorry. Here, let me write down the address of the apothecary for you. Just tell Mr. Robert that the Finches sent you and he'll help you with whatever you need."

"Thank you."

"My pleasure. Anything else I can help with?"

Mary smiled at her friend. "Not unless you know a good

way to cool off a metal man." She tapped a single finger on the counter as she thought. "Cooling from the outside didn't work. If he were a house, I'd say he could use my air cooler, but… Oh!" She clapped a hand over her mouth as the idea formed.

"Thought of something good?" Callie grinned. "I've seen that same expression on my husband's face a time or two."

"Yes, and I know just the book I want to grab." Mary bounced on the balls of her feet. "This is perfect. I've got to get to work making notes. Thank you, Callie!"

Mary waved at her friend and rushed off into the stacks. Mecha-Man would soon walk the streets. She had the answer.

* * *

Victor stepped through the front door of the club and handed off his hat and overcoat to the man at the cloakroom door. A small mechanical device rolled over the rug where Victor had wiped his feet, sucking up the dirt and snow. He fought off the urge to glare at it. No need to be jealous of automatons that worked, simply because his own didn't.

Mary was right. He ought to be at home, in bed, catching up on all the sleep he'd missed lately. The exhaustion had percolated through his system, leaving every muscle with a slight, dull ache. Or maybe that was the result of a night lying awkwardly in a bed of straw in a freezing truck.

Victor headed downstairs to the bar and ordered a single glass of Old Tub bourbon. This would be it for the night. Any more and he'd probably fall asleep here at the club and get written up as a troublemaker. God knows he didn't need that.

On his way up to the usual haunt of the Mad Scientists Society, Victor passed card players puffing on cigars and philosophers searching for enlightenment at the bottom of their glasses. In the library, a group of young men tinkered with a machine of indecipherable purpose. The atmosphere here usually brought Victor a sense of comfort. Today, he only felt tired.

Mary was *definitely* right.

He stepped into the alcove to find Hal and Nemo in conversation.

"I would expect you to be unusually sensitive to any such rumors," Nemo was saying. "Given what happened last year. But that doesn't mean you're wrong."

"It's worrisome, is all," Hal replied. "Finding strange substances at the same time we're reading about poisoned apples in the papers."

Victor winced. Not that again. "I had nothing to do with the apples," he insisted.

Hal and Nemo both looked up at him.

"I never meant to imply you did," Hal said. "But you seem unusually defensive about it. Want to sit down and tell us what's going on?"

Victor typically spent most of these gatherings standing, but today he grabbed a chair and put it between the others, making a semi-circle in front of the hearth.

"Sorry. My father was certain I had a connection to that apple incident, all because I knew Pilz from years ago. Made me a little twitchy."

"You don't have enough interest in chemistry to do anything that might poison people accidentally," Hal replied. "And you'd never do it on purpose. We know you're not the culprit. But you could have an unintentional connection. What if that unlabeled serum you found is the poison?"

Victor's eyebrows shot up. "That… what? What the hell makes you think I found anything at all?"

Hal sipped his tea. "I talk to my wife."

"And how would she know what I have or haven't found?"

Victor knew the answer, even as he asked the question. Mary had been talking about it. Everything Victor knew of her proclaimed her to be a highly private person. But Callie Finch was a friend, and potentially a trusted confidant.

"Mrs. Clay was looking for a referral to your apothecary?" he guessed, before Hal could say anything. Victor sincerely hoped that was all Mary had talked about. He didn't want his friends knowing the lurid details of last night's adventure. They didn't need to know the trouble his impulsive behavior had caused. Most of all, Victor didn't want to share the private time he'd spent with Mary. Nor did he want to dwell on why that might be.

"Yes," Hal confirmed. "Callie told me Mrs. Clay is looking to analyze an unidentified substance found at her family's factory. It was implied that you and she had found it together."

"Yes, we did." Victor swirled the bourbon in his cup, not drinking it. He wanted to confirm the information Mary had already imparted without adding too much. But how, when he couldn't know what she'd said?

"Sounds like you two had an adventure," Nemo observed. "How did you come to be at the factory with her? I thought she was avoiding the place because of her odious husband."

"The odious husband she suspects of smuggling," Hal added.

"What?" Nemo's brows rose in surprise. "Did she tell Callie that? Usually she avoids saying anything about him at all. As if she'd prefer no one remember he actually exists. He must be making a real nuisance of himself."

Victor stared down into the amber liquid at the bottom of his glass. Or else Mary would rather focus on Clay's offenses than last night's misadventure. Dammit. He had to remember that he was the only one who would jump at the chance for another night snuggling in a freezing truck.

"He might be, yes," Victor said. "I was driving her home, and she spotted lights at the factory after hours. We stopped for a look and saw some unknown men moving things about. I snatched a bottle because it looked like smuggling. I have no idea who they are or what they might be doing. But I'd hate to see Mrs. Clay come to any harm because of this. I suggested we analyze the substance in hopes that it would tell us more, and I mentioned Hal's apothecary friend."

Victor clamped his mouth shut. Dash it all. Had he said too much already? His story sounded woefully incomplete. Any fool would know he was holding back.

Hal and Nemo both appraised him for a time, probably considering all the holes in the story and how best to push for further details.

Hal shook his head, then spoke. "I'm not going to bother asking about all the things you're obviously not telling us. But you want my advice? Stay out of it. If you find out that serum is at all suspicious, hand it over to the police and walk away. Don't go back to the factory, don't let anyone know you suspect something. Return to your work and stick to that. And suggest to Mrs. Clay that she do the same."

"Right. Thanks." Victor nodded as if he agreed, but his insides churned. He was too late to stay out of it. The men unloading the truck had to have seen him and Mary as they drove away, even if only briefly. Clay wouldn't have any difficulty guessing the petite blond woman to be his wife. And apparently, it was common knowledge where she went every day and whom she was with.

God-fucking-dammit.

Now Victor had even more to atone for.

Chapter 13
A Slippery Slope

Nine a.m. was an odd time for Victor to be both awake and feeling refreshed, yet here he was. He'd stumbled home from the club after a disheartening recounting of the troubles with his mechanical man, fallen into bed, and slept for ten hours straight. A part of him wondered if someone had dosed his bourbon with laudanum.

The long sleep and a hearty breakfast had left him in a peculiarly chipper disposition, despite the troubles of the day before. Mary had been right about needing rest. Maybe her belief that they'd find a solution would prove true as well. Certainly, he was ready to get down to work. That had to count for something.

Mary was, as usual, hard at work when Victor stepped into the laboratory. She had opened Mecha-Man completely, exposing all his innards at once. In her hands, she held a thin copper pipe, bent into a peculiar serpentine shape. Carefully, she worked it down in between Mecha-Man's internal components and adjusted the placement.

"Good morning," she greeted Victor cheerily. She reached for the soldering iron. "You're looking refreshed."

Victor nodded. He must have looked like hell yesterday, to be so changed she would remark upon it. He couldn't recall her mentioning his appearance at any time in the past.

Then again, she was very proper, and would avoid saying anything that might be considered too forward. Maybe she'd become comfortable enough around him to move past such restrictions.

Or maybe he really had looked like hell.

"What are you working on?" he asked.

"A water cooling system, inspired by my air cooler. Fill it with cold water, which is pumped through pipes that run to all parts of his body. As the water moves through the system, it picks up the excess heat, then runs through a radiator which disperses that heat out into the air. I'm thinking we'll put the radiator up by his mouth. He'll seem to breathe out warm air, just like we do."

Victor stared at her, wonderstruck, unable to think of words suitable to express his admiration. He walked closer and peered down at her work, marveling at the elegance of her solution. Her slim, dextrous fingers moved with practiced ease, joining the pipes and securing them in place. The desire to have those same fingers moving across his skin surged to life, as strong as it had ever been.

"You're brilliant," he breathed.

She looked up abruptly, a blush turning her pale cheeks a rosy pink. "Thank you. I'm happy to have found a solution." She reached for another length of pipe and began bending it, holding it above Mecha-Man to get the curves exactly right.

Victor pulled up a stool and sat beside her. "Why on earth are you wasting your brain on my projects? I should be assisting with yours."

Mary shook her head. "I like your projects. They're fun. I like that science doesn't have to be dry and boring. It can be fanciful and unique. You're good at dreaming up those ideas."

Victor was one hundred percent certain she was more

fun, fanciful, unique, and beautiful than anything else he'd ever seen. He wanted to buy her flowers and books. To kiss her until she sighed and make love to her until dawn. Most of all, he wanted to know how Augustus Clay could be such a colossal fool that he couldn't appreciate her magnificence.

Mary blushed even redder under the weight of Victor's stare. He hurriedly looked away.

"Sorry," he muttered. "I'm rather in awe of your skills *and* the fact that you're willing to use them to improve my ideas. I didn't mean to embarrass you."

"It's fine. It's only that I'm unaccustomed to admiration."

"You shouldn't be," Victor replied adamantly. "You deserve to be admired every day."

Admired. Loved. Adored. I would praise you every day, if you were mine.

He hopped up from his seat, using the pretext of gathering some additional tools to put a safe distance between them. Every day he spent with her he loved her a little more and his control slipped a little further. He couldn't afford to do something rash. He'd already caused enough trouble.

Victor didn't even know if she was safe here. Would she be better off somewhere else? He hated to endanger her reputation. But he couldn't leave her alone if physical danger was a possibility. Not now, not ever.

He took up a new seat at the opposite side of the table, with Mecha-Man between them. Following her directions, he began bending and fitting pipes. With the work to occupy his hands and his mind, his worries faded. His body, though, could never be entirely at ease. Every time her hand came close to his, he tensed in anticipation of a touch, both fearing and craving it.

Despite this, the morning quickly became one of the

happiest in recent memory. Time seemed to fly by. All too soon the hands on the wall clock had moved past noon and Victor's stomach had begun to rumble. Mary paused in her work, stretched, and rubbed her neck.

"I think I'm ready for a break," she said. "How about you?"

"Absolutely. Would you like some lunch? I'd be happy to take you out for a sandwich. We can stop at the apothecary after and have our mystery substance analyzed."

She beamed at him and his breath caught in his throat. "That would be lovely, thank you. And I do want to get to the apothecary sooner rather than later."

Shortly thereafter, they were comfortably settled at a small table in an ice cream parlor with a light lunch of soup and sandwiches. Mary chatted on about her plans for the radiator portion of the water cooling system, her face alight with scientific excitement.

Victor nodded and made occasional sounds of agreement. He had to concentrate to keep from twisting around in his seat. Why hadn't he had the sense to pick a corner table? In their present location, he had his back to almost the entire room.

Intellectually, he knew the patrons behind him had their own concerns. They weren't staring at him, waiting for him to accidentally expose his feelings and embarrass Mary in public. Still, he couldn't escape the prickling sensation crawling up his spine.

To make matters worse, the only people he *could* see in the restaurant were a young couple at the next table over. They gazed adoringly into one another's eyes, taking full advantage of a rare socially acceptable location for them to be together, unchaperoned.

"What do you think?" Mary asked.

"I have nothing to contribute at the moment," Victor replied truthfully. Even if her idea did have a flaw in it, he wouldn't be able to find it given his current state of mind.

Her animated expression faded, and a tiny crinkle appeared between her eyebrows. "You seem distracted." She leaned across the table, almost too close for propriety. "Are you worried about that bottle in your pocket?"

"A bit." He gave her his customary smile to reassure her. "But don't let that keep you from your scientific musings. I like seeing you excited about your work."

She dropped her gaze. "I do tend to become over-enthusiastic about things that spark my interest."

"Appropriately enthusiastic, I'd say." He'd embarrassed her. Damn. And all he'd meant to do was compliment her. He picked up what was left of his sandwich to avoid saying anything else.

"Thank you." Her eyes still didn't meet his. "I love the work we're doing. And I'm grateful to have something to focus on besides my husband's suspicious behavior."

"Agreed."

Unfortunately, they couldn't avoid that topic forever. Lunch was soon over, and they departed on foot for the apothecary shop, both of them quiet and sober.

Mr. Robert, a tall Black man with graying hair and a bright smile, waved them toward the counter the moment they entered.

"Dr. Franklin, isn't it?" he greeted Victor. "I was told you might be stopping by."

Victor shook the man's hand. "Thank you. This is Mrs. Clay."

The apothecary gave Mary a slight bow. "A pleasure, ma'am. What can I do for you?"

"We need an unknown liquid analyzed," Mary explained. "Mrs. and Dr. Finch recommended you."

Victor placed the small bottle on the counter. Robert picked it up and examined it for a moment, then popped the cork and sniffed.

"Hmm," he murmured. "Follow me."

He led them into a back room filled with racks of ingredients and a long, narrow workbench. An array of cups, vials, droppers, and spoons lined the small wooden shelf just above. Robert poured out several small samples of the mystery liquid, then began to add ingredients, one by one.

On the third try, the liquid turned a bright red and began to bubble. Victor bit back a curse. He recognized that reaction all too well.

"Oh, dear," Robert fretted. "You've found yourself a bottle of Sobridyne."

"Sobridyne?" Mary blurted. "Isn't that illegal?"

And with good reason. The nasty mixture of cocaine, laudanum, castor oil, creosote, and tobacco—and God knew what else—had proven both addictive and highly dangerous.

"Not yet in Canada, I'm afraid," the apothecary sighed. "Too much of it sneaks across the river."

Mary looked up at Victor. "Wasn't Sobridyne the drug discovered in Becher's Tonic Water last year?"

He nodded, his jaw tight. "Yes."

Mr. Robert dumped the remainder of the Sobridyne into a bowl and added a few ingredients. He let it bubble and smoke for a few seconds, then poured the mixture down a small sink at the end of his workbench.

"That will take care of that. I suggest you contact the police and tell them where you found this bottle. Hopefully they can put a halt to the smuggling."

"I hope so too," Victor replied. Once more he shook the apothecary's hand. "Thank you for your assistance."

"My pleasure. You youngsters take care. We've had strange things happening around here of late."

"We will, thank you," Victor assured him. He motioned for Mary to lead the way, and they headed for the exit.

"Sobridyne," she murmured once they were outside. Her hand clenched on the edge of her cloak, wringing it between her fingers. "How could he do something so foolish?"

Her entire body vibrated with agitation. Victor walked as close as he dared, cursing the rules that wouldn't let him comfort her. He couldn't even ask if she wanted comforting. All he could do was stand by helplessly while she wrestled alone with her grief and fear.

Damn the rules.

"What can I do to help?" he asked. "What do you need? Do you want to go to the police? A train ticket out of town? A bodyguard? A hug?"

She spun around so suddenly Victor sprang back in surprise. His left foot hit a patch of ice and skidded. In the split second before he lost his balance, Mary's hand shot out and grabbed hold of his coat. It was enough to keep him upright, but not enough to prevent him from stumbling. Right into her.

Their bodies collided. Instinctively, Victor caught her in his arms.

They stood there, frozen, bodies molded together the way they had been in the truck. But this time they had no excuse for remaining like this. No excuse but the wild desire pounding through his veins.

Mary's chin lifted, her pink lips parting slightly, her blue eyes fixing on his face. On his mouth. A tilt of his head and he could kiss her. Taste her. Show her how much he ached for her.

His head dipped toward hers. Slowly. Inexorably.

"Victor," she gasped.

Cursing internally, he tore himself away from her and took a deliberate step backward, this time watching his footing.

"I beg your pardon." His voice was too low, too lusty.

"O-of course." Once again she began kneading her cloak in her hands. "It's slippery."

"Yes. I'll hail a cab. Take you home."

She gazed at him a long moment, her blue eyes riveting him to the pavement. "I'd rather go back to the laboratory," she said at last.

Victor nodded, not trusting himself to speak. He needed to get away from her, needed space to recover from the fact that he'd been a breath away from kissing her. He'd use the ride home to think up excuses to take himself somewhere else.

When he stepped out of the autocab in front of Franklin Castle, however, he still hadn't thought up a single damn one.

Chapter 14
Coping Mechanisms

Mary threaded the piece of copper piping down into Mecha-Man's arm, joining it at the wrist with its mirror image. Excellent progress. They would have most of the piping installed by the end of the day.

Victor slid the soldering iron across the table to her without a word. They'd settled into a rhythm this afternoon, working in parallel, saying very little. With her mind and hands busy, Mary could contain the agitation roiling inside her. Work was comforting, familiar. She would work through dinner and late into the night, if that's what it took to calm herself. No thoughts about going home. No thoughts about Clay and his smuggling.

She straightened up, rubbing her neck to keep it from tightening up. Across the table, Victor concentrated on the pipe bender in his hands, making precise adjustments to the setting.

No thoughts about their near kiss in the street.

If that's what it had been. Part of her believed it must have been nothing more than her fevered imagination. The other part…

The other part kept reliving the memory over and over. His flushed cheeks. His liquid brown eyes boring into hers. His lips so close she could feel his breath.

In that moment, it had seemed so inevitable, so right.

So foolish, she chided herself. To succumb to his charms in the middle of the street? Thank goodness he'd had the presence of mind to pull away. If his lips had met hers, only God knew what might have happened.

Mary reached for another length of pipe. Breaking from work, even for a moment, led to entirely too many unwanted thoughts. She snapped off the metal covering for Mecha-Man's left leg and threw herself once again into the world of science. Everything else slipped to the back of her mind.

"Aren't you hungry?"

The question, coming some indefinite amount of time later, startled Mary from her trance-like focus. She looked up into Victor's fathomless eyes and all the nervous butter-flies came fluttering back. The man was so blasted beautiful. Drat, drat, drat. Hours of work and none of her worries had subsided. They'd only been pushed temporarily aside.

"Hungry?" she repeated. Now that she said it, her stomach did feel a bit empty.

"Yes." She wouldn't have called Victor's expression troubled, but the corners of his mouth bent the slightest bit downward. "It's nearly seven. My stomach has been churning for an hour. If you swoon from hunger in my lab-oratory because I didn't provide dinner I'll never forgive myself."

On an ordinary day she would have interpreted such a statement as a joke, but this evening he lacked all signs of his usual humor. He was anxious too. Hopefully about the Sobridyne and the smuggling and not about the not-a-kiss.

"Ah. Yes. Food would be welcome," Mary replied evenly. "I don't need a substantial dinner. Something small will suffice."

"I'll have something brought in." He walked over to

press the button that rang the bell. A short time later, a knock sounded at the door.

"A light supper for myself and Mrs. Clay, please," Victor requested.

The servant nodded and departed.

"Do you intend to keep working after you've eaten?" Victor asked Mary. "Or are you finished for the night? I appreciate your determination to complete the project, but I'd hate to see you overexert yourself. I can drive you home at any time."

"Yes," Mary murmured. She kept her eyes on Mecha-Man. It was easier to avoid thinking about kissing Victor when she didn't look at him. The other topic she'd been avoiding, however, had to be addressed. "I..." She paused, took a slow breath, and composed herself. "I don't feel comfortable going home at the moment."

Victor cursed softly. "You're worried about Clay."

"The house belongs to him, and he does have a key. Knowing he's involved in something dangerous..." She shivered.

Victor was at her side in an instant. "Stay here. I'll drive to the house and fetch anything you need. We have plenty of rooms. You can stay as long as you like."

The offer was tempting. Acutely tempting. Despite her foolish attraction to him and her frustrations with his habitual lack of forethought, she felt safe with him. She would sleep easier knowing he was nearby. But it would not make her increasingly complicated life easier.

"I can't stay here. I'm already around you too much as it is. People are talking. I know they are. We were lucky our adventure the other night didn't draw notice. We won't be lucky forever. And even though your parents are here, my staying in the house overnight would be a step too far.

I bend the rules by being a scientist. I need to maintain my reputation if I want to continue pushing those boundaries."

Victor rubbed his hand across his brow. "You're right. There must be another way. I won't let you go anywhere alone if there's a possibility of danger. Maybe you could stay with a friend." His eyes brightened and he smiled. "Hal and Callie! They have room. We'll go there straight after dinner."

A weight eased inside of Mary. Yes. The Finches would welcome her. She would feel safe with them. And as much as she hated to impose on anyone, she couldn't go home. Not until she had a better idea of what exactly Augustus Clay had gotten himself into.

"Perhaps you might telephone Dr. Finch to ask first?" she suggested.

Victor shook his head. "Hal doesn't have a telephone. He hates machines. It doesn't matter. They won't mind."

Which was how Mary found herself standing on the front porch of the Finch townhouse at nine p.m. with several bags of clothes and other necessities. Despite the surprise appearance, the housekeeper quickly ushered Mary and Victor into the front parlor and offered them tea or brandy.

"Nothing for me, please," Mary replied. Tea would only make her more jittery, and she never drank anything as strong as brandy.

"Brandy," Victor said at nearly the same time. "A large glass."

Dr. Finch appeared a minute later, carrying a tray with a crystal decanter and four glasses. Callie followed close behind. Dr. Finch set the tray on a side table and poured out a glass for Victor, then one for his wife and one for himself.

"Are you certain you won't have any?" Callie asked Mary. "It might help settle your nerves. You must be worried for you to have come here so suddenly."

Mary eyed the decanter of amber liquid. "A small glass, perhaps." It couldn't hurt to try a bit, especially since Callie was drinking as well.

Callie poured out a portion that to Mary's mind was much larger than "a small glass" and handed it over. Mary took a careful sip.

She had expected the brandy to burn, but instead it felt smooth down her throat. The drink had a deep fruity base beneath the strong bite of the alcohol. Surprisingly pleasant. The burn did come, a second or two after she swallowed, but it wasn't nearly as harsh as she would have guessed. She dared to take another sip.

"Tell us why you've come," Callie urged. She and Mary settled side-by-side on the sofa, and the gentlemen moved armchairs to sit facing them.

"We visited the apothecary this afternoon," Mary explained. "The mystery liquid was Sobridyne."

Dr. Finch jumped and his brandy sloshed. "Not again!" He glanced at his wife. "That swill nearly killed us both."

Mary nodded. "You can see why I'm concerned. I don't know if my husband knows what he's smuggling or how deeply involved he is. But he's meddling with dangerous things and it's possible he knows I've discovered that."

Those men unloading the truck had likely seen her and Victor as they drove off. She wouldn't be hard to identify, and Clay would be furious that they'd disrupted the transaction. Her fingers tightened around her brandy glass. Fully explaining her concerns would mean divulging details of that night she preferred would remain private.

To her great relief, neither Callie nor Dr. Finch pressed for more information.

"Mrs. Clay shouldn't be alone in a house Mr. Clay can

access at any time," Victor insisted. "And she can't stay with me. So I suggested she come here."

"Sensible," Callie agreed. "I would be worried, too, in your position. I wonder if Mr. Clay had any connection to the incident last summer. Do you think he could have been Becher's supplier?"

"Then what is he doing now?" Victor wondered. "Supplying someone else? Shipping long distance? Didn't Becher go off to California or someplace?"

"Yes." Dr. Finch took a gulp of his drink. "And then died shortly after in a crash when the boiler in his steam car exploded. The circumstances were noted to be peculiar at the time. They're seeming even more suspicious now."

Mary, too, took a larger sip of her brandy. She needed that sensation of warmth and the relaxation the drink brought to her muscles.

"Clay isn't a murderer," she declared, though she wasn't one hundred percent certain of that. "He's selfish and greedy, but I can't imagine him going to all the trouble of killing someone thousands of miles away. Too much work and planning. He prefers the easy way. And he only recently took charge at the copper works. If he'd been smuggling for years, why change to doing that now? I think this must be a recent development."

"He's a minion, then," Callie guessed. "He's working for someone else. Which means maybe Becher was also working for someone. Some mastermind who's using greedy men as part of what can only be a nefarious scheme."

The four of them looked at one another, not speaking. A heavy weight seemed to settle over the room. Mary took another drink of her brandy, surprised to find it was almost gone. Dr. Finch rose and without a word began to refill everyone's glasses.

Victor broke the silence. "Who hired Clay? And for what purpose? Will the Sobridyne begin showing up in other foodstuffs, like it did in Becher's Tonic Water? Is this connected to that damned poisoned apples incident?" He ran a hand through his hair. "My father is going to kill me."

"Have you gone to the police yet?" Dr. Finch asked.

Victor shook his head. "Not yet. But I'll send them a note tomorrow."

Mary stiffened. They couldn't simply divulge all the sneaking and truck-stealing they'd done. They had to have a straightforward story as close to the truth as possible. "We will tell them the workers reported concerns about activity at the factory after hours and then we found a suspicious bottle out back. I can ask Mr. Gage to write down on paper the things he told me, if that would help."

"I'm sure it would."

Mary sipped more brandy. Callie had been right. It was helping settle her nerves. She didn't like the idea of going to the police, but she wasn't panicking about the prospect, either. It made sense to involve the authorities.

And she had to do something. She couldn't let Clay destroy the copper works through some foolish, illegal money-making scheme. Not only was the copper works her family legacy, it was the source of her income. Her livelihood depended on it, as did those of all her employees. She had to protect it.

The conversation turned from speculation about the smuggling to the practicalities of Mary's visit to the Finch household. She'd brought enough clothing for a week, but naturally Callie offered to let her stay indefinitely.

"I will pick you up every morning and drive you back at night," Victor said, in the most commanding voice she'd ever heard from him. "Don't walk or take the trolley until we're certain it's safe to do so." He caught her gaze and held it, his expression uncompromising. "Don't even think about it. Your safety is the absolute top priority."

Under ordinary circumstances, Mary would have objected to being told what to do. Tonight, she couldn't even utter a word of protest. The ferocity of his concern was making her stomach do strange flip-flops. She'd known he was worried. He'd been tense since the apothecary. But right now he looked ready to wage war on her behalf. And that thought was at least as unsettling as the fact of her husband's criminality.

"I won't go anywhere alone," she promised.

All her friends nodded their approval.

By the time the conversation wrapped up with thank yous and farewells, Mary had finished her second glass of brandy. The room didn't quite sway when she stood, but her legs were definitely less steady than usual. Perhaps she ought to have eaten more than a small salad for supper.

The group walked to the door to see Victor out. He shook Dr. Finch's hand, tipped his hat to Callie, and then turned to Mary.

"I will be here at eight a.m. sharp. I promise." He stared at her face for what felt like an abnormally long time, though it couldn't have been more than a few seconds. Somewhere in the back of her mind lurked a sense that she should have been embarrassed by the intensity of his gaze. She wasn't. She returned the stare with equal ardor, lingering on his lips, remembering how close they'd come to hers. Wondering what he would taste like.

Victor tipped his hat again and gave a polite nod. "Good evening to you, Mrs. Clay. I will see you in the morning." He turned and hurried out the door.

"You must be tired after your long day," Callie said once the door closed. "Let me show you up to your room."

Mary nodded. She was definitely tired. Tired, achy, and a bit tipsy. The tipsy was nice, though, because it hid her worries away behind a pleasant haziness. They couldn't reach her. She could be happy for a while. But also a little sad, because Victor had gone and she could no longer gaze at those pretty eyes and that kissable lower lip.

The stairs were difficult. Strangely tall, perhaps, or unusually narrow. Mary had to concentrate on each step, her hand gripping the handrail.

"Are you all right?" Callie wondered. She took hold of Mary's arm. "Too much brandy? Did you eat supper this evening?"

"Only a salad. But it's fine. The brandy was nice. I feel warm now."

"Mmm-hmm."

The stairs ended abruptly, and Callie had to steady Mary as they stepped into the oddly swaying hallway.

"I think I'm a little tipsy," Mary observed, the words a touch slurred.

"I think you're a lot tipsy," Callie replied. "But you're almost to bed, so not to worry. I'll help you with your buttons and things."

The two women entered a room at the end of the hall. Mary's bags sat at the foot of a lovely, large bed. It looked cozy. Like Victor's warm body in the truck. Except this bed probably didn't smell like oil and cedarwood. She giggled.

"I'll help you with your buttons and corset laces, and then you can get some rest," Callie assured her. Her nimble fingers made quick work of the fastenings. Which was good, because Mary's own body didn't seem to want to work right now. In fact, all it wanted to do was curl up in that bed.

The moment she was down to her shift and drawers, she climbed—stumbling a bit—onto the bed and burrowed beneath the blankets.

The sheets smelled of laundry soap. Victor's smell was nicer. It was too bad he'd gone away.

"I should have kissed him," she sighed.

"Victor?" Callie's voice asked from somewhere in the vicinity of the doorway.

"Yes. I bet he tastes nice. I almost tasted him."

Callie's laugh was soft and gentle. "There's always next time. Goodnight, Mary."

"Night," Mary mumbled.

The door closed with a gentle snick.

Chapter 15
Try, Try Again

He needed to stop hovering. Victor forced himself to take a step back while Mary made the final adjustments. No one was going to hurt her here. He had no excuse for being so… nannyish.

He'd been entirely too forward yesterday. Yes, her situation carried the potential for danger. But that was no excuse for ordering her about. He was not her husband, nor any relation to her. Protecting her was not his duty.

If I don't protect her, who will?

Victor flexed his fingers. There was the catch. She'd been too alone, for too long. She deserved a champion.

And if she doesn't want one?

Mary set down her screwdriver and reached for the large metal plate that would cover Mecha-Man's torso. She snapped it in place, checked that it was secure, and nodded. Done. And without a word of satisfaction.

Victor bit his lower lip. Mary was always a quiet person, but today was abnormal. She'd made a few remarks regarding the specific wording of the missive they'd sent to the police that morning. She'd asked him to hand her a tool or two. Nothing else. No observations on her work. No excitement over her accomplishments. She was ill at ease.

Ill at ease around *him*. Victor cursed his foolish behavior for about the hundredth time that day. Why had he let himself get so close to kissing her? Why had he stared at her so long and so often? He'd made her uncomfortable.

She turned to face him, frowning. "Well?" she asked.

He blinked. "Well, what?"

She gestured at Mecha-Man. "He's done. Do you truly have nothing to say? Aren't you at least a little bit excited?"

"I…" Victor's mouth couldn't form words. All day he'd been fretting that she wasn't talking. Worrying over the silence. A silence he could have broken at any time. If she was unusually silent, what did that make him? Extraordinarily silent? Mind-bogglingly silent?

He ran a hand through his already untidy hair. "Sorry. I'm… a little off today."

"Up too early?"

Their eyes locked for a moment, and Victor had to tear himself away before he once again stared inappropriately.

"Yes." *Among other things.* "But I am pleased with our progress. Let's take him out for a test."

"He's going to work this time," Mary vowed.

Together they hefted Mecha-Man from the table and carried him out the door. They stood him on a clear, flat section of the stone path that ran along the side of the house, his legs apart for good balance. When he was steady, Victor took a small key and slotted it into the hole at the back of the neck.

"Here goes nothing," he murmured, and turned the key.

The machinery started up with a gentle whir. Mecha-Man's mouth opened, expelling a small cloud of steam. He took a single step.

Victor checked his watch. The slim second hand moved smoothly across the face. No immediate overheating. Mary's cooling system was working.

Mecha-Man took a second step and exhaled again. He paused, his head turning left and then right.

Victor's heart leapt. His creation was working. It was moving and looking around on its own!

He dug his nails into his palms. He couldn't celebrate prematurely. Perhaps they would get minutes instead of seconds, but a thousand other tiny things could still go wrong.

Mecha-Man turned slowly in a circle, looking here and there. He paused when his artificial gaze fell on Victor.

Victor raised a hand and waved.

Mecha-Man's arm stretched upward, his fingers uncurling. He waved back.

"Oh, my God." Victor's hand shot out toward Mary, as if needing her to steady himself. His good sense kicked in before he could touch her and his hand froze in midair, then dropped to his side.

Mecha-Man mirrored the movement. His head bobbed up and down, taking in Mary.

She clapped her hands.

He clapped.

She crossed her arms.

He did the same.

"Let's take a walk," she declared, starting off down the path toward the front of the house. Mecha-Man followed.

Victor snapped out of his stupor and hurried to join them, watching from a few yards away. Mecha-Man walked smoothly—no tripping or balance problems, no creaking or grinding of parts. He didn't falter, didn't spark, didn't smoke. As he walked, he continued to breathe out small puffs of hot air. Mary's cooling system was magic.

"Oh, my God," Victor blurted again. "Oh, my God, he's working!"

Mecha-Man slowed, turning toward the sound. He looked at Victor, raised a hand, and waved.

Victor staggered. "We did it. My God, we did it. He's alive!"

Mary walked over, her mouth curved in a wide smile. "Well, he's operating and seems to be learning. But he's still a machine."

"Alive-ish," Victor amended. But he couldn't stop an ear-to-ear grin from forming. He bent down and picked up a rock from beside the pathway. "Catch." He tossed the stone to Mary, and she caught it easily.

She tossed it right back, needing no explanation. After a few times back and forth, Victor turned to his creation.

"Here you go, Mech. Catch." He threw the rock and the metal man snagged it out of the air. A moment later, he hurled it back at Victor.

The flying stone stung Victor's palm when he caught it. Mecha-Man didn't know his own strength. That would need some work. But it couldn't dampen Victor's excitement. He wanted to jump up and down for joy. He wanted to spin Mary into a celebratory dance. They had done it. They had really, truly done it.

"You are so brilliant," he gushed, beaming at his marvelous scientific partner. "A simple, ingenious cooling system, and he's off without a hitch! And he's balanced and moving and doing everything right, and it's all because of you. My God, I could—" *Kiss you.*

Mary moved closer. "Could what?" She looked up at him, blue eyes sparkling, cheeks flushed. From the cold, naturally. Not from bashfulness and certainly not from arousal.

Victor couldn't look away. No matter how he'd berated himself for all the staring yesterday, he'd fallen back into the same trap. She was just so fucking glorious. He was powerless to resist.

"I want to hug you," he admitted. "I want to haul you into my arms and dance up and down the street in celebration."

Her blush deepened. For a moment, he thought she might back away and give him a thorough tongue-lashing. But then she stepped right up to him, wrapped her arms around him, and crushed her body against his.

"I'm so happy for you," she murmured.

Happy couldn't begin to describe Victor's own feelings in that moment. She had catapulted him into some new plane of bliss. She'd joined in his work, fixed his man, and now she was holding him in her arms. Holding him like she cared. Looking up at him as if she genuinely wanted him to bend down and taste her tempting lips.

There was definitely a reason he shouldn't be doing that, but right now damned if he knew what it was.

"Mary," he breathed.

She opened her mouth to say something, but her words were lost beneath the furious snarl of a new voice.

"Get your filthy hands off my wife!"

Chapter 16
Throwing the Gauntlet

Victor went stiff as a board beneath Mary's hands. She relaxed her grip on him and turned to face the scoundrel who called himself her husband.

"Augustus." She kept her tone even, though she couldn't force a smile. "We were merely celebrating a remarkable achievement." She waved a hand at Mecha-Man, who mimicked the gesture. Perhaps it was a good thing her impulsive embrace had been interrupted. It would have been awkward if the automaton had decided to join in.

"You were engaged in an indecent embrace with your illicit lover in a public space," Clay retorted.

Victor glared at him. "The embrace was only friendly, we're not lovers, and this is private property. You're not welcome here. Go away."

"I have a right to come here and claim my wife. It's reprehensible, the way she's been carrying on with you. Practically living here, under the guise of 'scientific research.' An appalling pastime for a lady, even if it were true."

"It *is* true. She helped me build *him*." Victor picked up the rock again and tossed it at Mecha-Man, who caught it and threw it back. "Mary is a genius, and I refuse to allow you to slander her."

"That's 'Mrs. Clay' to you, you arrogant cad."

Victor huffed. "No." He folded his arms across his chest. "No, I think not. I think she deserves better than your foul name."

"Enough!" Clay stalked toward Mary. "Mary, you're coming with me."

She skittered backward to avoid his grasping hand, knocking into Mecha-Man. The automaton attempted an awkward backward shuffle of his own, but slipped and fell to the ground, his metal body clanging against the pavement. Victor rushed over, and together they hauled Mecha-Man back to his feet.

"No more fooling around with ridiculous giant toys," Clay snarled. "No more sneaking about at night. No more turning my own employees against me. I'm taking you away from here and you're not coming back, is that understood?"

"No." Again, Mary stepped away when he tried to grab her arm. "You don't get to touch me."

Something inside her had snapped. Maybe it had happened when Clay had booted her out of the copper works. Or perhaps when she'd discovered his smuggling scheme. Maybe it had only happened last night, when her brandy-loosened tongue had blurted out hidden feelings.

She was tired. Tired of holding back. Tired of bottling up her rage and frustration. Tired of keeping herself so tightly controlled she felt she might explode. How much of her tirade at Victor all those weeks ago had been anger at him, and how much the weight of too many unexpressed emotions? No more.

"You're my wife," Clay retorted. "You have no choice in the matter."

She had plenty of choices. Maybe none of them were perfect, but they were there. He had already stolen one laboratory from her. She wouldn't let him take this one, too.

"Oh, I'm your wife am I?" she shot back. "You clearly have an extremely loose definition of the term. Tell me, Augustus, is there a single marriage vow you *haven't* broken yet?"

"You're a fine one to talk, you insolent slut. Spending day after day alone with—"

"I have done nothing wrong," she interrupted. "Nothing. I've given you every courtesy you didn't deserve. Though it hardly matters. I've never been your real wife. You stopped pretending to want me the moment the ink was dry on the contract. So why the sudden interest in this sham of a marriage? I can only assume it's because I've become an inconvenience to you."

"I have every right to—"

Mary talked over him. "It's time to be done with this. You don't like me and I don't like you. I'm not asking anymore. I'm demanding. I want a divorce."

"No."

"Say whatever you want. You've been neglectful, adulterous, and cruel. I'm filing for divorce whether you like it or not."

Victor stepped up to Mary's side. "And keep in mind, she has plenty of friends willing to assist with legal fees if you decide to cut off her funds. I suggest you give the lady what she wants."

Clay ignored him, keeping his attention solely on Mary. "I'm afraid I cannot agree to any such thing. All I want is for you to be home where you belong."

Mary squared her shoulders. "The only way I'm stepping foot in that house again is over your dead body."

Clay kicked at a stone on the ground, sending it bouncing along the path to stop at Mecha-Man's feet. The metal man peered at it, then kicked it back. The rock struck a bump in the pavement and shot upward, smacking Clay in the temple.

Clay yelped in pain. "That monster attacked me!" He clamped a hand over the wound. "Just you wait, Mary. You'll be sorry you ever defied me." He spun around and dashed off, muttering curses.

"Bastard," Victor growled.

Mary's shoulders sagged. It had been satisfying, standing up to Clay, but it had taken more out of her than she'd expected.

"I can't understand it," she sighed. "He dislikes me. Maybe even despises me. Why not agree to a quick divorce? What does he stand to lose? It would be *my* reputation ruined, not his."

"The man is an ass," Victor replied. "He can't handle not getting his own way."

Mary shook her head. "It's more than that. He needs me for some reason. He ignored me for so long, the way he ignored the copper works. Now he insists on controlling both it and me."

"The smuggling."

"It must be." She rubbed the back of her neck. "He wants me locked away in the house because he's afraid I know something."

"Well, he's not wrong about that."

"I don't know enough, though. I need to look into the books for the copper works. I need to unravel his scheme before it drags the company and myself down with it."

"I'll take you there anytime you like," Victor replied. "But you shouldn't go alone. And if you ever need to leave Hal and Callie's, my offer for you to stay here remains. Better scandalous than in danger."

Mary smiled at him. "Thank you." She hugged him

again, though only for a second before letting go. Even that brief contact sent waves of desire coursing through her body. Curse her inconvenient attraction. Why did it have to get out of hand when so many other issues needed her attention?

Mecha-Man extended his arms and reached for Victor. Victor yelped and dodged, narrowly avoiding being crushed in a mechanical embrace.

"Careful, there, buddy." He stepped behind the automaton and turned the key to shut him off. "Let's make some adjustments before you go hugging people." He gestured at the laboratory door. "Would you like to join me, Mrs. C—" He broke off, frowning. "What's your family name?"

"Amesbury."

"Well, then. Would you like to join me in the laboratory, Miss Amesbury? We can talk divorce papers and industrial espionage while we tweak our boy, here." Victor's smile was as charming and roguish as any Mary had ever seen. Her knees went weak.

"Thank you, Dr. Franklin," she replied, slightly breathless. "I'd like that very much."

Chapter 17
Papers, Please

Shit, shit, shit.

Victor snatched up the newspaper before his father could get a look at it. He took a seat at the dining room table and did his best impression of a man who habitually began his day with coffee and the morning paper. He probably looked ridiculous. Maybe he could arrange to spill the coffee all over the paper before anyone questioned his abnormal behavior.

"Good morning, Victor," his father greeted him. He pulled out a chair for Victor's mother and they both sat.

Victor took a large swallow of coffee to avoid replying. The hot liquid burned the roof of his mouth, but the pain hardly registered. The printed headline near the bottom of the front page mocked him.

Local Factory Owner Attacked by Mechanical Man

"It's *so* nice to have you joining us for breakfast in the mornings," Victor's mother cooed. Gweneth Franklin was, as always, impeccably turned out. Her loose morning dress could have come straight off the pages of a Paris fashion magazine, though no one would ever see it, since she would change before going out or receiving any visitors. Even at this early time of day, her hair had been pinned up into a terrifyingly complicated confection of twists and curls.

Victor lowered the paper momentarily. "Good morning,

Mother. Father." He nodded to them, then went back to reading.

Detroit businessman Augustus Clay fell victim to a peculiar accident yesterday, while out for an afternoon stroll. The owner of Clay Copper, Ltd. was walking down Atwater Street, when a humanoid automaton assaulted him. According to Mr. Clay's report, the monstrous creation had the look and proportions of a man, only made of brass and steel.

"It came stalking toward me," Clay said, "staring me down with hollow, empty eyes, devoid of any human feeling, looming over me, as malevolent a machine as I've ever encountered."

Fortunately, Mr. Clay escaped the harrowing encounter with only a minor gash to the temple and is now resting comfortably at home. He cautions all citizens of Detroit to be on the lookout for dangerous automata and implores any scientists or engineers working on such projects to keep their work safely locked away and to reconsider the consequences of "playing God."

Victor wanted to crumple the paper in his fist. That lying bastard! He wouldn't get away with this. They'd find proof of his smuggling and see him behind bars.

"You see, Edward, dear? I knew he would outgrow that working at night nonsense," Victor's mother said. "It was merely a holdover from his school days."

Victor gulped more coffee. He hadn't outgrown it, he simply wasn't sleeping much any more. Hence the coffee. He didn't even particularly like coffee, but he needed its stimulating effects. He folded the paper to hide the offending article and stabbed a piece of sausage, though he didn't have much appetite.

His mother beamed at him across the table. "It's good to see you taking a responsible approach to your life. I hope this means you're thinking of settling down. I would like to see you married to a nice girl."

Victor forced down a bite of the sausage. If this was what he could expect from a typical morning, he'd never rise before noon again. By "nice girl" his mother no doubt meant "rolling in money and trained from birth in the arts of hosting elaborate parties and dressing to impress." Which was fine for someone whose life revolved around the social whirl of Detroit's most prestigious families. Victor's only social activities were the meetings of the Mad Scientists Society, and he preferred it that way. Besides, he'd already met the lady he wanted.

A momentary fantasy flitted through his mind of Clay in prison and Mary happily clutching an official notice of divorce. Which, unfortunately, led to Victor imagining his mother fainting when he told her he was courting a divorcée.

And what if Mary wanted nothing to do with marriage ever again? He'd hardly blame her if that were the case.

"Not planning to marry any time soon," he mumbled, quickly shoveling another bite of sausage into his mouth.

"You should introduce him to Hackenburg's daughter," Victor's father suggested. "She's a brainy girl. Victor likes the smart ones."

"Yes, like that friend of his," his mother agreed. "Miss Majhi, isn't it?"

Victor picked up the newspaper again, as if it could shield him from the conversation. The last thing he needed was for his parents to begin prying into his relationships with his schoolmates. Certain points of that history were not fit for polite society.

His father cleared his throat. "What's in the paper today, son? Something caught your interest?"

Dammit.

Victor pulled out his pocket watch. "Oh, dear. Look at the time. I'd better run or I'll be late picking up Miss Amesbury. Good day!" He hopped up and hurried from the room, leaving his breakfast behind, but taking the newspaper with him.

As he rushed down the hall, he just caught his father's voice in the distance. "Who the deuce is Miss Amesbury?"

* * *

"You want to go to the copper works *now*?" Victor stopped the car only a few feet from where he'd started. He twisted in his seat to frown at Mary. Though frowning was difficult when she looked so adorable in her fuzzy hat with her cheeks turning pink in the cold air.

"Yes. Mr. Gage told me Clay has been staying after hours, which makes sense if he's interacting with the smugglers. It also means he won't be there early in the morning. We should be able to get in, look through the books or take some of them with us, and leave. He'll never know we were there."

"And you don't want to leave the matter to the police? They did tell me patrols in the area would be increased."

"But what if the smugglers start taking more care to go unnoticed? We don't have enough information for the police to act yet. We need to keep investigating."

She needed to know for herself, Victor suspected. She didn't trust men, and that included the police. Hell, it even included himself.

"Very well," he allowed.

"Thank you. This," she tapped the newspaper, "suggests we need to act quickly, to stop him before he does anything else damaging."

Victor had to agree with that. He nodded. "And he won't have much luck contesting your divorce claim from a prison cell."

Mary's gaze fell to her lap. "I hope not." She sighed. "I'm so ready to be done with it all."

"I'll drive you to a lawyer as soon as we're finished at the factory. And then stand guard outside in case anyone comes along to try to stop you."

She looked back up, and the shyly affectionate smile she bestowed on him made his pulse race. He turned his focus hastily back to the road and put the car in motion once again.

Business at the copper works was in full swing when they arrived, but Mary expertly wound her way around people and machines, her rapport with the workers evident in every nod and smile. The men greeted her, doffed caps, and waved as she passed by. Mary addressed several of them by name and even asked after wives and children. She wasn't merely a familiar face. She had deep ties to this business and the people who ran it.

"How long have you been coming here?" Victor asked. He walked close behind her to avoid accidentally knocking into anything in the crowded, unfamiliar space.

"Oh, my whole life. I visited with my father regularly when I was a girl. Once he retired, I took his old office as my laboratory, and stayed there until Clay kicked me out."

"This should be your factory, not his."

Mary stiffened. "Yes, well, my father thought he was picking a good man to run the company. And I thought I was getting a kind, attentive husband. Turns out we were both mistaken."

She paused in front of a door with a placard reading, "Management & Accounting," and knocked.

"Come in," a voice called.

Victor and Mary entered, closing the door behind them.

"Good morning, Mr. Lyle," Mary addressed the gray-bearded, dark-skinned man seated behind a large desk. "This is my friend and scientific collaborator, Dr. Franklin. He is assisting me in an investigation into Mr. Clay's unusual activities of late." Mary took a seat in one of the two empty visitors' chairs and motioned for Victor to do the same. "Victor, this is Mr. Lyle, the company accountant."

Victor gave Mr. Lyle a nod.

The accountant stroked his bushy beard. "You want to see the books, I assume?"

"Correct," Mary replied. "In particular, I wish to know if you've noticed any changes leading up to or since Mr. Clay returned to town. Or any irregularities at all, really."

"None," Lyle replied. He turned his open ledger book around so Victor and Mary could look at it. "Everything's been quite normal, even since he arrived. Let me grab you last year's book to help you compare." He rose, unlocked a filing cabinet behind him, and selected an identical book to the one on the desk.

Victor made a quick scan of the numbers from the last few months as Mary flipped pages. Nothing stood out to him, but he wouldn't claim to be any sort of expert on financial matters. She appeared to have a better grasp of the situation, nodding as she read and asking an occasional comment of the accountant.

"It's possible it was the dip in earnings in November that drew your husband's attention. A long-time customer went under." Lyle pointed out some notes to that effect in the book. "But, as you can see, things went back up in December and have remained up. I entered the January totals only yesterday. Overall, the company's doing well. Clay's been receiving his percentage, and ought to have no complaints." The accountant leaned over the desk and lowered his voice. "Rumor is he's hiding here to avoid debts associated with his other business. Maybe skim a little off the top while he's here. But it won't happen on my watch."

Victor gave Lyle a puzzled look. "Can't he simply order you all to increase his percentage? He's in charge, isn't he?"

"Financial changes have to come to us through the company's attorney," Lyle replied. "Something about the way Mr. Amesbury arranged things. Clay can make recommendations, but someone else has to approve. Mr. Amesbury, probably." He frowned at Mary. "I thought you'd know about that."

Mary shifted in her seat, her mouth twisted in confusion. "No. The entire transfer was done without my participation, and my father told me none of the details. Clay would take care of me, was all he ever said. He was so certain of it. And eager to retire someplace warm." She closed last year's ledger book. "Thank you for this. Do you have any of the records from when Clay took over? Anything that might clarify the situation?"

"Not here, no. I believe those documents will be with your father's attorney, Mr. Biggs."

"Well." Victor turned to Mary, a broad grin spreading across his face. "I believe we had plans to visit the attorney anyway." He rose from his seat and offered her a hand up. "Come, my lady. Your carriage awaits."

She accepted his hand but didn't look him in the eye. She gave the accountant a polite nod. "Thank you, Mr. Lyle. I feel better knowing the company is in good financial standing. I would appreciate it if you would not disclose our conversation to Mr. Clay if he comes asking."

"I don't recall you ever stopping by, Mrs. Clay."

"Thank you."

Victor and Mary took their leave, returning to the car in silence. He smiled at her as he helped her into her seat, but didn't say anything. Her expression had turned contemplative rather than surprised or confused, and he didn't want to intrude on her thoughts. Each new discovery brought new questions, and—knowing Mary—her brain would be running at top speed searching for answers. She gave him the address of the attorney's office, and within a few minutes he rolled the car to a stop in front of a well-maintained stone edifice.

Mary hopped from the car without waiting for assistance, and walked around to stand at the bottom of the steps, staring up at the entrance.

"I'll stand guard here," Victor assured her. "If anyone is following us or wishes to interfere, he'll have to go through me."

He hoped the offer sounded more confident than he felt. He was tall and relatively fit, but he was a scientist, not a fighter. As a youth he'd charmed his way out of any trouble, unlike those who relied on their fists.

Mary laid a hand on his arm and gazed up at him. In the morning sunlight, her eyes sparkled a crystalline blue. "No," she said softly. "No." The second time the word was more resolute. "I'd prefer to have you accompany me."

First the factory and now a law office. Word would get around, no doubt, and it would only fuel the rumors of an illicit affair. The decision was ultimately hers, though, and Victor would deny her nothing.

"As my lady wishes." He looped their arms together and started up the stairs.

* * *

Mary had only met Mr. Biggs twice that she remembered, and both times he'd struck her as a level-headed, unflappable sort. Today, though, she had rendered him nothing short of flabbergasted. His jaw hung open for an awkwardly long time, and he started and stopped three full times before getting his words out.

"But, Mrs. Clay, *you* are the owner of Amesbury Copper Works."

For a moment the words didn't quite make sense. Beside her, Victor flinched. He'd been sitting with his chair tipped slightly backward, and now the front legs slammed against the ground with jarring force.

The sound startled sense back into her. "*I* am the owner?" she gasped.

"Didn't your father tell you?" Biggs scratched his balding head. "Didn't he show you the documents?"

"No." A sudden flash of anger tempered her shock. "He trusted Clay to handle everything. I think it's past time I was properly informed, don't you?"

"I do." Mr. Biggs pressed a button on his desk and a moment later a young man appeared at the office door. "James, please fetch the file on the Amesbury Copper Works transfer from the Amesbury family records."

"Yes, sir." The youth scampered off.

Mr. Biggs folded his hands and rested them on the desk. "It is… an unusual circumstance for a woman to be granted sole ownership of a company, and I understand why your father and husband may have wished to shield you from the rigors of the day-to-day operations of the business. But to leave you in absolute ignorance as to your role? It's unconscionable."

Mary's jaw tightened. Clay had deliberately kept her in the dark, letting the whole world think him the owner. Her father, in his haste to leave the world of business behind, had placed all his trust in a scoundrel, rather than in her. And wasn't that the crux of all her problems? Even the men who cared for her let her down.

She kept her voice calm despite her inner turmoil. "What do you know of my role, Mr. Biggs?"

"Let's see." Biggs scratched his head again. "You own the company, but Mr. Clay was given controlling rights over everything but finances and sale, I believe. As soon as James returns, we can delve into the specifics."

The young assistant didn't take long in returning. Biggs took the papers from him and shuffled them around for a few seconds before spreading a few pages on the desk.

"Here's what I was referencing." He tapped a finger on one of the pages. "Full ownership of the company to Mrs. Mary Clay, nee Amesbury. Controlling rights to Mr. Augustus Clay. His rights are then detailed below. You can read it for yourself, but these are standard managerial rights over day-to-day operations." He added another page to the pile. "Moving on to restrictions on his controlling rights, you can see here that he can give input as to any large financial changes, but that such changes require the owner's written approval. The same holds true for any sale of the company."

"I'm surprised Clay hasn't brought you random documents over the years and asked you to sign them," Victor muttered.

"He knows I would have read them first. And then discovered all this." Mary waved a hand at the papers. "I imagine he's been content to let the company sit and pay him an undeserved salary while he dreamed up possible ways to further exploit the situation."

"The company earnings is another section of the agreements," Mr. Biggs explained, showing her yet another document. "Here is the percentage meant for your own personal use."

Mary nodded at the familiar figures. This bit she knew, since her modest stipend funded her scientific projects.

"A larger percentage goes to your household accounts."

The number made Mary cringe. Clay was pocketing more than she would have guessed. And it still wasn't enough for him? Scoundrel.

Biggs removed one final paper from the file. "Lastly, we have some contingencies. Some of them cover issues such as if the business fails. It also states that if you die without heirs, ownership reverts to your father or mother, and after them to the nearest living relative. If Mr. Clay should die, all controlling rights fall to you. The same holds true if there is a dissolution of your marriage for any reason."

"Damnation," Victor swore. "That's why he's so against divorce."

"I imagine he would be," the attorney replied. "He would lose everything."

Mary's pulse raced. Sweat slicked her palms. This handful of papers had upended her entire world. After years of hiding herself away and making do, she'd discovered a path to something better. She only had to screw up her courage and take it.

"Well, then, Mr. Biggs," she declared. "In that case, I would like to file for divorce."

Chapter 18
Planned and Unplanned

"I'm reluctant to test him outside again after that article in the paper." Victor rubbed a hand across his temple in the habitual motion Mary had come to know so well. In the last few weeks, she'd spent more time in close proximity to him than she'd ever spent with her husband. A disconcerting realization. And one that reinforced her conviction that insisting on a divorce was the right path.

She folded her arms and looked down at Mecha-Man. "I agree. No sense drawing negative attention to ourselves. The talk will die down eventually. What alternatives do we have? I wouldn't want to test him in here."

"No, certainly not," Victor agreed. "Too many dangerous things about. And I'm not sure testing him in the house is any better. My parents won't be happy if he accidentally knocks over a vase or punches a hole in a wall."

"*Hmm.*" Mary pursed her lips. They needed a wide open space, but they also needed to keep Mecha-Man hidden from public view. Perhaps outdoors, but obscured. "What if we dress him?"

Victor's nose wrinkled. "Pardon?"

"Dress him up. In proper clothing. From a distance he'll look human. Then we keep to a relatively secluded location."

Victor's lips slowly curved into an appreciative smile. "I

like that plan. He'll need a suit, a greatcoat, and a hat. He's shorter than me, but about the same breadth of shoulder, I think. We can pin up the trousers if necessary. Galoshes will work well over his wide feet." He started for the door, waving for Mary to follow. "Let's go."

They headed into the house proper, where Mary once again found herself gawking at the lavish world Victor inhabited. Elaborate electric wall sconces lit their path, even though the sun shone brightly outside. Carpets so ornate she feared to step on them lined the halls. The wide central staircase looked so much like something out of a grand gallery or opera house that she was halfway to the top before she thought to ask where they were going.

Mary swallowed the question before she could say it aloud. Logically, if they were to fetch clothing, they would have to go into the family's personal chambers. If Victor told her they were headed to his bedroom, she might turn and flee out of… what? Embarrassment? Nerves?

Even worse would be if he asked her to leave, after realizing the impropriety of the situation. As long as she remained silent, though, she could claim ignorance.

"Shirt, tie, trousers," Victor murmured, ticking off the list on his fingers. "I think we can do without a vest and jacket because of the overcoat. Obviously he doesn't need underthings."

Mary's cheeks flamed. The last thing she needed as she marched toward Victor's bedroom was to think about his underthings. What they might look like. What he might look like in them. Or without them. She studiously stared straight ahead, avoiding both Victor's gaze and any hall mirrors that might confirm her girlish blush.

Victor hadn't even paused to question the idea, as if

showing a woman to his bedchamber were a perfectly ordinary occurrence.

Maybe it was. Probably, even. Victor's heart-stopping smile and charming manners surely won him ladies on a regular basis. He would think nothing of welcoming a woman as prim and ordinary as Mary. Of course nothing untoward would happen.

Disappointment knotted her stomach. For once, she wanted to be glamorous and sensual like Callie. Or comfortably non-conforming like Nisha. The sort of person who would not stumble over her own feet at the thought of a handsome man's large, inviting bed.

She was not that sort of person. Victor caught her arm to steady her. Warmth radiated out from his fingertips, seeping deep inside her, all the way down to her most private parts.

If only she had kissed him the other day. It would have been glorious. If mere fingers through clothes could set her aflame, then lips on lips or the touch of a tongue…

She stepped away from him, breaking contact. Better to keep such thoughts firmly in the realm of fantasy. In her dream world there was no possibility of the other potential outcome. No chance he'd find her so cold and boring that he never wanted to touch her again.

"Are you all right?" Victor asked, his voice gentle and concerned. "I know we've had a hel— heck of a day and it's not even mid-afternoon." His expression softened into a smile. "You're not second-guessing your plan, are you? I kind of jumped right into it, but you know me." He shrugged one shoulder.

"I still like the plan. It's only…" She waved a hand. "I can't enter your private rooms. It's… indecent."

"Oh!" His brows shot up, then his smile turned sheepish. "Sorry. I didn't think. I'll gather what we need. Be right back." He disappeared through the door, leaving her in the hall at the top of the stairs.

Mary rubbed the cloth of her skirt between her fingers as she waited. Why, oh, why did she have to be such a ninny? Poor Mary, whose husband didn't want her. Foolish Mary, who had raging sexual feelings for a man who could pick a thousand people more interesting than she was.

Victor saved her from further moping when he returned holding a crisp, white shirt.

"One old shirt," he declared.

For an "old shirt" it looked remarkably perfect. Unlined and unstained. The attached cuffs and collar attested to his wealth. He could afford to change shirts every day. Honestly, with a house like this he could probably afford to change suits every day.

"Which tie do you like?" Victor raised his other hand. Several colors of silk dangled from his fingers.

"Uh, the red?"

"Great. Here." He handed over the shirt and the red tie, and Mary took them, not knowing what else to do. How had she ended up here, standing in the middle of the hallway, holding his clothing? It hadn't been long ago that her life had been entirely ordinary. Now it was almost incomprehensible.

Victor vanished once more, reemerging a moment later with a pair of dark-gray trousers. Attached suspenders dangled nearly to the floor.

"These should work. We can grab an overcoat and galoshes from the coatroom downstairs, and then he'll be dapper as Beau Brummel." He gestured toward the stairs. "Shall we?"

Mary bobbed her head in agreement. Best to get back to work as soon as possible.

They had just reached the top of the staircase when

Victor froze and uttered a low curse. Mary glanced up at him before following his gaze down to the hall below.

Oh. The man standing at the base of the stairs could only be Dr. Edward Franklin. The resemblance between father and son was remarkable. The same light-brown hair. The same aristocratic nose. He even stood with the same relaxed posture Victor adopted when keeping his emotions in check.

Dr. Franklin waved a folded newspaper. "I've read the morning paper, Victor, and I'd like an explanation." His voice was calm, but brooked no argument. "Both of the incident mentioned and…" He waved a hand toward Victor and Mary. "Whatever this is."

The only thing that kept Mary from dropping Victor's shirt and tie, clapping her hands over her flaming cheeks, and fleeing the premises was the knowledge that it would make her appear even more guilty than she must look now. Instead, she swallowed hard and started down the stairs in as proper a manner as possible.

Victor stalked past her, reaching the bottom at a far less decorous pace. He jabbed a finger at the offending newspaper. "*That* is nothing but a vicious pack of lies."

His father made a slight huffing noise. "I certainly hope so." Up close, the family resemblance was even more striking. He, too, possessed those expressive deep-brown eyes. And the way his lip curled into a near smile was so like Victor that Mary had the jarring sensation she was looking at a man speaking to a future version of himself.

"I did nothing wrong," Victor insisted, apparently too agitated to mimic his father's composure. "My project isn't dangerous or damaging, and no one was 'attacked' in any way."

Dr. Franklin nodded. "But *something* happened, Victor. This sort of article does not appear without a reason. I assume Mr. Clay has some rationale for disliking you?" He carefully did not look at Mary. Too carefully.

"Victor has been assisting me with a matter at the copper works," Mary jumped in. Victor had been nothing but a gentleman, and she hated that anyone—especially his family—might think otherwise. She couldn't simply blurt out all the trouble with the smuggling and the Sobridyne, but she had to say something. "We accidentally uncovered some recent mismanagement on the part of Mr. Clay. As owner of the business, it is something I needed to address, and I've greatly appreciated having the perspective of an outsider with no stake in the matter. Mr. Clay, however, seems to have taken exception to our attempts to correct his error."

Dr. Franklin did turn to look at Mary now. For a moment he assessed her silently. What must he think of her, standing in his house with her hands full of his son's clothing. Working all day every day with a man she wasn't married to. Addressing that man by his given name.

Drat. Her peculiar, vague explanation had probably made everything worse. It had to sound as if she were simply making up a story to cover her illicit tryst. Improvisation didn't suit her.

"Thank you for the clarification," Dr. Franklin replied.

Mary flushed harder.

"We ought to be getting back to work," Victor said, regaining his cool. He held up the pair of trousers. "As you can see, we are in the process of making our automaton as respectable and unobtrusive as possible. The next time you see him mentioned in the papers it will be with nothing but respect and admiration. Please excuse us."

Victor's father didn't quite scowl, but his mouth set in a hard line. "We will talk later, Victor. Good day to you, Mrs. Clay." He gave Mary a nod, then departed.

Victor swore under his breath again. "He hates everything I do. I can never do anything right."

Mary's nose wrinkled. "I didn't get that sense. But I do think he worries about you. I'm sorry for all the trouble."

Victor spun to face her. "It is *not* your fault. It's Clay's fault and all the blame should fall squarely on his shoulders."

"Absolutely. But I meant just now. I must have come across as terribly awkward and, well, guilty. I didn't mean to make it seem like we were… you know." She shrugged with the arm that still held his shirt and tie, then thrust the garments at him. "Please take these. I feel so strange holding your personal items." The instant he had hold of the clothing she whirled away. "I'll meet you in the laboratory."

A few brief minutes to herself did little to settle her nerves. She paced the laboratory, her silly brain unable to stop. And what was it obsessing over? Not the automaton people thought was dangerous, her smuggling husband, her impending divorce, or any number of other more important issues. No, all she could think about was how unfair it was that Victor's father and probably half the world thought she and Victor were having an affair. They'd been nothing but proper. Even when they'd been forced to snuggle together for warmth there had been no kissing, no groping. If she were to be branded a harlot and he a Lothario, didn't they deserve at least a kiss?

Really, she deserved more than that. She deserved ardent embraces, words of adoration, a grand passion. All the things her husband had never given her.

But she would settle for a kiss.

What could it hurt, anyway? Her reputation was already in question, and soon she would be a scandalous divorcée. All she had to do was ask.

Right. Ask. As if she were a practiced seductress and not

a mortifyingly inexperienced wallflower. How appallingly unfair. She seemed doomed to receive all of the censure and none of the reward.

Mary was facing away from the door when Victor arrived. She could hear his confident strides, and for a brief moment she imagined him crossing the room to her, sweeping her into his arms, and giving her the kiss she so longed for. Her hands trembled. She forced a slow breath before she turned toward him.

Victor didn't cross the room to her, but instead carried his armload of clothing to the table and dumped it beside Mecha-Man.

"That's everything." He gave her an affectionate smile that made her breath hitch. "Should we dress him now, or—"

"I want you to kiss me," she blurted.

Chapter 19
Give and Take

Victor took off across the laboratory as if someone had lit an explosive underneath him. Years of fantasies replayed in his head. Memories too. Her body pressed to his. The scent of her hair—plain soap, nothing fancy or fussy. Simple. Straightforward. Just like her demand for a kiss.

He jerked to a halt. What the hell was he doing? She couldn't possibly have said what he thought she'd said. He'd imagined it. Conjured it up out of his fevered brain. It was the result of too much stress. The smuggling, Mary's discoveries about the company, her divorce, the article in the paper, and his father's disapproval on top of it all. No wonder he wasn't thinking straight.

Mary stood only a few steps away. Her fingers were clenched in the top layer of her skirts. Her wide blue eyes gazed up at him with an expression he couldn't quite decipher. Hopeful? Victor took another step forward.

No, no. There was something else there. An uncertainty. Or was that his own feelings intruding?

He rubbed his temple. "I'm sorry, what did you say?"

Best to clear this up. She'd explain that she'd said, "I want you to dress him," or something similar, and he'd go back to work and shove his fantasies back into the depths of his mind where they belonged.

Her gaze dropped to the floor. "Never mind. You… you don't have to…" She trailed off as she turned away.

Victor took another step, his hand automatically reaching out to comfort her. He checked himself before he could touch her.

"No, please. I only want to be certain I didn't misunderstand you. You, er, want me to kiss you?"

The act of saying it out loud brought him firmly back into the realm of reality. His entire body trembled with a combination of excitement, desire, and terror that he would bungle the whole thing.

Mary glanced back at him. Her cheeks were pink again, the way they'd been in the hall during that agonizing conversation with his father. Dammit. He hated that he'd embarrassed her.

"Yes," she replied. "If you want. I thought it might be nice, and I've officially filed for the divorce, and…" She turned away again. "I understand if you don't want to."

"No, I do." Victor lunged forward, and this time he did take her arm. "I very much want to." She trembled in his grasp and he immediately released her. *You fool*, he cursed himself. "Unless *you* don't."

Time came to a standstill, the breath sawing in and out of his chest the only motion in a frozen world.

Until she moved.

Slowly, so slowly she was halfway around before Victor believed it wasn't his imagination, Mary pivoted to face him. Her chin crept upward, bringing those sky-blue eyes up to look into his. Lifting those perfect lips into kissing distance. Lust roared in Victor's veins, but his limbs remained motionless.

Mary's words came in a near whisper. "If I didn't want to, I wouldn't have asked."

Victor leaned in, until he could inhale her scent and feel the warm caress of her breath on his lips. "You can always change your mind," he murmured.

One delicate hand rose, her fingers brushing against his chest before closing tightly around the lapel of his jacket.

"Not this time," she declared. She rose up on her tiptoes and sealed her mouth to his.

Victor almost fell over. In all his fantasies, he'd always been the one to kiss her. He'd been prepared, in control. Instead he was... "stunned" seemed too mild a word for it. Ensorcelled, perhaps. Wholly undone. Her lips were the softest, sweetest thing he'd ever tasted. They stroked over his in a gentle exploration that sent electric shockwaves out to the very tips of his fingers and toes. Even the air around him seemed to prickle with energy.

Mary broke contact as suddenly as she'd initiated it. Her grip on him relaxed, but she didn't quite release him. "I'm sorry. Was that bad?"

Bad? Victor tried to shake off the daze the kiss had left him in. Why would she think...?

You didn't kiss her back, you dolt.

"No." He reached for her, setting his hands lightly on her hips. "It was lovely. Please do it again."

She lifted toward him once more, tentatively, and this time Victor met her halfway. Again, electricity jolted through him, but now he was prepared. He slid his mouth over hers, matching her soft strokes. Her body relaxed beneath his hands and she inched closer. Encouraged, he let his hands slide around to her back, caressing her, urging her closer still.

Mary's kiss was hungry, but she made no attempt to deepen it, or to part her lips for him. When Victor let his tongue sweep over her bottom lip, she flinched, though she neither pulled away nor broke the kiss.

Damnation. She kissed like a wide-eyed innocent. Or how he imagined an innocent would kiss, since he'd never kissed anyone inexperienced before. Shouldn't she have *some* experience? She was married. How could it be possible she'd never had a proper kiss?

Victor traced the seam of her lips with his tongue. She made a noise of pleasure, her body pressing into his, but still she didn't open for him. He pulled away.

"Do you want to stop?" she asked, gazing up at him with a slightly dazed expression.

"No. I was hoping we might go further. It can be even better if you open your mouth and use your tongue."

Victor tried not to wince. Did that sound weird? How did people talk about these things? When he'd been a teenager, he'd just fumbled his way through until he learned, and since then he'd known more or less what he was doing. Except now it had been years. Maybe she was only tentative because he was a terrible kisser.

"I know that's what people say," Mary lowered her lashes, turning shy again. "But Augustus did that to me and it was unpleasant."

Victor's jaw clenched. That fucking bastard. He should have been showering her with love and affection. Instead, he'd probably pressed forceful, intrusive kisses on her and made her uncomfortable. Mecha-Man should have hit him with a boulder.

"It's extremely pleasant if you do it right," Victor assured Mary. "It should feel like how we just kissed, only deeper and…" *Wetter? Hotter? Wilder?*

"More passionate?" she suggested.

"Exactly. I'd love to show you, but I don't want to do anything that makes you unhappy or uncomfortable."

She nodded, worrying her lower lip between her teeth. Even their fairly chaste kisses had left it stained a deeper pink than usual. Good God, how he wanted to taste it again. To taste more of her mouth. More of her body.

"You didn't like it when he put his tongue in your mouth, is that right?" Victor couldn't even bring himself to speak Clay's name.

Mary nodded again.

"So I won't do that. But, would you maybe like to try doing that to me?"

Her eyes grew wide.

* * *

Kissing Victor somehow managed to be exactly how she'd imagined and nothing at all like she'd imagined at the same time. It was everything sweet and gentle and comforting. It also left her body humming with longing for more. Mary wanted to rub her suddenly sensitive breasts against his solid chest and run her hands all up and down him. She wanted to kiss his lips and the stubbly jaw he hadn't shaved this morning. And possibly more.

She stared up at him, contemplating his offer. Did she dare attempt it?

"Are you sure?" Mary's face was burning. "I'm not... I mean... I'm sure you've had many other ladies—"

He gently cupped her cheek. "Some, yes. Gentlemen too."

"Oh." Mary thought suddenly of the times a pretty woman had caught her eye. Of the school friend whose hand she'd held while thinking about kissing. "I'm that way too. Oh, not that I've kissed any ladies, but, well, I've..."

"Darling, you don't have to have experience to feel the way you feel. You are who you are and you like who you like. That's what I was saying, really. I don't choose my partners because they look a certain way or have certain experience. I pick them because I like them. And I like *you*. So when I say you're welcome to kiss me, I don't mean just anyone is welcome to kiss me. I mean you. Specifically. I would be happy and honored to be kissed by you, Mary Amesbury."

Such pretty words. She wanted to sway into his embrace and stay there forever while he murmured more pretty words.

But Clay had wooed her with pretty words and gentle kisses, once. When he'd decided it was time to take things further, the kisses had turned rough and disagreeable. He'd blamed her, of course.

"You're cold and hard."

The words had seeped into her soul, no matter how many times she told herself he was probably lying. The insidious fear twisted inside her, warning her that every step further risked discovery that those words were true.

They're not, she told herself. *They're not. They're not.*

So far Victor didn't appear to think her either cold or hard. And while he'd made his desires clear, he had left it up to her to decide when to stop and what to do. He'd handed her the power to make new memories. Maybe she did dare.

"Here," Victor said. His hands still on her hips, he steered her across the room, then lifted her up to stand atop a metal toolbox. The new position brought them eye-to-eye. And lips-to-lips. "That should make things easier. Do whatever you'd like. You're in control."

A breath rushed out of her. *You're in control.* She could do this.

Mary wound her arms around his neck, brushing her fingers up into his hair. She pressed a kiss to his jaw, the way she'd imagined. The stubby beard hairs scratched her lips, but she found the sensation intriguing rather than unpleasant. Emboldened, she continued along his jawline.

Victor made a low noise that was almost a growl, and leaned in, pressing her against the cabinet behind her. He braced himself with a hand to either side of her, but the knowledge that this was *her* exploration of *him* made the position protective rather than confining.

Mary tugged him closer. Her breasts crushed into his chest, and she squirmed a little, enjoying the friction against her stiffening nipples. By the time her mouth reached his, her entire body was taut with yearning. Tentatively, she ran her tongue over his bottom lip, the way he'd done to her.

"Mary," he groaned. The husky timbre of his voice made her insides quiver.

Desire made her bold. She slipped her tongue between his parted lips, eager for a deeper taste of him. She almost jumped when their tongues touched, but the sensation, though shocking, was also arousing.

She broke the kiss just long enough to say, "Show me what to do."

He did, with great enthusiasm, stroking his tongue across hers, coaxing her lips further apart, urging her to do the same to him.

"Tell me when it's okay to be inside you," he breathed.

She kissed him again, sliding her tongue inside his mouth until he made another noise of pleasure.

"Now," she whispered. "Please now."

He obeyed her command, sweeping between her lips in a slow, tender caress. Only when she responded in kind did he push further, deeper.

It *was* glorious. This was what a kiss was meant to be.

Not an invasion, but a dance. A back-and-forth, a give-and-take, shared equally between partners.

Mary's fears dissolved beneath the passion of the kiss. Her fingers tightened in his hair and strange noises rose unbidden in her throat. She kissed him wildly now, plunging into his mouth and straining against him. When at last they broke apart, she was breathless and hot all over.

"You," Victor gasped. "Are a very quick study." His brown eyes had darkened, and his lips were quite pink and perhaps a bit swollen. A slight flush colored his pale cheeks. She'd done that to him.

His mouth curved into a grin, and he rubbed the tip of his nose against hers. "More?" he asked. "Or stop?"

"A bit more, ple—"

A knock at the door interrupted her. Victor's smile morphed into a frown of puzzlement and suspicion.

"I'll chase them off," he murmured.

As he walked toward the door, Mary took stock of herself. She traced one finger over tingling lips that were surely bright red. Her clothing was a bit rumpled from the embrace, so she shook out her skirts and smoothed the fabric down with her hands. Better. She patted her hair, checking that everything was in place.

"Is a Mrs. Mary Clay here?" asked an unfamiliar voice. "I have an urgent telegram for her."

"I'll take it to her, thank you," Victor replied.

An urgent telegram? Mary trotted across the laboratory, meeting Victor in the center of the room. He handed her the paper and she studied it.

"It's from Mr. Biggs."

"The attorney?"

Mary tore into the envelope. "What could he want? Was

there some problem with the divorce papers?" She yanked the paper out and scanned the printed words. "Oh, my God."

She swayed, and Victor grabbed her arm.

"What? What's wrong?"

"It's… I…"

A storm of conflicting emotions engulfed her. She flung herself against Victor's chest and wept.

Chapter 20

Bad News First

Victor folded his arms around Mary and ran his hands up and down her back in slow, soothing strokes. He'd never comforted a crying woman before, but it seemed the thing to do.

What on earth had happened? Was it wrong to ask? His heart ached for her. Her sobs went on and on, but at least today he could hold her.

"I'm here," he murmured. There. That was the right sort of thing to say. "Is there anything I can do to help?"

She kept her face buried in his shirt, but lifted the hand with the telegram. Victor accepted the paper and read the message.

"Oh, shit."

He read it a second time, more slowly to make certain he wasn't hallucinating.

Mrs Clay
Mr Clay found dead pls return to office directly
Biggs

Victor continued rubbing Mary's back as he tried to process the blunt message. This was bad, right? Except now she was free, without the stigma of a divorce. Was she mourning for that bastard who hadn't even had the courtesy to give her a decent kiss? Was she sobbing in relief? Confusion? All of the above? Victor didn't know what to think. It had to be all the worse for her.

They needed more information. Where had this happened? What had been the cause?

Dread churned in his stomach. Clay had looked relatively young and fit. A sudden medical issue seemed unlikely. Which meant foul play. A smuggling incident gone wrong?

"Do you want me to drive you to the attorney's office?" he asked softly. "When you're ready?"

Mary took a deep breath and nodded. A few moments later, she looked up. Tears still glistened in her eyes and streaked her cheeks, but her expression was calm.

Victor pulled out a handkerchief and handed it to her. "Are you all right?"

She dabbed at her eyes. "I think so. Shocked."

"Who wouldn't be? Let me get your cloak, and then I'll drive you to see the attorney. Whatever you need, you tell me."

"Thank you."

As was happening all too frequently of late, the drive passed in complete silence. Victor focused on the road in an attempt to keep himself from fretting. Now that the tears had stopped, Mary appeared unflappable. She'd ruthlessly shoved all her emotions behind her stoic shell. Inside, she had to be restless. If the last month had taught him anything, it was how intense her inner passions were. She liked to keep them tidy and controlled, but that didn't mean they were lacking.

"You want me to go inside with you again?" he asked when they arrived. He wished he had more to say. But "I'm sorry" didn't seem appropriate and "it's all right" sounded like a lie. He settled for being at her side in case she needed anything.

"Yes, please." Mary waited for Victor to walk around and help her out of the car. "I'm not sure what to expect, and I appreciate having someone along for support."

He offered his arm and led her inside.

They were ushered immediately into Mr. Biggs' office, where the lawyer waited with brandy at the ready. Victor pulled out a chair for Mary while Biggs poured.

"Mrs. Clay," the lawyer greeted her solemnly. "Please, have a drink. I'm sorry for the urgent summons and the distressing news, but I thought it better you heard it from me."

Mary took a delicate sip of the brandy. "Thank you. What—" She shivered and Victor scooted his chair closer, in case she needed a shoulder to cry on again or a hand to hold. "What happened?"

"That is unclear," Biggs replied. "Mr. Clay was found late this morning, behind Amesbury Copper Works. I'm afraid it looks like foul play. Mr. Lyle telephoned me, and I sent you the message at once. The investigation is ongoing while the police interview the employees at the factory. As attorney for both your family and the copper works, I would advise you not to answer questions about the matter without consulting me. At least not until we know more about the situation."

Victor clenched and unclenched his fingers. Dammit. This was one of those times when he hated being right. Clay's involvement with the smugglers had turned deadly. Which meant Mary could be in danger. He took a gulp of brandy. Mary took another dainty sip of hers.

"Did they say how he died?" Her voice held a hint of a tremble.

"Strangulation, it appeared," Biggs replied. "But we

should not assume that to be a certainty until the police inquest has been completed."

Mary reached toward Victor, and he caught her hand and gave it a squeeze.

"The police are likely to wish to speak to you about his whereabouts last night, since you are his wife… er, widow. I can arrange to be present for the interview."

"It won't help them," Mary replied. "I've never known his whereabouts. And the last two nights I've spent at the home of my friend Mrs. Finch."

The lawyer pursed his lips. "Do you know anything at all that could be relevant?" he asked. "Anything that might explain why someone would target him?"

Mary's fingers tightened on Victor's. "I believe he may have been smuggling. I saw unfamiliar men loading a truck after hours at the factory one night. I informed the police about it."

Victor kept still and silent, waiting to see if she would elaborate further, but she made no mention of the Sobridyne. For now, he agreed. Best to divulge the details of that night to as few people as possible. The police already knew the important information.

Biggs steepled his fingers. "I see. That certainly could explain the matter, if he had dealings with the criminal class. Thank you, Mrs. Clay. I will keep you informed if I hear more. And I will make certain that official notice of death is recorded and everything is clear for you to take full management of your company. I will notify you as soon as the papers are prepared."

"Thank you."

"Only doing my job, ma'am. In the meantime I would advise you to return to your friend's home to rest and re-cuperate from your shock. Callers should not trouble you, as you are in mourning." His gaze dropped to Mary and Victor's entwined fingers. "I suggest you take care to be as circumspect as possible."

Mary didn't withdraw her hand, but Victor could feel the stiffening of her muscles. Dammit. They'd shared one kiss, and that only after she'd begun the divorce paperwork. But the whole world seemed determined to judge them guilty.

He stood up. Enough of this. He was taking her away where no one would make innuendos or look at her suspiciously. Biggs was right in one respect. She needed to be safely ensconced with her friends so she could have the time to process all of this.

"Allow me to drive you home, Mrs. Clay," Victor said. When she nodded, he helped her to her feet. "Thank you for the information, Mr. Biggs. We'll leave the address where Mrs. Clay is staying with your assistant. I hope this matter can be resolved as quickly as possible."

Biggs rose. "I hope so too. Please let me know at once if you think of anything else that might be important."

That was clear enough. He didn't believe them.

"Of course," Mary replied. "Good day, Mr. Biggs."

"Good day, Mrs. Clay. Dr. Franklin."

Victor escorted Mary back to the car, his mind whirring as he contemplated their next steps. He would drive her to Hal and Callie's, of course. Though at this time of day Hal would be in his laboratory and Callie running her library. The library had several quiet spaces where Mary could relax, but it *was* a ladies' library. Would it cause trouble if Victor stayed with her? They could always use the back entrance, and go up to one of the third floor trysting rooms that Callie rented out to women in need of a private location.

That thought conjured up an image of Mary sprawled across a bed, her lips rosy from his kisses and her skin flushed with arousal. Not the direction his mind ought to be going right now.

Dammit, had it truly been less than an hour ago that he'd been standing in her embrace, feeling as if he'd found heaven?

"Drive me to the copper works, please," Mary said softly.

Victor flinched. "What?"

"The copper works," she repeated, louder. "I'd like to talk to Mr. Lyle and Mr. Gage."

Victor gaped at her. "But there's an investigation happening. It will be chaos. The bod—" He cut himself off and tried to be more tactful. "You wouldn't want to see Mr. Clay in that condition."

She kneaded her cloak between her fingers. "Please, Victor. I can't go home yet. I need to know what's happened. As much as possible."

She gazed up at him with eyes still slightly red from crying and his resistance crumbled. Whatever she asked, he'd do it. He started up the car.

"All right. Let's go."

* * *

Deep breaths, chin up, relax your shoulders.

Years of maintaining her composure when she'd wanted to scream had served Mary well. After that brief, embarrassing flood of emotion in the laboratory, she'd been able to carry on in a reasonably controlled fashion, even if her stomach roiled with nausea and her every limb tried to tremble.

Her feckless, worthless, buffoon of a husband! She'd had her life under control. No. More than that. She'd *taken* control of her life. She'd set herself on the path to independence and happiness. And now this. Everything was in chaos. All because Clay had been such a greedy bastard that he'd allied himself with dangerous people.

Instead of the woman who'd demanded her freedom, she'd now be a woman in mourning, burdened by new expectations and responsibilities. She wanted to weep with pain and fury. This acute sense of loss frustrated and confused her, especially since it did come with some amount of sadness for her late husband. She'd wanted him out of her life, but she hadn't wanted him dead. And murder was a terrible way to go.

Worst of all was that Clay's harebrained actions might have put her and Victor—and perhaps even Callie and Dr. Finch—in danger.

She had to know more. She had to know what had happened and why and who had done it. Only when she was fully armed with information would she be able to feel safe. Or to take the steps necessary to ensure her safety and that of her friends.

Victor had surprised her with his swift acquiescence to her request to visit the copper works. She'd expected him to insist that she shut herself away immediately. She'd seen his protective side many times in recent days. As a gentleman, he'd feel duty-bound to see to her safety and comfort.

His tension was clear in the clenching of his hands on the steering wheel and the hard set of his jaw. Yet he said nothing. Only drove them though the streets toward the factory.

They arrived to find the street outside the copper works abuzz with activity. Two steam cars with police markings sat in front of the building, along with several ordinary vehicles. A pair of uniformed men stood on the sidewalk to either side of the factory, barring curious pedestrians from approaching. Across the street, people gawked and chattered.

"Go around to the back," Mary instructed.

Victor glanced at her with raised eyebrows. "Wasn't Clay found out back? We won't be allowed anywhere near."

"It's my factory and he was my husband. If anyone should be allowed back there, it's me."

Victor didn't look convinced, but he pulled the car around the side of the building regardless. A temporary wooden barricade blocked off the drive to the rear of the factory. Victor stopped the car in front of it, and Mary hopped from her seat.

"We can walk from here."

Victor scrambled after her, falling into step at her side, mere inches away. He wasn't stopping any of her plans, but he was in full protector mode.

"Police business only," a gruff voice called out. "You can't come back here." A beefy officer with a thick, curling moustache stepped into Mary's path.

"I'm Mrs. Mary Clay," she explained. "The owner of this factory. Mr. Clay is… w-was my husband."

The policeman's expression softened. "I'm so sorry, ma'am, but we cannot allow you entry until the investigation has concluded. I can send someone out to talk to you, if you like."

Mary gave him a polite nod. She would have preferred to go inside herself, but this would do. "Yes, please. I would like to speak to my accountant, Mr. Lyle, and my foreman, Mr. Gage."

The man's moustache twitched. "Oh, sorry again, ma'am. We're not allowing anyone from inside to leave until the initial questioning is finished. Have to be certain we have proper testimony from anyone who might have seen something. But I can have one of our detectives speak to you."

Victor leaned closer. "Not without a lawyer," he whispered.

"I would appreciate that, thank you," she replied to the police officer. Maybe she could convince the detective to escort her inside.

The officer jogged off. Mary peered past the barrier, considering taking the opportunity to walk behind the building. She waited only because interfering with an investigation could lead to her arrest. That would help nothing.

Victor turned to face her. "Are you sure you want to—"

"Mrs. Clay?" a new voice interrupted from somewhere behind them.

Mary spun to see a pale, red-cheeked face peering out from beneath a wide hat. The man held a notebook with a pencil poised. A reporter, clearly.

"The man found dead was your husband?" the reporter asked. "Did he have any bad relations with anyone at the factory? Any enemies? Are you familiar with his business dealings?"

Mary gestured for the man to leave. "I'm sorry. I have no comment at the moment."

"I understand you and Mr. Clay have been estranged for some time and he has kept several mistresses over the years. Is that true?"

Victor stepped between Mary and the reporter. "The lady said she had no comment," he snapped.

"Your name?" the reporter asked Victor. "Relationship to Mrs. Clay?"

"Get lost."

Another man came rushing over. "Did I hear that correctly?" he asked Mary. "You're the widow?"

A woman followed quickly on his heels. "Move aside, gents. She'd much rather speak to a woman, wouldn't you, dear?" Her gaze raked Victor from head to toe and her mouth curved in a speculative smile. "Who's your vigilant friend?"

Panic clawed at Mary's chest. She didn't like talking to strangers on a good day. All these people hurling their intrusive questions at her threatened to snap her tenuous self-control.

"Dr. Franklin?" guessed the woman reporter. She set pencil to paper. "From the peculiar family with the castle house? How long has Mrs. Clay been living with you?"

"I have *not* been living with him!" Mary exclaimed. She seized Victor's arm before he could do anything rash. "We should leave."

Her hands were shaking now, her heart racing. *Deep breaths, chin up, relax your shoulders*, she told herself, but this time the technique failed her. This was too much. Too many questions she didn't want to think about. Too much emotional upheaval for a single day. Her fingers tightened on Victor's arm.

"Please, take me home."

Victor used his body to shield her from the reporters while she climbed into the steam car. Instead of walking around to the driver's side, he hopped up onto the hood of the car, then jumped down into his seat. He was starting the vehicle before he'd even settled.

The reporters sprang out of the way as the car reversed, still calling out questions and making marks in their notebooks. Victor spun the car around and tore off down the road, away from the press and police alike.

Tears pricked Mary's eyes. She blinked rapidly, trying to clear them away. She'd failed in her quest to learn more, she was likely in danger, and she'd become an object of titillation for the newspapers.

The brief moments of happiness from earlier now seemed like a dream. For a few minutes, there, she'd actually believed she could have a life of freedom where she made her own decisions and received magnificent kisses from a charming gentleman. Now the world had reminded her that sort of life was not for her.

Go back to your quiet corner, all alone. It's the only place you're safe.

The tears broke free again, washing away what little remained of the wall she'd built to guard her heart.

I can't. I won't. I deserve to be acknowledged and respected for who I am.

But how did a shy, modest, bookish woman face down scandal and criminals?

"I'll take you straight to Hal and Callie's," Victor said. His voice was tight, his knuckles white on the steering wheel. "We'll get you a hot meal, a hot bath, and anything else you need."

"Thank you," she sniffed. "That's a fine plan."

And there it was: her answer. How did she face all her obstacles? With a plan.

Chapter 21
Friendship

Mary settled onto the sofa and adjusted Callie's warm, fuzzy dressing gown to wrap fully around her. She'd dressed fully before joining them, so she didn't strictly *need* to close the dressing gown for modesty. Being in the company of others, even friends, meant wearing a proper dress. It didn't matter that none of them would care what she wore, or that she'd just had a bath and her hair was still damp. She minded. Bashfulness over her appearance would interfere with talking to her friends and crafting a plan.

The robe, though, was cozy and comforting, its big sleeves falling to cover her hands. So she wore it and snuggled into it as she tucked her legs up beneath her. Going without shoes was her one nod to informality.

Victor didn't hesitate to sit beside her, sprawling onto the sofa and draping his arm across the back of it. He didn't touch her, but he was close enough to put an arm around her with only a slight shift in position. Either he was still determined to be her knight in shining armor or that kiss had left him hoping for more.

Opposite them, Callie lounged on a fainting couch, her stocking-clad legs scandalously draped across her husband's lap. Dr. Finch dragged a finger absently up and down her calf, as if unaware of what he was doing.

The door opened and Nisha strode in, swiftly covering the distance to the Finches' best leather armchair. She settled herself, pulled a flask from a pocket in her vest, and took a swig.

"Sorry I'm late," she said. "I wanted to check with my father, in case he had any relevant news."

Mary's spine straightened. Nisha's father was chief of police. A high-profile murder potentially connected to a smuggling ring would certainly garner his attention.

"Did he?" she asked.

"Not much that he could reveal to me," Nisha replied. "Cause of death appeared to be strangulation by someone with large hands, based on the markings on the body. Doctors will still perform an autopsy. They think he died early this morning. No one from the factory has been arrested. Investigation is ongoing. When I asked about smuggling, he ended the conversation. Which makes me assume they're investigating that aspect of the situation."

"Thank you," Mary replied. "I'm relieved to hear they don't suspect anyone from the copper works. And if they're looking into the smuggling, I believe they're on the right track. No one else had a motive to kill him."

Callie raised an eyebrow. "Oh?"

Mary wrinkled her nose. "What do you mean by that? Do you mean *me*?"

"I believe close relations always fall under suspicion."

"I didn't want him dead!" Mary sat up straight, her stockinged feet sliding out from under her to hit the floor. The movement pressed her back into Victor's arm, but she pretended not to notice. "If anyone thinks I did, they're absolutely wrong. I hate that he's dead. I'm… I'm so *furious*." Speaking the word aloud unclogged the emotion that had festered inside her since she'd read that awful telegram. "I had demanded my freedom," she explained. "I had taken charge of my own life and thrown him out of it. Now he's ruined everything! Now people will pity me. They'll tell me not to speak ill of the dead if I tell the truth about him. I'll be stuck with his rotten name! I can't even feel glad that he's gone!"

A tremor wracked her body. Victor's hand settled on her shoulder.

"I will never use his name again, Miss Amesbury," he murmured. "You don't need to dress in black for him, and even though your freedom didn't come through your own efforts, I'm absolutely certain you can make it into what you want."

Only the presence of the others prevented Mary from twisting around into his arms. The fervor in his voice not only sparked desire deep in her abdomen, but instilled her with a confidence that she could reclaim her path forward.

"And there's another suspect," Nisha drawled. She waved a hand at Victor, who stiffened and abruptly withdrew his hand.

Mary curled up on the sofa again, hugging her knees to her chest beneath the voluminous dressing gown. "Not you, too," she lamented. "We are scientific colleagues! What's so wrong with that? Why must everyone insist that we're having an affair?"

"Because Victor hovers around you like *he's* your husband?" Dr. Finch suggested.

"I think it's more in the way they look at each other," Callie argued. "You know, that 'if we were alone we'd be humping like rabbits' look."

Mary pulled the collar of the dressing gown higher to hide her flaming cheeks. Since the robe was scarlet, it probably didn't help much. "That is not true," she insisted. "We've been very... platonic."

Except for that kiss earlier. Which had been the most liberatingly carnal event of her life, to be honest. And most likely an aberration, not to be repeated again.

"Really?" Callie shook her head. "That's unfortunate."

"Clearly everyone is mistaking friendship for something else," Mary said, determined to seize control of the conversation before she melted into a puddle of mortification. "Which leads to the first part of the plan I'm working on. How do I avoid and refute scandal? I can stay out of public, of course. That part is easy. I'm accustomed to not going out. But what about my work? Those reporters knew enough that they'll surely swarm Franklin Castle and see me going in and out."

"Simple." Callie grinned like a child given an ice cream soda. "You stay there. Then the only going and coming will happen inside the house."

Mary couldn't even pretend she didn't understand the innuendo. She'd been friends with Callie too long for that.

"I *can't* stay with Victor," she argued. "People would know and that would only lead to more talk. Besides, what would his parents think?"

"That you need a safe place to stay while recovering from a traumatic moment in your life?" Victor suggested. "My parents are decent people, even if they think I'm a menace to good society."

"We can sneak you over there in the dead of night," Nisha stated, as if she did this sort of thing all the time. "That house is huge. No one ever needs to know you're there, and you can carry on with your work until everyone's found something new to talk about."

It was a good plan. If Mary kept out of sight, people

would forget eventually. But to be perpetually locked inside? How could she assist with Mecha-Man? Or visit the library?

"It's a possibility," she admitted. "Though I'd rather find a way to prove all the gossips wrong." Which wasn't likely unless she gave up working with Victor, and they all knew it. "Let's move on to part two. Find out what Clay was up to so we can keep ourselves and my company safe. First, I want to talk to the men at the copper works so I know all the details of what happened this morning. After that, I'm not sure."

"Let the police handle it?" Dr. Finch suggested.

Callie ran a finger down his cheek. "The way you did, darling?"

He blushed.

"Break into Chief Majhi's office and read all the reports?" Victor joked. When Mary turned to frown at him, he gave her his impish smile.

She heaved a sigh. "Maybe there's nothing else I can do until I know more. Maybe I'm doomed to be frustrated."

Victor's expression turned serious, and he brushed a finger along her arm in the briefest of caresses. "Frustrated for today, perhaps. But after a good night's sleep and a hearty breakfast in the morning, you'll feel better. You'll figure out your plan. You always do." He looked over at Dr. Finch. "We *are* having a hearty breakfast in the morning, right?"

Dr. Finch's eyebrows arched. "What do you mean 'we'? Are you planning to stay the night?"

"You honestly think I'd leave when Mary could be in danger? You have an extra room."

There was indeed an extra room. Right next to hers. This was not going to curtail the gossip. Though she would sleep better with Victor here. If the smugglers believed they both knew too much, he was in as much danger as she was. Whoever Clay had tangled with, they weren't playing games.

"We'd love to have you," Callie said firmly. Mary looked down to avoid meeting anyone's gaze, but she had to smile even so. Callie was unashamedly the matchmaker. Embarrassing as it was, it came from a good place, and it warmed Mary's heart that her friend wanted to put fun and happiness—and a bit of wantonness—into her life.

Not that Mary intended to engage in any wantonness tonight. She was exhausted and emotionally drained. Her brain was having difficulty formulating the plans she needed. A few more minutes with her friends, and then she'd turn in early.

When she did lay down in her bed, however, sleep wouldn't come. She tossed and turned, trying to make herself comfortable. Trying to will her thoughts to quiet. Every time oblivion neared, some new worry would flash in her mind, dragging her back to wakefulness.

Around her, the house was silent as the grave, everyone abed for the night. The Finches would have everything locked up tight, and Mary had locked her own door for extra security. Still, a trace of fear lingered. Was it possible someone would come after them? Had Victor remembered to lock his door?

She slipped out of bed and headed next door. The knob turned easily in her hand. He hadn't remembered. The door swung open. A shaft of light from the streetlamp outside illuminated the room just enough for her to see Victor bolt upright in bed.

"Mary?"

"I'm sorry," she whispered. "Did I wake you?"

"No. Couldn't sleep."

"Neither could I." Shutting the door behind her, she thought back to his words from earlier.

I'm absolutely certain you can make it into what you want.

She could be bold, the way she'd been when she'd asked for a kiss. Slowly, she walked toward the bed.

"Victor?"

He pushed back the blankets. "What do you need?"

"Would you…" She fortified herself with a deep breath. "Hold me? The way you did in the truck that night?"

He opened his arms. "Absolutely."

Mary rushed into his embrace, and he scooped her up onto the bed, tucking her against his body and wrapping the covers around them both. She ought to have felt bashful, snuggling with a man who wore nothing but a union suit. She'd never even *seen* a man in so little clothing before. Granted, she couldn't see much now, but she could feel the soft flannel and the shape of his lean body beneath. Maybe in the morning she'd wake up shy and awkward. Now, though, she could only feel relief that he was here and they were both unharmed. At long last, her body relaxed.

Chapter 22
Part of the Solution

Waking with Mary in his arms under awkward circumstances was still preferable to not waking up with her at all, Victor decided. And a comfortable bed where they were both barely covered was infinitely preferable to straw on the floor of a truck. With luck, this would be a pattern in a series of steady improvements, culminating in passionate love-making.

He scooted back, putting a bit of space between them before his body could get too excited. She'd come here for comfort, not for sex.

Mary stirred and scrunched closer to him, destroying his attempt at chivalry. When she snuggled against his chest, his cock throbbed in response. Dammit. But what could he do when she clearly wanted to cuddle?

You could get out of the bed.

No. He wasn't that noble. Not after the way she'd kissed him yesterday.

"Victor?" she murmured.

"Morning, beautiful." He tucked a stray curl behind her ear. Even fully stretched out, her hair would hardly fall to her shoulders. He liked that she wore it unfashionably short. She was a rebel at heart. A quiet rebel, but one with a lot more inner courage than the world—and perhaps even she—realized.

Victor's heart thumped in his chest. He loved her so damn much. More and more with each secret she revealed and each obstacle she faced down. Bizarre as it seemed, he had a chance to be with her now. If he could keep being a friend to her and not fuck everything up again.

She lifted her chin to look at him, and he dared to brush his lips across her cheek. Immediately, she twisted to bring their mouths together.

Her kiss was sweet and warm, as gentle and soothing as a good morning kiss ought to be. Victor reveled in it, sweeping his lips over hers, tasting the little indentation in the center of her top lip and the very corners of her mouth.

He thought he might go on this way for hours, in case he never had the opportunity to wake up with her again. But then she twined her arms tightly around him and plunged her tongue into his mouth.

Groaning into her, he clasped her to him, returning the kiss with unchecked abandon. Her hands began to wander—over his arms, down his back. He allowed himself the same freedom, caressing a soft body hidden only beneath a single layer of woolen nightgown. He stroked down her spine and over the plump curves of her buttocks. When she wriggled into him, he ground his hips against her in response.

Mary flinched and let out a squeak.

Victor sprang back. "Sorry. Sorry." He scrambled out from beneath the bedclothes. "Got carried away. Too far?"

She stared up at him. "Well… no. But…"

But what? Her gaze was riveted on him, her expression slightly dazed. He must look utterly ridiculous, standing there in a horrendously ugly red and yellow striped union suit. It wasn't something he'd ever meant for anyone to see. But he hadn't brought a change of clothing, and it was February. Too cold to sleep naked.

But apparently not cold enough to quell the raging erection that strained the bottom buttons of his undergarment.

Victor contemplated ways to apologize for his appearance as Mary's eyes tracked up and down his body. She didn't frown at him, though. Nor did she laugh, so perhaps he didn't look as ridiculous as he feared.

"You have a very nicely formed body," she said, then averted her gaze as if she'd embarrassed herself.

Victor's jaw worked up and down, but no words came out.

"I would like to touch you more," she continued softly. "But I'm not ready for…" She looked back at him, her gaze lingering for a second on his groin. "For everything."

"Right." One word. A slight improvement. He took a step toward the clothes he'd left draped over the back of a chair. "Another time." Two. Maybe someday he'd be able to manage complex sentences again.

"Yes."

Mary slipped from the bed and hugged her arms to her chest. "I should return to my room. Thank you for… keeping me company."

Victor nodded. "You're welcome."

"I'll meet you downstairs for breakfast?"

"Yes."

She scampered away and he set about attempting to make himself presentable with yesterday's clothes.

The dining room was silent when he arrived, though Hal and Callie were already there, with food in front of them. They turned toward him together, their mouths set in identically grim lines.

"What's wrong?"

Hal pushed a newspaper across the table. "We might

want to implement that plan of keeping out of sight as soon as possible."

Victor picked up the paper and scanned down the page until he found the relevant article.

"Fucking hell. Not again," he moaned.

"What is it?" Mary hurried into the room. She came to stand at his side and they read the article together.

KILLED BY AN AUTOMATON: GENTLEMAN DIES GRUESOME DEATH

Mr. Augustus Clay, who only recently survived an assault perpetrated by a mechanical man, did not survive a second encounter with such a creature. The unfortunate businessman was discovered late yesterday morning behind his copper factory. The cause of death appeared to be strangulation. According to our sources, bits of gears and other scraps of metal were found in the vicinity of his body. Doctors who examined Mr. Clay believe the markings seen on his person could only have been made by large hands with superhuman strength. The likely culprit: the same metal man who has been terrorizing the waterfront neighborhood.

Was this some terrible accident or a deliberate attack by the automaton's creator? The motive for the attack remains unclear, but an inside source tells us this may not be the first such incident to occur. Of particular concern is the nature of this monster, which moves under its own power with no assistance from its creator. Is it truly all machine, run on a futuristic power source? Or are we seeing the effects of occult magic? Could the monster be harvesting pieces of its victims to power itself? Unless this aberration can be captured, we may never know.

Victor dropped the newspaper on the table and turned toward the door. "Please excuse me. I need to go talk to my father."

* * *

Mary had to run to catch Victor before he hopped in his car and drove away. Holding her skirts nearly up to her knees, she vaulted into the passenger seat. Victor said nothing, his mouth set in a firm line. He started up the car and it rolled into motion.

"You didn't need to come along," he said. "I expect reporters will be watching the house. We'll incite more talk."

"I don't care," she retorted. "I'm not letting you go alone. None of this was your fault, and I can verify that."

He shrugged and fell silent.

No one accosted them when they pulled up to the carriage house behind Franklin Castle, but a crew of servants awaited them. Victor left them to clean and stow the car and led the way inside.

The butler greeted them with a slight bow. "Master Victor, your father awaits you in his study."

"Of course he does," Victor sighed. "Thank you, Sakai."

In the study, to Mary's surprise, they found Victor's father seated not behind his desk, but in an armchair, sipping a cup of tea. A pot and additional cups rested on a small table beside him, and two more chairs had been placed nearby to form an intimate circle. He motioned for them to sit and began to pour tea into the empty cups.

"I can explain," Victor blurted, not bothering to sit.

Mary took a seat and accepted a cup of tea, adding a single lump of sugar. Her stomach was rumbling from running off without breakfast, and a drink was welcome. "It's not his fault," she said calmly.

"Of course not," Victor's father replied. "He would never do something that would bring you grief or hardship. Not intentionally, that is. Though he can be rather rash, and sometimes that can lead to trouble."

"*He* is right here!" Victor protested.

Dr. Franklin sipped his tea. "It might be nice if he would join us for a civilized conversation."

Victor slumped into the vacant chair with a grunt of frustration.

His father handed him a teacup. "Have some tea, my boy. You seem agitated."

"Damned right, I'm agitated!"

"You needn't be." Victor's father paused to pour himself more tea. "I have everything under control."

Victor stilled, his brow furrowing in confusion. "I'm sorry?"

"I suppose I'm getting ahead of myself. Let's begin with your explanation of the situation."

"I—" Victor rubbed a hand over his face.

"He had nothing to do with this incident," Mary jumped in. Victor was a victim in this, and she refused to allow his family to believe anything else. "As you know, I've been working with him on the mechanical man. We've made great strides, and the automaton is functioning as he should. He is in no way a danger to the public. Not only has he been locked in the laboratory this entire time, he cannot be started without the key that only Victor possesses."

"But even if he were running, he wouldn't attack anyone," Victor added, sitting up straighter. "He's still learning, mimicking what we do. And that nonsense about how he's powered? He's electric, with batteries, like my car. Whoever is behind this knows nothing about our actual work. Someone killed Clay and is using salacious news stories to cast suspicion on us."

Mary suppressed a shiver. That same thought had been rattling in her head since she'd read the paper, but now that Victor had stated it aloud, she had to face it. Someone wanted her, Victor, or both to take the blame for Clay's death. Even without evidence against them, the press would hound them and censure them, until they were guilty in the eyes of the public. All the worry about people assuming they were intimately involved suddenly seemed silly. She'd happily take that scandal over accusations of murder.

Victor's father lifted the teapot. "More tea?"

Mary accepted a second cup.

"Your explanation is what I expected," Dr. Franklin said, still entirely unruffled by the situation. "I suspect you know more, though. You have some idea of who may have done this and why?"

"If I knew who'd done it, I wouldn't be here!" Victor gulped down half a cup of tea at once and shifted restlessly. "I'd be with the police giving testimony or with a lawyer suing for slander."

"Libel," his father corrected. "But back to the point. You know *something* or this wouldn't have happened. Tell me about it. It will help me as I craft the next portion of my plan."

"Plan?" Mary leaned forward in her seat. "I've been working on a plan. This morning's news has shifted it, but only somewhat. We need to discover who killed Mr. Clay. That will prove our own innocence."

"Exactly. Tell me what you know."

"Clay was smuggling. He appeared in town, supposedly to take charge of the copper works, but he didn't do much and he kept odd hours. Victor and I caught men loading crates onto a strange truck after hours. The crates had an unusual easy-open mechanism and contained bottles of an illegal drug called Sobridyne."

Victor swiveled to look at her, his eyes wide. Mary gave a tiny shake of her head to reassure him. She wouldn't tell anyone about the rest of that night.

Victor's father set down his teacup and rubbed his chin. "Ah. That explains a lot. I'd been wondering what you two had gotten up to that time you disappeared all night."

"We got locked in the truck," Victor exclaimed. "It wasn't my fault. I didn't do anything inappropriate."

Mary cringed. *Deep breath. Relax.*

Dr. Franklin momentarily lost a bit of his cool. "We will discuss this matter further at another time," he said sternly. "For now, we will address the more pressing matter. You, and your automaton, need to keep out of sight—both for your own safety and to avoid public scrutiny. Simply staying here in the house will invite unwanted guests, as would staying with friends. Fortunately, I have a solution. Come with me."

A solution? Mary hopped up from her seat, eager to learn Dr. Franklin's plan. A boat to carry them to another city? Train tickets out of state? A machine that could turn them invisible?

Sadly, an invisibility machine was probably impossible. It would be by far the most practical option.

"You have a solution?" Victor rose slowly, staring at his father with lifted brows. He'd entered the room frustrated and defensive, but now he looked baffled and defeated. His shoulders slumped and the furrow in his brow had deepened.

Mary would have put a hand on his arm to soothe him if his father weren't in the room.

She didn't quite understand why Victor fretted so much about upsetting his father. Dr. Franklin was a bit stern, and had definite ideas about appropriate behavior, but he didn't seem unreasonable. He was calm, thoughtful, and business-like. And he had a plan. Mary quite liked him.

"I would love to hear your solution," she said, giving Victor's father a genuine smile. At last, she could smile without forcing it. As much as she loved her friends, they'd been entirely unhelpful with planning. Now she'd finally met someone who thought the way she did. Even if his plan wasn't perfect, she could use it as a starting point. "It's so kind of you to offer your assistance."

"Happy to help, young lady. Please, follow me."

They started for the door. Victor jogged to keep up.

"I don't understand," he babbled. "Why are you doing this? Aren't you angry at me?"

Dr. Franklin huffed. "Angry? Why would I be?"

"Because I made a mess of things?"

Victor's father shook his head and looked at Mary. "He always blames himself. Have you noticed that tendency, Mrs. Clay?"

"Yes, I have."

"Right this way. I have everything taken care of. I always expected this sort of thing would happen."

Behind them, Victor stumbled to a halt. "You *what*?"

Chapter 23
Bunker Down

Victor hardly even registered where they were going, he was so flummoxed. What the hell was going on? There was no scolding, no glower of disapproval. Instead, his father was acting like the valiant hero, come to save the day.

"What do you mean you 'expected this'?" Victor demanded. "You thought I would be framed for murder?"

"Please don't shout, Victor. It's uncivilized. And, no, I obviously didn't expect this exact scenario. But I knew someday you would stumble into trouble, and I do like to be prepared. Watch your step, please, Mrs. Clay. These stairs are steep."

"Miss Amesbury," Victor corrected. He hurried ahead to offer Mary his arm as they descended the stairs to the cellar.

"Yes, thank you," she replied. "I would like to distance myself from Mr. Clay if possible."

"Miss Amesbury it is, then," Victor's father said.

Mary beamed at him. She seemed oddly pleased with him and his bizarre solution, whatever it was.

"Where are we going?" Victor wondered. He hadn't been down here since he was a boy, when the castle had been one enormous playplace. The few basement rooms were only used for storage, primarily of food and wine.

He sincerely hoped his father didn't expect him to hide out among the turnips and spiders.

"Right here." His father stopped beside a shelf of canned goods. He reached up and plucked a can of tomatoes from the shelf.

For a moment, Victor wondered if this was going to be the start of some strange lecture. The noise that assaulted his ears, however, was not a scolding but the clank of chains and pulleys. The wall in front of him swung ponderously open. His jaw dropped.

"A secret tunnel!" Mary peered through the entrance, eyes shining. "Where does it lead?"

Victor made a quick assessment of their position. They were facing the back of the house, toward the river. The carriage house? The boathouse?

Victor's father stepped through the entranceway and flipped a switch. A series of round lights running along the top of the tunnel flared to life. Smooth white walls reflected the light, illuminating a corridor that sloped steadily downward into the distance. Well past the outbuildings. Under the river.

"What the—" Victor cut himself off before he could swear again in front of Mary and his father.

A wheeled vehicle the size of a small car sat on a track that ran down the center of the tunnel. Wires connected the box-like trolley to a cable running the length of the ceiling. The trolley looked to be made for hauling cargo, but four chairs had been loaded into it for holding passengers.

"Dad?" Victor took two steps toward the trolley. "What is all this?"

"My contingency plan, of course." His father set the canned tomatoes on a small shelf, and the secret door closed behind them. "In case of danger in the city, temperance laws, severe weather, a son who needs to avoid the scrutiny of the press, and so forth. Allow me to give you a hand up, Miss Amesbury."

Mary took hold of his hand and, using one of the trolley's wheels as a step, climbed up and into the vehicle. Still smiling, she seated herself in one of the chairs.

"What an ingenious little cart," she enthused. "And an incredible tunnel. It must have been quite the undertaking."

"Thank you. It's been many years in the making, but the entire project is near to completion." Victor's father climbed up into the trolley and took a seat beside Mary. "Come along, Victor. You can gawk just as well while we drive."

Victor snapped his jaw closed and joined them. His father threw a simple switch, setting the trolley in motion. The cart rolled smoothly and quietly down the track, neatly powered by the electric lines running the length of the tunnel.

Mary launched into a series of questions about the apparatus: was it direct current or alternating current, was it also powered through the tracks or only the wires, and any number of other questions Victor missed entirely. He couldn't concentrate. Was his father really a smuggler? He'd been joking when he'd said that. But why else would anyone need a secret tunnel beneath the river?

The trolley continued on at a speedy clip. Barely a minute into the journey, Victor's father waved a hand at a wide black stripe painted on the wall and announced, "Welcome to Canada!" Shortly thereafter, the ground began to slope upward.

Their trip ended at the entrance to a large, open room lined with shelves of all sizes. About half the shelves were empty. The remainder held casks and bottles of liquor.

"Here we are," Victor's father announced. "My underground laboratory and wine cellar. Hop out and have a look."

Victor clambered out of the trolley and reached up to give Mary a hand, but his father was already assisting her.

"We're in Windsor now?" she asked.

"Indeed. Let me show you around. This main room houses my drink collection. I've been stocking it gradually in case those temperance protesters manage to get laws passed banning the things I like. I have a number of wines, brandy, bourbon, scotch, and a few others."

Victor gaped at the array of alcohol. It was nearly enough to open a liquor store. The Franklins could hold parties for years with all of it. Maybe that was the plan.

"Living quarters are through those doors to either side," his father continued. "Victor's rooms aren't furnished yet, I'm afraid, but the ones I made for my wife and I are quite habitable. This door directly to my left is the workshop area." He walked to the door and opened it, reaching inside to turn on a light. "A simple table and storage for tools. Nothing fancy, but it should have most of what you might need."

Victor started for the small workroom, but his father shut off the light and closed the door, then headed for an identical door on the opposite wall.

"This, though, is what I'm most proud of. This is where all the power for the tunnel and this complex is generated." He threw open the door, and this time he waved Victor and Mary inside.

The room buzzed with the hum of machinery. Directly in the center and taking up most of the space was a spinning apparatus, four feet high and as many feet across. Thick wires ran from the device into a box on the wall.

"An electromagnetic generator?" Victor guessed.

His father beamed. "Exactly right, my boy! Hydroelectric power at its finest. Down underneath is a turbine spun by the power of the river itself. Do you like it? Took me months of work. Consulted with Nikola on the design."

Victor blinked at him. "Nikola Tesla?"

"Do you know another Nikola? He wants to build a power plant at Niagara Falls, did you know that? Could power whole cities with the force of that water!"

"Um…" Victor stared at the generator, his mind finally making sense of everything. His father wasn't a smuggler. His father was a Mad Scientist.

"Do you have a club?" he asked. "You and Tesla and, I don't know, Lewis Latimer, maybe?"

His father's nose wrinkled. "No. Never met Latimer, unfortunately. But all my light bulbs were manufactured using his processes."

Mary circled the generator, her eyes shining with delight. "This is fabulous! I'll have to study it more in detail. Do you still have the plans?"

"Of course, dear girl," Victor's father exclaimed. "I'll have them sent down while we're fetching all your things and getting you settled in. I can show you the plans for the entire complex, if you'd like."

"That would be wonderful!"

Victor scratched his head. For some strange reason, Mary didn't seem to think any of this was mad. Then again, she hadn't thought his Mecha-Man project mad, either. It made sense, in a way. Maybe she liked her men a little bit out of the ordinary. Maybe it meant he had a chance at a future with her.

"You two take your time looking around," Victor's father instructed. "I'll arrange to have Victor's things brought down, as well as your automaton. We will have to send for Miss Amesbury's things, of course."

"Mmm-hmm," Mary replied, distracted by a particular piece of the generator.

Victor caught his father before he could leave. "Um, Dad? I wanted to ask, *why* did you always expect that I would get into trouble?"

"Why?" He frowned and rubbed his temple in a manner that Victor had unconsciously learned to mimic. "We all get into trouble, son." The frown dissolved and he laughed. "You ought to know that. Ever since your great-great-great-grandfather flew that kite in a storm, we Franklins have been getting into trouble. It's a family legacy. Bound to happen to you eventually."

"So you…" He ushered his father out of the room and lowered his voice to keep from embarrassing himself in front of Mary. "You don't think I'm a disappointment?"

"Disappointment? I don't know where you get these ideas in your head. Clearly you received an extra dose of the fanciful side of our scientific heritage."

Victor's gaze darted over their surroundings. This bunker had been created by someone at least as fanciful as he was. Probably best not to mention that.

His father glanced back over his shoulder, to where Mary was still examining the generator. "It's a good thing you've found yourself a sensible girl. I like her. Glad she's not married anymore." He clapped Victor on the shoulder and then trotted off to hop back into the trolley.

"Yeah," Victor murmured. "So am I."

Chapter 24
Winter Warmth

Mary had never expected to have to hide out from nosy reporters and murderous criminals, but if she had, she couldn't have designed a more perfect location for it. The Bedlam Bunker, as Victor had dubbed it, was admittedly a tad outlandish. But it was also practical, ingenious, and cozy.

The main bedchamber was the finest room Mary had ever stayed in. The carpet was so soft she wanted to dance barefoot on it. The dark wood paneling and burgundy wallpaper gave the space a feeling of warmth and intimacy. A spindle-legged dressing table added practical beauty. And the large bed was heaped with thick quilts and downy pillows.

Best of all, the attached washroom offered sinks with hot and cold running water, a fully modern flush toilet, and a large, gleaming ribcage shower. Mary could already imagine herself standing inside it, bathed in steam as she washed her hair amid the jets of gloriously hot water.

She stretched out on the bed, looking up at the ornate plaster medallion that surrounded the glittering electric light fixture. Dr. Franklin had spared no expense when decorating his room. He was a peculiar man, but in an organized, cultured, and highly scientific way that appealed to her.

Victor was more like him than he thought, albeit more impulsive.

"Ugh." As if her thoughts had beckoned him, Victor appeared at the door, dragging a traveling trunk. "What the hell did they pack in here? Rocks?" With another grunt of exertion, he tugged the trunk fully into the room.

Mary sat up. "I wouldn't think your clothing would be that heavy."

Victor unlatched the trunk and threw it open. "Oh. Books. Dozens of books. I hope my father doesn't think we're going to be here *that* long."

"Well, he likes to be prepared, clearly."

Victor selected a book and set it on the bedside table. "In case we need something to read. I'll put the rest of these on the shelves in the sitting room." He returned to the trunk and began to gather an armload of books. "Is there room in the closet to hang my clothes?"

Mary barely contained a snort. The closet was nearly as large as the washroom beside it. One entire wall was dedicated to space for hanging garments, while the opposite was lined floor to ceiling with drawers and shelves.

"I think there's room to sleep in the closet, if you wanted to."

Victor straightened up, using his chin to steady the precariously tall stack of books in his hands. "It couldn't be worse than sleeping on that hard, tiny couch in the other room. Which is obviously what my father intended when he instructed everyone to leave my things out there."

"I suppose it would be a gentlemanly sacrifice to make."

He sniffed. "I think we can safely say I'm not a gentleman, given how I have twice now spent all night in your arms."

Mary felt her cheeks warming and fought to keep herself

composed. "But you never attempted to take advantage of the situation. You made me comfortable, not uncomfortable. I think that's very gentlemanly." She swung her legs over the side of the bed. "There's plenty of room for two in this bed."

His mouth quirked up at one side. "I was hoping you'd say that."

A tremor of nervous anticipation undulated through Mary's body. She rose and moved toward the closet door. The last few days had had too many ups and downs of emotion. She needed a bit of relaxation.

"Do you mind if I take over the washroom for a time? I'd like to try out the fancy shower."

Victor's eyebrows lifted slightly. "Please do. I'm sure you'll love it. I've used the one my parents installed in the main house. The water gets deliciously warm. Hot enough to turn you pink all over." He coughed. "Er, excuse me. I'll go put these books away."

Mary hurried into the closet to fetch her nightgown, then darted into the washroom. Victor would have plenty of time to get his things put away while she washed. Then they could… talk? Snuggle in bed? Kiss?

She spent a bit of time rearranging her personal effects on the shelf beside one of the two matching sinks. Next to her migraine tonic, she had a small bottle of a contraceptive draught that Callie had recommended. Mary liked the comfort of being prepared, even though she wasn't sure she'd ever use the concoction. Taking things that far would involve confessing her shameful secrets. She might never be ready for that, much as she liked kissing Victor.

Before she undressed, Mary spent some time familiarizing herself with all the knobs on the shower. After a bit of trial-and-error, she had the jets that sprayed from each of the c-shaped pipes pumping out water at a comfortable pressure.

Additional water rained down from the overhead sprinkler. She left it to warm up while she disrobed.

Victor had been absolutely correct. The shower was delicious. Hot water sluiced over her skin, soothing tired muscles as it stripped away dirt and grime. Mary scrubbed soap all up and down her body until she felt pristinely clean, then stood beneath the cascade of water until every part of her was warm, her limbs loose, and her mind at ease.

Like everything else in the bunker, the towels were of the finest quality, and Mary seriously considered simply wrapping herself in the fluffy fabric in lieu of a nightgown. But Victor would be waiting for her in the bedroom, and she couldn't be so undressed in front of him. She slipped into a clean pair of drawers, pulled her warm winter nightgown over her head, and buttoned it up to her neck, as always. This was who she was. So far, Victor seemed interested in kissing and cuddling her anyway, and she would take pleasure in that fact.

Mary gathered up her clothes and stepped out into the bedroom. The space was empty of any trunks, clothing, or people.

"Victor?" she called.

She took two steps, then froze. He stood just inside the closet, stripped down to his underwear, pulling what looked like a nightshirt from a drawer.

"Mary." He yanked the garment out and held it in front of him.

She ought to have apologized for startling him, or brazenly told him he didn't need to cover himself. Instead, what came out when she opened her mouth was, "Are all your union suits striped?"

Victor lowered the nightshirt to mid-chest. This particular suit was blue, with narrow green and white horizontal stripes. She liked that he didn't wear boring white or gray.

"I bought a whole set of various colors," he admitted. "I didn't anticipate that anyone would see them. They're rather silly, I'm afraid."

"I don't mind." Her mind spun over his words. He hadn't thought anyone would see his underclothes? But he'd already admitted to dalliances with men and women alike. He could charm and flirt his way to any number of affairs. Did he wear something different or special for a tryst? Her lack of knowledge on the subject made her squirm. She needed a long conversation with Callie.

Slowly, Victor relaxed his grip on the nightshirt. He folded it, stowed it away, and closed the drawer.

"I seem to recall you saying something about having an interest in touching me." His voice was calm, but his dark eyes bore into her with an intensity that heated her as much as the shower had done. "Does that still hold true?"

Mary's gaze roved up and down his body. She couldn't help it. The shape of him intrigued her, from the breadth of his shoulders down to his muscled calves. And then there was the bulge of his penis—not as large as when she'd last seen him like this. She could change that if she kissed him.

She hugged her bundle of clothing tighter, awed and somewhat fearful that she—plain, bookish Mary—could excite a man. She had no idea how to wield such power. Anything beyond kisses and she might reveal herself to be entirely boring.

The memory of those kisses spurred her on. As he'd done before, Victor had handed her an opportunity. All she had to do was seize it.

"It's still true," she answered.

Victor stepped from the closet, moving past her without

touching her. His eyes, though, watched her with the hungry gaze of a predator, and he licked his lips as he looked at her.

"I'll let you put your things away," he said. "Come join me on the bed whenever you're ready."

Mary quickly stashed her clothing, determined to accept what he was offering before she lost her nerve. A few moments later, she stepped out of the closet to find him sprawled on the bed, arms tucked up behind his head. He looked every bit the seductive rake.

"The bed is comfortable." He arched his eyebrows and grinned at her. "But a bit lonely. It could use a lovely lady."

Mary's heart beat faster. She couldn't take her eyes off him, especially with the way his blasted tongue kept moistening his lips. She circled around to the opposite side of the bed and climbed in, sliding toward him but not touching him.

"I appear to be the only available lady," she murmured.

Victor flipped onto his side to face her. "Perfect. You are the loveliest, most desirable woman I could ever imagine."

Instinctively, Mary hugged her arms across her chest. Her too-small chest that he could hardly see beneath the most modest nightgown known to mankind.

Victor's smile faded. "Am I making things awkward? Please tell me if I'm making things awkward."

She shook her head. "Everything is awkward with me. I'm not like you. I'm shy and I never know what to say. But you are so charming, with your quick wit and dazzling smile. You can flirt with anyone."

"Not with you." His gaze dropped from hers. "I never know what to say to you. Nothing works with you. I can make you angry or sad or annoyed, or I can talk about work. Everything else…" The shoulder that wasn't touching the bed rose and fell in a half shrug.

Mary gaped at him. "But your flirting *always* works." How could he not know that? She would have sworn it was flashing over her head in giant electric lights. "It works so well I have to try to hide it from everyone. Otherwise they'll all know how much I want to… to…"

Victor looked back up at her, catching her gaze and holding it. "Kiss me?" he suggested.

Yes. That was precisely what she wanted. She lunged toward him, fingers scrabbling for purchase on his clothing, lips seeking his. All day, she'd been longing for this. The warmth of his body. The desire pounding between them. The taste of him driving all doubt from her mind.

She could be brave. Because he had doubts and fears too, and she wanted him never to feel that way. Never to think she didn't ache for him.

"God, you smell good," he rasped, inhaling deeply and pressing a kiss to her neck. Wild shivers of pleasure shot up and down her spine. "I was going mad the whole time the shower was running. Thinking of you wet and naked."

Oh, my. That explained his odd reaction when she'd asked about the shower. Mary splayed her hands over his chest, losing the last of her nervousness to the thrill of wanting and being wanted. He was hard beneath her fingers, so different than the softness of her own body. But when she rubbed his nipples through the flannel of his union suit, he shivered. That pleasure, apparently, was one more thing they had in common.

"Don't stop," he sighed, still nuzzling her neck. "Touch me everywhere. Anywhere you like."

"Me too," Mary gasped in reply. "Touch me too."

Victor's mouth found hers again, capturing her lips in a deep, drugging kiss. His hands stroked over her, rising to cup her breasts. He explored slowly at first, tracing her curves with his fingers and fitting his palms to her. Mary arched into him when his thumbs grazed over her nipples. As glorious as it felt, she wanted more. Needed more. She wanted his skin against her own.

The words clogged in her throat, but she reached for the top button of her nightgown to show him. He responded with a noise of appreciation and undid the next button himself. Mary sucked in a sudden breath as his finger skimmed over the newly-exposed expanse of her throat, where her pulse pounded just beneath the skin.

He broke the kiss as he worked the next button. "When you unbutton me, you should start at the bottom."

Mary looked down without thinking. He'd gotten hard again, the thrust of his erection stretching the fabric. The sight of it caused a corresponding throb between her legs. Again, that sense of wonder surged through her. She inflamed his passions, but he was never insistent or intrusive. She could take what she wanted, when she wanted it.

Her explorations began carefully, her fingers sliding over and around his rigid shaft, learning the size and shape of it. His breath hitched. He liked this. And she loved that he did.

The junction of her thighs grew wetter as her strokes grew bolder. She cupped him and squeezed him, thrilling to every sound he made. At last, she dared to open a button, then another. His erection sprang free. She curled her fingers around it, knowing it was what they both wanted.

At the same time, Victor pried her nightgown open, exposing her breasts to the cool air. His hands covered her, kneading and caressing, sending pulses of longing straight to her core.

Yes. Yes. This was what she'd yearned for. No barriers. No worries. Only his flesh and hers.

She couldn't stop her fingers from clenching tighter around him, but the way he thrust into her hand said he wanted more. She pumped up and down from the base to the very tip and back again.

Victor squirmed. "God, yes, Mary, please." His breathing grew ragged, his confident caresses giving way to fumbling. The skin of his cheeks and neck was flushed, his lips pink and parted.

Mary stroked faster, enthralled by his reaction. Theoretically, she knew what she was doing to him. How could she not, with Callie's detailed lectures on human pleasure? Seeing it was a different matter. She, Mary, was the one to make this gorgeous man shake and moan. His pleasure brought her a profound, beautiful sense of joy.

"Mary," he gasped. "I-I can't—" His body went rigid, and his sticky seminal fluid spilled into her fingers. Gently, she uncurled her hand. He flopped onto his back, breathing hard. "Sorry."

"Sorry?" she repeated, frowning down at him.

"Didn't last very long," he explained. "It's been… a long time."

"I thought it was lovely." Yes, her cheeks were warm again, but this time it wasn't only embarrassment. Watching him come apart beneath her ministrations had been one of the most amazing experiences of her life. She couldn't wait to do it again. And to discover how it felt when he did the same to her.

Victor sat up. "It will get even more lovely. I promise. Don't go anywhere."

He hurried off to the washroom and returned a moment later with a damp cloth, which he used to wipe her fingers clean.

"Now, I intend for you to enjoy this evening at least as

much as I have," he said, his voice a low purr. "But I don't want to do anything that would make you uncomfortable. How would you like me to pleasure you? With my hands or my mouth?"

"Um…" Mary thought back to the erotic images she'd seen at the library. "Which is better?"

He laughed. "Maybe we'll try both." He grasped the hem of her nightgown and pushed it slowly up past her waist. "And you may stop me at any time."

Mary couldn't imagine any scenario where she would stop him short of the ceiling caving in. Her body sizzled at his slightest touch. Watching him find his pleasure had left her wet and needy. And tonight she wanted more than a brief touch under the covers that she could pretend had never happened.

Victor untied her drawers and slid them down her legs, murmuring words of appreciation.

"So beautiful." His fingers trailed up her thighs.

"So delectable." He kissed both her breasts, then laved one nipple with his tongue.

"So perfect."

Mary let out a gasp that quickly turned into a sigh as his fingers stroked between her legs. No wonder he'd been so enraptured when she'd touched him. This was… It was…

"Oh, God, Victor." The press of his finger against her clitoris was driving all rational thought from her mind. She had become one of those women in the erotic drawings, legs splayed wide open, mouth agape. Entirely unashamed.

Yes. More. Oh, please.

Soft lips trailed over her belly, steadily downward.

Please, please, yes.

"As my lady desires."

Had she spoken aloud? Her body arched and strained,

mimicking the pleading of her words. He'd made her wanton. And it. Was. Wonderful.

Mary didn't flinch or tremble or turn her head in embarrassment when his lips and tongue took the place of his fingers. Instead, she sighed, long and loud, giving herself over fully to the pleasure. His teasing mouth stroked and suckled her until she thought she might burst into a shower of sparks, like a frayed electrical wire. Her fingers dug into the bedding, anchoring herself against the pulsating energy inside.

Whether she said anything else out loud, she didn't know. She was lost in a whirl of physical sensation. Victor slid a single finger inside her, adding soft strokes and gentle thrusts to the feelings overwhelming her. When she lifted her hips into him, he thrust faster and suckled harder.

Close. So close. There. Th—

The climax surged through her, bolts of bliss rocking her body from head to toe. It was only when the orgasm began to fade that she realized the noise sounding in her ears was her own keening cry.

Victor crawled up beside her, a smile on his face that dazzled her senses almost as much as the passion had.

"It's a good thing we're in a bunker." His eyes twinkled in the electric lamplight. "You don't make any secret about your enjoyment, do you?"

Embarrassment crawled up Mary's neck, but Victor's hand closing around hers stopped the heat before it could reach her cheeks.

"It was magnificent," he stated, in a tone so reverent it brooked no argument.

"Thank you."

Mary rose briefly to wash up, but within minutes she was back in the bed, beneath the covers. Victor reached to turn down the bedside lamp to its lowest level, leaving only enough light to move around the room if they woke in the night. He wrapped an arm around her and she snuggled against his chest.

"Tomorrow we'll need to pick up where we left off with the testing for Mecha-Man," she said, her brain returning to its usual state of constant thinking. "And I need to talk to my employees at the copper works. I want to know what happened."

Victor stroked her hair. "We'll need to sneak out to do that."

"I know. I'm trying to come up with a plan."

His chest vibrated with his soft laugh. "You think you can do that before you fall asleep?"

"I can try."

"Good thing you're the planner. Because I'm not going to last much longer." He emphasized this point with a drawn-out yawn.

Mary yawned too. Drat that contagiousness.

"I'll see you in the morning, sweetheart," he murmured. "Maybe you can wake me with a kiss, like in the fairy tales."

A short time later, Victor's breathing slowed and his grip relaxed. Mary tried to work on a plan, but his warmth and his scent kept intruding on her thoughts. Oh, well. There was always tomorrow. For tonight, she would simply revel in the beauty of their evening together.

Chapter 25
On Ice

Some part of Victor knew he was dreaming. He ought to have been faster than the metal men chasing him, but he never seemed to make any progress. He rounded another corner, only to find himself back where he had started. A moment later, he collided with something. The creature or person fell atop him, smothering him.

He awoke with a start, jerking and flailing, trying to throw off whatever was atop him.

"I'm sorry."

Mary. The knowledge of where he was and who he was with flooded through his brain. She was half-curled against him. Soft and warm. Nothing like the hard metal of the enemies from his nonsensical dream.

"I didn't mean to startle you," she said.

Victor tried unsuccessfully to blink away the grogginess. His lips tingled. She must have tried to kiss him. "That was not the sweet and romantic awakening I'd imagined. Please don't do it again."

"Never," she promised. "I wouldn't have done it if I'd known."

"It sounded nice in theory. But maybe not so nice for someone as bad at waking up as I am." He closed his eyes and groaned. "I feel like I want to sleep for another million years."

"Maybe a hot shower will help," Mary suggested. "You can go ahead and use the washroom. I'll go out to the main room and telephone for some breakfast."

Victor gave her a flirtatious arch of his brows. "Will you be thinking of me in the shower, wet and naked?"

She flushed. "Probably."

The shower did help. Whether or not she was thinking of him, he was absolutely thinking of her. Thinking of how her body had molded perfectly to his hands. How she'd writhed unabashedly at his touch. The memory of her had etched itself onto all of his senses. When he gripped his cock, he recalled the explorations of her hand on him, the clenching of her elegant fingers. By the time he finished his shower, the hot water had faded to tepid.

Mary and a hot breakfast awaited him in the sitting room when he finally arrived. He took a seat and picked up his plate, grateful for the staff who had made and delivered the food. If he'd been stuck cooking for himself, they would be having jam on burnt toast. Which was admittedly better than anything Hal had tried to cook when they'd been college roommates.

"After breakfast I'd like to write down my ideas and come up with a plan for the day," Mary said. She stabbed a bite of eggs and slid the fork into her mouth in an entirely un-flirtatious manner. It roused thoughts of kissing anyway. She looked lovely this morning, in a simple light-blue shirt-waist and navy skirt. Her hair was pulled back into a small bun at her nape, a few wisps hanging loose.

"Plan," Victor agreed, determined to focus on what they needed to accomplish and not hustle her back into bed. "First we sneak out. Then we sneak there. Oh! I have an idea." Mary's eyebrows arched, but he plunged ahead. "It's a good one. Trust me. We can't just walk or drive down the street, because members of the press will be near the house or the factory looking for us. So, instead we'll drive off the street."

Her brow furrowed. "Is it safe?"

"It should be."

It should be safe, Victor repeated to himself, forty-five minutes later. The electric car bumped down the grassy slope behind Franklin Castle and out onto the ice. Mary had a tight grip on the door, but she hadn't yet condemned his idea as foolhardy. Hopefully she wouldn't come to regret trusting him.

The car slowly worked its way up to full speed, bouncing and jostling them without pause. Here along the shoreline, the ice was pitted and undulating. Victor steered a bit further from land, but didn't dare stray too far out. The ice was smoother there, but also thinner. Plus, they blended in better close to the docks and buildings.

"I apologize for the lack of comfort," he said, between bumps.

"I don't mind that." The ice creaked beneath them and Mary winced. "I'm only concerned about the safety."

"The ice is plenty thick," Victor declared, praying he wasn't mistaken. The weather had been cold, but it was February now. That meant more sun, more thaws. And the river's current could easily break up weak ice. "See, there's a fisherman's hut out further than we are." He pointed at the small temporary structure. "And this car is light and doesn't generate much heat." He swerved to avoid a particularly rough patch, and the car skidded and spun in a circle. "Sorry!"

Much to his surprise, Mary laughed.

"You find this funny?" he asked, coaxing the car back into the correct direction, using smaller movements of the steering wheel this time.

"It felt like a carnival ride. And sometimes I laugh when I'm nervous. It was the combination."

"Ah." Victor peered at the ice ahead, thankful for driving goggles that cut the glare. "I will do my best not to do it again. Unless you'd like to do it just for fun." He couldn't do his usual eyebrow wiggle with the goggles in the way, but he grinned at her regardless. Driving on the ice was odd, but he was beginning to get a feel for it. By the time they reached the copper works, he'd have it down cold.

"Maybe another time," Mary replied. "This is a stealth mission, not a whimsical drive."

"Someday I'll take you on a whimsical drive," he promised. "We'll go out all day and race around and be silly and have fun."

Victor darted a glance in her direction. Her posture had noticeably relaxed, and now she smiled.

"But maybe not on the ice. Though this is less scary than I thought it would be."

They bounced over a rough patch and skidded again, but this time Victor steered them through it and kept them on track. He was definitely getting the knack of this.

"Don't tell anyone," he pseudo-whispered. "But I think it's actually rather fun."

"You would think that!" Mary exclaimed, but she was laughing again.

After some careful steering around a permanent dock, the ride smoothed out, and within minutes they were trundling alongside the red-brick buildings of the industrial section of town.

"That's the copper works, up ahead," Mary said, pointing.

"Thank you. I wouldn't have recognized it from this side."

Victor eased off the throttle and let the car slow gradually, rather than making any attempt to use the brakes while on the ice. He'd save that for a time when they were only having fun. When they were directly behind the copper works, he turned them toward shore and bumped his way up onto the grass. He took a quick look around for anyone who might have spied them or followed them, but the area seemed clear.

Mary hopped out of the car. "Thank you, Victor. This was an excellent idea. Let's head inside."

He hurried to follow her, a warm pleasure spreading throughout his body. Rarely was he one hundred percent certain of his ideas, and he often grew more uncertain in the presence of thorough planners like his father or Mary. Her confirmation that his intuition had led him down the right path felt as comforting as the steaming spray of the shower.

The moment they stepped through the back door, Mary was inundated with condolences and how-are-yous. She nodded at her employees, assuring them of her well-being, but maintained a brisk pace through the factory.

"I thought you might be coming around," a tall, muscled white man with thick gray sideburns greeted them. "Let's go into Lyle's office and we can talk."

Mary smiled up at him. "Thank you, Mr. Gage."

They crowded into the office. Mary declined the offer of a seat, so Victor and Gage remained standing, and Mr. Lyle rose to join them.

"I'm sure you gentlemen know why I'm here," Mary said calmly. Any apprehension lingering in her mind had been smothered. She was all business. Serious, direct, determined. "We wish to learn as many details as possible regarding Mr. Clay's death in order to understand the situation to the best of our ability."

"None of the men seem to be involved, thank God,"

Gage informed them. "The police were thorough, and everyone cooperated fully. I can tell you for certain that Simmons had nothing to do with it. Poor man was terribly shaken after finding Clay. Offered him the rest of the week off, but he's back today. Says he's more comfortable continuing on as normal."

"I think most of the men are," Lyle agreed. "And I agree that I don't think anyone here was responsible."

"Good," Mary said. "Can we see where Mr. Clay was found?"

"Of course," Gage replied. "It was out back. Though I'm not sure if there's anything much to learn."

The two men escorted Victor and Mary back outside, leading them to an area where stacks of wooden skids and coils of rope sat neatly stacked, waiting for pipes or other materials to be bundled for transportation.

"Simmons found Mr. Clay back here," Lyle explained, ushering the small group around the transport materials. "Simmons had driven the steam-lifter out here to pick up some skids. Routine job. It happened shortly after eleven a.m."

"And Simmons was the only one here at the time?" Mary asked.

"Correct," Gage replied. "The new steam-lifter is a one-man machine. Simmons came running inside, bellowing, white as a sheet. I went out with him after that. Clay was lying right there. We telephoned the police immediately. No one touched anything before they arrived, and I don't think anyone has touched anything since."

"Good." Mary squatted down for a closer look.

Victor knelt beside her. Nothing in the area showed signs of a struggle. No furrows or scuffs on the ground. Nothing broken or knocked obviously out of place. The morning light glinted off a handful of small metallic objects. Mary scooped up several of them and examined them a moment before handing them over to Victor.

"The bits of metal mentioned in the paper?" he wondered.

"Probably. They're random scrap."

Victor assessed the collection. A tiny piece of brass plating. A screw with a stripped head. Two small gears. Random scrap, like she'd said. He handed them back to her, then rose to his feet.

"Tell me, Mr Gage." Mary stood up and passed him a gear. "Are these gears even remotely like anything we use or manufacture here at the copper works?"

The foreman turned the piece over a few times. "No, ma'am. Nothing I've ever seen."

"That's what I thought." She turned her gaze to Victor. "And they're not something that would have come from an automaton like Mecha-Man."

"Not at all," he agreed.

A tiny shiver shook her shoulders. It could have been mistaken for cold, if not for the flash of worry in her light-blue eyes and the slight wrinkling of her forehead. Victor stepped closer, putting himself in arm's reach. If she needed support, he was there. To clutch, to hug, to cry on, or simply to stand next to.

Her mask of calm slipped quickly back into place, and she faced her employees. "Thank you, gentlemen. I believe I've seen enough. Is there anything else you think I should know?"

They both thought for a moment, then shook their heads.

"I believe you know everything we know," Mr. Lyle said. "If we think of anything else, we'll send you a message. Or if the police contact us again about the matter. Where can we reach you?"

Mary hesitated only a moment. "Call Mr. Biggs. He will make sure the message reaches me. Thank you. We should be going now."

Lyle nodded. "Good day to you, Mrs. Clay. If there's anything we can do for you, you let us know."

"And I'll make certain the proper Amesbury sign is hung up on the building again," Gage added.

A slight smile touched Mary's lips. "Thank you."

Lyle and Gage returned to the building, and Mary and Victor started for the car.

"Clay wasn't killed here," Victor stated. "Someone drove in, dumped him where he'd be found eventually, and left. Probably in the dark. Maybe they even came over the ice, like we did."

"Maybe." Mary chewed her bottom lip for a moment. "Either way, they left him here, and they left those bits of scrap along with him."

Once again, her eyes locked with Victor's. Neither of them needed to say more. They weren't merely victims of a scandal-hungry press, or convenient scapegoats. Whatever the reason for killing Clay, the disposal of his body had been done with one clear intent: to deliberately point the finger at them.

Chapter 26

It's a Wash

Mecha-Man, now clothed like a gentleman out for a stroll, tipped his hat in greeting as Mary walked past.

"Very good," she praised him, even though he had no language processing capabilities. Perhaps a future project could involve teaching him to understand and speak. Such a thing might not even be possible, but it would be fun to discuss the matter with Victor and contemplate the potential.

"He's definitely beginning to behave more like an ordinary person," Victor agreed. "To really fine-tune him, though, we're going to have to take him out into the real world. There's only so much he can learn from the two of us."

Mary shuddered, reminded of why they were working here in an underground laboratory-cum-wine-cellar on the Canadian side of the river. They'd been sabotaged. Clay had been killed for his involvement in an illegal enterprise, and the culprit knew she'd been asking questions. Was the murder meant to scare her off, or was she the next potential victim?

She ruthlessly pushed the thought aside in favor of more work. Work kept her focused. Work gave her something to do that wasn't crying in helpless frustration.

She dropped a handkerchief on the ground. Mecha-Man bent to retrieve it, bowing as he handed it back to her.

"Such a gentleman. Someday everyone will see you like this, and they'll see there's nothing to fear from you." Her last few words came out more forcefully than she'd intended. The impotent rage at the person or people who had killed Clay boiled inside her. She wanted to throw things and scream the way she'd done that day in the laboratory. That day seemed so far in the past now.

"We'll show everyone," Victor agreed, his voice tight with determination. "This is only temporary. Here, let's take Mech into the sitting room and have him practice the proper way to sit and stand."

A bit of Mary's anger subsided. Victor seemed to understand her need to keep busy. Maybe he felt the same way. They had so much in common, and they were in this mess together, after all.

Mecha-Man took swiftly to the lessons, and soon they were moving on to the more complicated task of sitting at a desk or table. Mary and Victor each demonstrated twice, then let the automaton make an attempt. Mecha-Man gripped the chair to pull it out, as they had done, but he pulled too hard, and it toppled to the floor.

"Oh, dear," a lady's voice spoke from the doorway behind them. "Am I interrupting anything?"

Mary spun around. Victor's mother stood inside the entrance to the sitting room, dressed in a cream and peach tea gown, a covered basket in her hands.

"Mother!" Victor exclaimed. "What are you doing here?"

"Is that any way to greet a lady?" she chided.

Victor righted the fallen chair and Mecha-Man sat. Victor patted his shoulder. "Stay right there, buddy." He turned his attention back to his mother. "Sorry for the outburst. We weren't expecting you."

"Of course not, dear, but I had to come by and see how you were doing. Miss Amesbury, in particular."

Mary started at this use of her maiden name. The Franklins had been discussing her, it seemed.

"I'm quite well, thank you," she replied, though inside her mind spun at a fevered pace. Why was a paragon of high society elegance like Mrs. Franklin showing even the slightest concern for a mousy girl widowed in a scandalous fashion? Especially one who did unladylike things such as build automatons.

"Oh, that is good to hear," Mrs. Franklin cooed. "I know Edward has been fancying up the rooms, but it's still such a dark and unladylike place. I brought you some goodies to make you more comfortable." She walked toward Mary, whipping the cloth off the basket as she approached. "Here you are, dear."

Mary accepted the offering and peered inside. Two dainty bottles of perfume winked up at her, both probably more expensive than any she'd owned in her life. The generously-sized jar of cold cream would be soothing for her dry hands. And the bars of soap meant she could take many hot showers.

She selected a bar and lifted it to her nose. Her nostrils filled with an enticing aroma: rose and sandalwood and something else she couldn't discern.

"Those soaps are all the rage," Victor's mother explained, a broad smile playing across her features. "Absolutely everyone is buying them. The ladies simply can't get enough! You'll love them."

Mary sniffed the soap again, then looked at the paper wrapper ringing the bar. Simpson Fine Soaps and Lotions. Where had she seen that name before? It had been recently. A sign, in dim lighting…

When the memory crystallized in her mind, she flinched so hard she nearly dropped the soap. Victor was at her side in an instant, not touching her, but clearly ready to offer his assistance. She handed him the soap.

"Do you recognize this soapmaker?"

His eyes widened as he took in the printed words. "Mother, when you say people can't get enough of this soap…"

"They're buying it by the crate-full," she replied. "And I can understand why. It's simply divine. Smell it for yourself. The scent wraps itself around you and makes you want to fill your whole house with it."

Victor took a tentative sniff. His brow furrowed. "Shit," he muttered.

"Victor!" Mrs. Franklin put a hand to her brow, as if she might faint from his language. "Good heavens!"

"Don't use this," he commanded, waving the soap. "Ever. Don't sniff it. Don't even touch it if you can avoid it. Throw it all out."

"Throw it out? What on earth are you talking about?"

Mary carefully lifted the remaining bars of soap from the basket, trying to hold them by the wrappers. Even now, her nose twitched, wanting another sniff of that alluring aroma. Too alluring, she now realized. The Sobridyne. She didn't know much about the tonic water scandal from the summer before, but Victor did. Given his reaction, she had to assume he believed these soaps had been similarly adulterated.

Mrs. Franklin recovered from her confusion enough to give her son a stern frown. "Is this related to the smuggling?"

The Franklins had definitely been talking.

"Yes," Victor admitted. "I think it is, and I think the

soap might be dangerous. Get rid of any we have in the house and tell all your friends to do the same."

"Oh, dear. I suppose I'll have to explain all this to your father."

Victor blinked at her, his head cocking slightly to the side. "You don't think *I* have to do that?"

"I bought the soap, dear. I suppose I ought to have taken a bit more time before joining in with the new fashion. I will simply have to look for another brand and set a new trend. I wager if I can convince Mrs. Ackner all the other ladies will follow." She turned to Mary. "I'll send down some replacement soaps. And if you need anything else at all, please don't hesitate to ask. We want you to be safe and comfortable." Her gaze roved the room, lingering for a moment on the couch where Victor was supposed to be sleeping. "I trust my son is behaving himself?"

"He's a perfect gentleman," Mary replied. *Except when I ask him not to be.*

"Good. You stay safely down here until all this smuggling and soap and murder nonsense is over." Mrs. Franklin nodded at her son. "You be a good boy, Victor. I'll tell your father about the soap. He'll take care of everything. Good luck with your metal man. He sits in a most genteel manner. I approve."

"Dammit," Victor blurted, the moment his mother was out of earshot. "It's that nasty, addictive stuff all over again. I should have known this would happen the instant we discovered the Sobridyne." He chucked the bar of soap he held into the small wastepaper bin.

Mary did the same with the rest, then took the bin and set it outside the room, where they'd be less likely to catch a whiff and be tempted to use it. What a waste. She would have loved to have pretty soaps with bright, fresh scents for her showers. Happy, relaxing things were of greater than usual importance in her current situation.

Victor motioned at Mecha-Man to stand, and the automaton obeyed. "Let's get you put away for the evening," he said in a dispirited tone.

Mary set down her basket and walked with Victor to see that Mecha-Man was properly shut down and stored in one of the empty rooms at the other side of the bunker. "We'll get back to work with him tomorrow. He was doing well. I think his knocking over the chair was similar to throwing a ball. He needs practice to understand his own strength."

They started back to the sitting room. Victor's mouth remained turned downward, his shoulders slumped.

"Are you all right?" she asked. "You seem bothered by this new discovery."

"I am." He closed the door behind them once they were inside, then slumped on the couch. "Someone is manufacturing addictive products again. Why? To make people buy them? Or something worse?"

Mary took a seat beside him. "I don't know. But maybe we can find out."

Victor's brow furrowed, his frown changing from glum to puzzled. "You're taking this awfully well. Doesn't it bother you? Whoever's doing this must be powerful and dangerous."

She edged closer to him. "Yes. That does bother me. Although, I believe we are safe here. But as disturbing as the discovery is, I can't help but see it as an opportunity."

"How so?" Victor straightened up, bringing his shoulder into contact with hers and his mouth within easy kissing distance.

Focus on the problem at hand.

"We have a lead," she replied. "All day I've been frustrated that the visit to the copper works told us so little. It felt hopeless. But now?" A giddy hope washed through her and she couldn't prevent a smile. "Don't you see? We have a new direction to explore. A new path that could lead us to the answers."

"True."

"We can make new plans," Mary continued, the excitement growing. She wouldn't be here forever. She could find the killer and gain her freedom. "We'll investigate the soap factory. Look up records. Discover who owns it. Establish a link to Clay. This opens an entire avenue of investigation!"

Victor's lips at last twitched upward. He gazed at her silently, his brown eyes soft. "You're right. I think we do have a good opportunity."

Her smile broke into a full-fledged grin. "Let's get started, then. You might have to think of another sneaking technique, but first I'm going to begin with a telephone call to Mr. Biggs. He can tell us where to find information on the company. Then we may have to visit the library or city hall. We'll make lists of any owners, shareholders, or other prominent people at Simpson Soaps and cross-reference them with Clay's known business associates." Victor made a tiny noise of amusement and she paused. "What?"

He looked her straight in the eye. "You are the most adorable person I have ever met in my entire life."

Mary's heart thumped wildly. That was the sweetest thing anyone had said to her. She flung her arms around Victor's neck and kissed him.

Chapter 27
Fair's Fair

Victor scooped Mary up into his arms and carried her into the bedroom. Much as he disliked the circumstances that had them holed up here, he would forever be grateful for the opportunity it had given him for these intimate moments. He set her on the bed and lay down beside her, brushing a brief kiss to her lips.

"I'd love to see you completely naked," he murmured. "To hold you with nothing between us. To touch and taste every delectable part of your body."

Her fingers skimmed over his chest, touching the buttons of his vest, but not unfastening them.

"I enjoyed what you did to me last time," Mary replied. "Would you, maybe, like me to do something similar to you?"

Victor almost laughed. "Yes. Yes, I would." Very much so. *Hell, yes,* might be a better answer. Or even, *Fuck, yeah.*

She toyed with one of the buttons, staring absently at her fidgeting fingers. "I've seen pictures in Callie's books. Some had instructions. It seemed… exciting."

Good God. Lust roared through his veins. Her determination to be bold despite her shyness had him entirely undone. He feared to let her touch him, lest he spend as quickly as he had last time. On the other hand, if she didn't touch him, he might explode from sheer desire.

Victor climbed out of bed and began to undress, taking his time, focusing on maintaining his self-control. Mary sat up and began to unfasten the buttons of her shirtwaist. Then the ties of her skirt and petticoat. Victor's fingers stalled on his vest buttons, his body nearly frozen in awe as she shimmied out of one layer after another.

"Must you go so slowly?" she asked. She worked each clasp of her corset loose. *Pop. Pop. Pop.*

"Huh? Oh, sorry. You're—"

He lost his train of thought again as she discarded the corset. A woolen navy blue chemise and matching drawers comprised her bottom layer. Modest, practical, and warm. She looked utterly delectable.

"I'm distracting you?" Mary guessed.

Victor hurried to remove his vest. "Very much so."

"I wasn't trying to."

"Well." He worked quickly to undo all the fastenings of his shirt. "Clearly, you're a natural."

She shook her head, and an expression of uncertainty furrowed her brow, but only for a moment before she smothered it. She doubted her ability to entice? She needn't worry. Victor went to work on his trousers. In a moment, she'd see exactly how enticing she was to him.

"That's better," Mary said, the moment he was down to his union suit and stockings. "Now it seems fair."

"Fair, hmm?" Victor didn't like messes and had no desire to ruin his clothing, or else he might have ripped open the undergarment and sent buttons flying. "I like the level of fair where neither of us have a stitch on." One button at a time, he worked his way down.

"Please hurry. I'm getting very—"

"Wet?" Victor suggested. "Aroused?"

"Yes," she admitted. She pulled off her chemise and tossed it aside. A flush colored her pale skin down to her breasts, and her rosy nipples stood erect, just waiting for his fingers and tongue to play.

Victor stripped off his union suit and stockings all in one motion, then scrambled onto the bed right as Mary wriggled out of the last of her own clothing.

"You are so fucking gorgeous," he breathed, tracing the underside of one round breast before palming it and rubbing his thumb across the taut nipple.

She reached for him, her fingers trailing lightly across the hairs on his chest. "You say the nicest things."

"I say the truth as I see it," he replied. "Others may overlook you. Clay may have ignored you. But to me, you're impossible to overlook or ignore. You're so damn beautiful, Mary."

For the second time that evening, she lunged at him, staggering him with the hunger in her kiss. Victor sprawled on his back, and she straddled him as they kissed, running her hands up and down his torso. Exploring him. This time without any barrier. He cupped both her breasts, kneading and teasing until she groaned her pleasure into his mouth.

Yes. His sweet, sensual beauty. Watching her give in to her passion was nothing short of glorious. He couldn't wait to see her lips parting again in a gasp of bliss. To hear her cries of ecstasy as she came.

Mary broke their kiss and inched downward, pressing her lips to his throat, then his shoulder, then his chest. Her name rasped from his lips.

"Tell me if I do anything wrong," she said.

He didn't think it possible for her to do anything wrong. Every touch of her fingers sparked pulses of delight. Each press of her lips, a searing pleasure. She'd teased him for undressing slowly, but now she was killing him with her leisurely explorations. She seemed determined to touch every inch of his torso, creeping her way down his ribcage, across his abdomen…

Victor groaned when her fingers at last curled around his cock. "Taste me," he gasped.

Mary did, first a slight brush of her lips, then a stroke of her tongue across the crown of his shaft.

Victor writhed. "Fuck."

"Good?" she asked. "This is all a sort of experiment for me."

"More," he choked out. "Please."

Again, she complied, licking him with curious lashes of her sweet tongue before she mercifully opened her mouth to draw him inside.

Victor clutched the bedsheets and fought to keep himself from arching into her. Christ, she was divine. The gentle suction of her mouth made his balls tighten and his muscles clench. He *would not* spend in her mouth after five seconds like a randy teen. But, Lord above, she was torturing him.

She'd read books. She'd absolutely read the right kind of books.

By her own admission, this was new to her, but she knew to tighten her grip. To stroke him up and down in concert with the motions of her mouth. To swirl her wicked tongue over the head of his cock. Sucking. Teasing. His bookish beauty. Her eager curiosity was more thrillingly erotic than any seasoned professional.

Victor didn't know when he'd begun thrusting in time to her movements. His body screamed for release, even as he willed himself to hold back, to let the pleasure carry him higher and higher, on and on. Forever.

His will wasn't as iron-clad as all that. With orgasm imminent, he quickly twisted away, pushing gently on her shoulders to move her off of him.

"That's enough," he panted.

Mary rose up to a seated position and peered down at him, a furrow of confusion forming on the bridge of her nose. "But you haven't, um, finished."

"I know." He took a steadying breath. "But I can't neglect you. I was hoping we might try something where we could finish together."

"Oh. I'd thought we would take turns." Several heartbeats passed before she continued, a note of hesitancy in her voice, "I don't know if I'm ready to go further."

A coil of apprehension knotted in Victor's gut. Mary was a widow. She understood coupling. She clearly enjoyed other sex acts. Yet she remained reluctant to engage in intercourse. His blood boiled. If Clay had been rough with her, if he had hurt her, Victor was going to dig up the man's body, bring him back to life, and kill him again.

Victor grasped Mary by the waist, pulling her back on top of him for a long kiss. "There are other things we can do that don't involve penetration."

"Like what?"

"Here." He adjusted their position until her slick folds rubbed across his cock. Pleasure speared through him and he inhaled sharply. Damn, she felt good. He ached to slide inside her, to feel the tightness of her vaginal walls squeezing him. But for now, while she didn't want that—even if she never wanted it—he would be creative.

He flexed his hips, rubbing himself back and forth until she let out a little squeak of pleasure. "That's it, love. You can ride me, just like that. Rub your sweet clit all up and down my cock. Use me until we both can't stand it any longer."

Mary stared down at him, her eyes glazed with lust, her hips already rocking. "You are wicked," she sighed.

"Yes."

Her eyes slid closed and her tempo increased. She was perfection, from the swipe of her pink tongue across her parted lips to the bounce of her breasts to the triangle of golden hair where their bodies came together.

"I love it," she moaned. She rocked harder and harder, her breath quickening, mewls of yearning pouring from her lips. "Oh, Victor. I want to be wicked, too. I want… I want…"

She screamed as she climaxed, thrusting her pelvis into him again and again, prolonging her pleasure. She swept Victor up in her ecstasy, and this time he didn't try to fight it. His body convulsed and he lost himself between her thighs.

Mary sank down on top of him, resting her head on his shoulder. Victor toyed with her hair, which had almost entirely come undone from its knot and now twisted and curled around her face.

"You are so lovely," he murmured. "Anything and everything is lovely with you."

Her fingers snaked along his arm. "You make me forget that I'm supposed to be shy and modest."

Victor kissed her forehead. "Sweetheart, you can be anything you want with me. You can bashfully ask me to show you something or you can wantonly demand that I pleasure you every which way. I'll take everything you'll give me. But I'll never pressure you. Wherever we go from here is up to you."

Mary said nothing, though her hand continued to stroke his arm. Beneath her cheek, his heart hammered. Had he said too much? Not enough? She seemed content, but he feared he might be embarrassing her with his enthusiasm. She'd just been widowed, for God's sake. And some villain was trying to pin a murder on them. He needed to watch what he said. She didn't need a lovesick lab partner on top of her other worries. He would not pressure her. And if that meant keeping his feelings to himself, so be it.

Mary lifted off of him. "We should clean up. Stay here. I'll go get a warm cloth." She hopped from the bed and disappeared into the washroom.

"I love you," Victor whispered. Maybe someday, in the far, unknown future, he'd be able to say it to her face.

Chapter 28
One Thing After Another

This was not the time. It was absolutely, completely not the time. Mary's heart, however, appeared not to respond to logic. It had chosen now, of all times, to fall in love.

She hadn't recognized her situation right away. All evening she'd been basking in the euphoria of her latest intimate encounter with Victor. They'd cuddled in the bed, reading to one another and discussing ideas for future scientific endeavors. Her happiness had been all-encompassing. Like floating on a cloud of bliss, up where her doubts and worries couldn't reach her. Every word Victor had said about how beautiful or desirable she was had carried her higher. Every touch had made her snuggle closer, as if she could burrow deep inside him so they'd never be apart. She'd fallen asleep with his taste on her tongue and his warmth enveloping her.

It was only when she'd woken this morning, awash with happiness to have him beside her, that she'd been able to put a name to the feeling inside her. She was in love.

Warm water cascaded down her body, washing away any sticky remnants of their lovemaking. The heat of the shower relaxed her muscles and soothed her body. It also, unfortunately, fully woke her brain.

She'd always possessed a highly active mind. In her

scientific pursuits, it was invaluable, helping her think up new ideas, correct mistakes, and puzzle through difficulties. Times like now, however, it felt more of a curse, whirling and swirling with scenarios and possibilities, many of which were out of her control.

"What a perfect time to go to pieces over a man," she muttered.

Mary let her head fall back against one of the curved pipes, the metal warm to the touch from the water pumping through it.

Why now? Why him? And what on earth was she going to do about it?

Nothing. She would do nothing. What mattered was proving that she and Victor were in no way culpable for Clay's death. They would discover who was responsible. They had to investigate Simpson Soaps. Burying her feelings was nothing new. What did it matter if this was a different sort of feeling than the ones she usually hid?

She shut off the water and toweled herself dry, determination growing with every swipe of the cloth. Wipe away any inconvenient emotions. Be her usual calm, sensible self.

She'd only brought a dressing gown into the washroom with her, but she tied it snuggly to preserve her modesty. No sense inflaming Victor's desire and distracting herself from what needed to be done. Prepared to conduct herself exactly as she always did around him, she stepped out into the bedroom.

"Good morning, darling," he greeted her.

Mary almost tripped over her own feet. Victor sat in the bed, the blanket slung low across his hips, his naked torso on full display. He held a dainty teacup in one hand, a saucer in the other. A shadow of stubble coated his cheeks, and his mouth hitched in a smile so provocative that Mary reflexively checked her clothing to see if she'd accidentally shown any skin.

"I made us some tea." Victor set his cup on the bedside table and began to pour a cup for her. "You like it with one lump, correct?"

Mary's heart beat wildly beneath her breast. Yes, she did like it with one lump of sugar. How did he even know that? She didn't recall ever telling him how she took her tea. Somehow he'd noticed. And remembered.

He had to stop. Enticing nakedness, sweet words, kind gestures. How could she resist it all? How could she focus on what needed to be done when all she wanted was to fly into his arms and kiss him forever?

Gingerly, she reached for the teacup he held out to her, making sure not to let their fingers brush.

"We need to get to work," she said curtly. "Please get dressed. Thank you for the tea." She whirled around and rushed into the sitting room, closing the door behind her.

* * *

Mary's plan for gathering information on the soap company still had a number of holes, but by the time she and Victor had both dressed, she'd settled on a first course of action. They would visit her attorney for an update and any information he could provide, then continue on to look up any public records and news reports about Simpson Soaps. Since they'd been out of sight for a few days now, she hoped the press had moved on. But in case they hadn't, she would ask Victor's father if they could use the enclosed steam carriage. Bundled up in their winter gear they wouldn't be easy to identify, and with a driver operating the vehicle they could stay hidden in the back.

Victor voiced no objection to any part of the plan. He

hadn't even questioned the way she'd run off and ordered him out of bed. An arched eyebrow here or there was the only indication that he found anything peculiar in her behavior. He remained his usual, solicitous self, assisting her in and out of the tram that carried them through the tunnel and offering his arm to escort her up the stairs from the cellar.

It's just an arm and he's fully clothed, Mary told herself as they started up. She'd keep repeating the words as long as necessary. And once they reached the top, she could let go without being rude. She had only to breathe normally for eight more steps. Seven. Six.

Mary almost squeezed her eyes closed to stop herself from counting. For heaven's sake, she was behaving like a silly schoolgirl.

The hallway at the top of the stairs came as a blessed relief, and she slipped away from Victor, putting more than the usual space between them. Not touching him, however, made it easier to look at him. Which led to the memory of him a short time ago, sipping tea while naked in bed.

"Did I do something wrong?" he asked. "Because you seem suddenly reluctant to touch me. If I did something to bother you, please tell me so I won't do it again. I don't want to do anything to upset you."

Mary hugged her arms across her chest. The poor man. Of course he was confused, after how brazenly she'd touched him last night. And she couldn't blurt out the truth.

Well, you see, I've fallen in love with you and I'm trying to keep my emotions in check, which is greatly aided by maintaining physical distance and avoiding anything that might even hint at romance.

"It's me," she explained. "I'm anxious today." That was true enough.

"Of course." He scrubbed his hand across his face, and

his usual calm demeanor returned. "Pardon me. It's only natural that you'd be on edge, and I ought to be helping instead of thinking only of myself."

Himself? He'd been as thoughtful and attentive toward her as anyone ever had. Mary couldn't imagine how that could be construed as thinking of himself. And she had no time to puzzle over the matter, because Victor started off down the hall at a brisk pace.

"Let's put your plan into action, shall we?" he declared.

She hurried to catch up.

Mary still didn't entirely know the layout of the massive house, but she recognized the corridor leading past Victor's father's study. As they neared the door, Dr. Franklin's voice rang out.

"I'm afraid they are not here."

Mary and Victor both froze.

"It is imperative that both your son and Mrs. Clay come to the station as soon as possible," a stern voice replied. "Would you happen to know their current whereabouts?"

"I'm afraid not," Victor's father said.

Mary swiveled to look at Victor. His eyes were round with alarm. He jerked his head in the direction they'd come from.

Mary nodded, and together they hurried back toward the cellar as quietly as possible.

Once downstairs, Victor yanked on the magnetized can that triggered the secret door. He helped Mary into the trolley and flung the throttle into the "go" position.

"Goddammit," he muttered, when they were nearly halfway down the tunnel. "My father is lying to the police. He must think we're in serious trouble."

Mary's plan crumbled. "We have to turn ourselves in. It's the only way we won't look guilty. We go to the station, we tell them everything we know. We can give them the soaps for testing. That will prove someone else was responsible."

Victor mulled over her words for a moment. "Yes. I think that's a good idea. I don't want to do anything that would make people suspect you."

"Or you, either," she added.

His mouth hardened into a tight line. "Better me than you."

Mary's heart skipped a beat. No. That was absolutely not better. No one was going to harm Victor on her watch. Ever.

* * *

Despite her insistence that this was the right thing to do, Mary couldn't help but tremble as she peered up at the imposing red-brick facade of police headquarters. Victor stood quietly at her side, ever patient. She'd given herself plenty of time to prepare for this. Not wanting to rush out suspiciously soon after Victor's father had claimed no knowledge of their whereabouts, she and Victor had remained in the bunker until mid-afternoon.

Most of the time had been spent teaching Mecha-Man. The automaton could now sit properly at a table, use glasses and utensils correctly, and pull out a chair for a lady before seating himself. He responded well to all of Victor's hand signals and most of Mary's. The day had been a smashing success from a scientific standpoint.

From an emotional standpoint, however, it had been exhausting. Victor's enthusiasm for his work was endearing, and she'd caught herself smiling foolishly at him nearly a dozen times. Whenever she'd grown excited, he'd beamed at her. Once, those looks would have been nothing more than his usual charming smile. Now, they had a wicked edge that said, *I'd like to take you to bed right now.* Maintaining her cool had taken all her resolve.

She rubbed her temple. Her migraine tonic kept the headache from becoming debilitating, but a dull throb still plagued her. Between that and her uncertainty of what awaited her inside, the fifteen stone stairs between the ornate iron rails looked positively mountainous.

"Ready?" Victor asked. He crooked his arm.

Mary placed a hand on his forearm. "Yes."

She kept her grip light as they started up the stairs, though her fingers itched to cling to him. The small bag containing the incriminating soaps dangled from her opposite hand. Would the police believe their story? Maybe they should have gone to the apothecary for testing first.

Step after step she made her way up to the wide, trapezoidal porch, then finally through the large entrance doors. Was she a fool for doing this? Would they throw her in a cell, assuming she'd killed her husband?

"Mrs. Clay?"

Mary jumped. A lanky, pale-haired man walked briskly toward her.

"And Dr. Franklin? Thank you for coming. We've been expecting you. Right this way, please."

Mary exchanged a glance with Victor. Maybe her worry was for nothing. This certainly didn't seem like the greeting of someone expecting to arrest her.

They followed the man into a small room containing only a simple table and three chairs. He motioned for them to sit before taking the place opposite them.

"I'm glad to see you received our message," he said. "My name is Detective Daide, and I'll be asking you a few questions this afternoon."

Mary set the bag of soaps on the table. A faint hint of

floral wafted up from the bag, and she had to fight down the urge to lean in and sniff. She nudged the tote a bit further away.

"We will do our best to assist you, Detective," she replied. "We have some information we wanted to pass on, as well."

The detective pulled out a notebook and pencil. "Do you? I should very much like to hear that."

Mary upended the bag, spilling the soaps onto the table. "These are Simpson Soaps. The latest craze. People are buying them at an unusually high rate. We believe the soaps may contain Sobridyne to make them addictive."

Daide pursed his lips and made a note. "Really. How interesting. And how did you reach this conclusion?"

"The truck the smugglers were using," Victor cut in. "I assume you know that we reported having found Sobridyne in a situation that suggested smuggling?"

"I do," the detective replied.

"The truck had a Simpson Fine Soaps and Lotions logo."

Mary almost kicked Victor under the table. After he complained about his father lying to the police, he went and did the same thing? And for what? To protect her reputation? People thought she was an adulterous murderess. What difference would it make if the police knew they'd spent a night locked in a truck together?

"Hmm." Detective Daide picked up a bar of soap and examined it for several seconds before setting it down. "We'll have these analyzed. Thank you. Now, if we could go over a few questions regarding your whereabouts near the time of Mr. Clay's death?"

Despite the lingering headache, Mary wrapped a mantle of calm around herself and answered every query as simply and truthfully as possible. Victor didn't say much more except to agree with her, but his presence at her side steadied her. She was not in this alone.

Daide nodded and wrote, maintaining the same serious yet amiable demeanor he'd greeted them with. Not once did he glare at them, raise his voice, or in any other way resort to intimidation tactics. As the interview wore on, Mary's shoulders began to lower, and even her migraine ebbed slightly.Whatever this result of this meeting, she hadn't been called in to be mistreated.

"I think that's everything." Daide snapped his notebook shut and pocketed it. "We will compare your story with our information, of course, but I believe we have what we need from you." He picked up the bars of soap and stashed them in his outside coat pocket. "I will see these are analyzed. Thank you for your assistance." He rose from his seat.

Mary and Victor also stood and shook hands with the detective. He walked them to the front door, where he thanked them one last time.

"That wasn't so bad," Victor declared. Mary once may have taken such a statement at face value, but now she knew him well enough to catch the note of relief in his voice. He'd been nervous, and perhaps still was.

"No, it wasn't."

Would Victor notice the same slight hesitation in her own voice? They hadn't been arrested. The police had the soap for evidence and could further their investigation into the smuggling. Still, something nagged at her. This had been almost too easy.

The back of her neck prickled, and she looked around. People walked down the sidewalk as usual, but no nosy reporters lay in wait. Her shoulders lowered again. This was almost over. The walk to Victor's house wasn't long.

They hadn't even gone a single block before the prickling

sensation returned. Not wanting to obviously look all around her, Mary stopped and bent as if to tie her bootlace. As she twisted to adjust her cloak and fiddled with the shoe, she was able to take a surreptitious glance. Across the street and not far behind was a man with a top hat tilted to shadow his face. Mary recognized him as one of the people who had been walking down the street when they'd departed the police station. But now that she'd paused, he had too.

Victor took her arm when she rose to her feet. "Everything all right now?"

She gripped him tightly and spoke in a low voice. "No. It's not."

Chapter 29

Hold on to Your Hats

Victor had run through every swear word he knew and was on the verge of making up new ones. He had yet to get a good look at the man following them, but he didn't dare stop to look or turn around.

"We can't go home," he murmured, leaning toward Mary as if flirting. "We can't put the household in danger."

Mary didn't turn her head, but her eyes darted back and forth. "We need to stay in public. If people are watching, he can't harm us."

"It's a lovely day for some shopping," Victor said aloud. He steered toward Cadillac Square. "Valentine's Day is just around the corner, after all."

Mary flinched. Damn. He oughtn't have said that. Implying she might be his Valentine was not part of the "do not pressure her" plan.

"I would be happy to help you select a gift for your sweetheart," she said brightly. Victor hoped her superficial cheerfulness was to mask her worry about the man following them rather than anger at him.

Carriages and steam cars trundled along the wide street on either side of the Cadillac Square park. Individuals and couples strolled the criss-crossing park paths and sidewalks. The leafless trees left clear sightlines from one side of the square to the other. Lovely for people-watching. Not ideal when someone was following you.

"That looks like a good place to start." Victor pointed at a random shop on the opposite side of the square and turned to cross toward it. The change of direction finally afforded him a glimpse of their pursuer.

The man wore a black suit, with his hat tilted forward. The awkward angle of the headgear shaded his eyes, while the rest of his face was obscured by a bushy beard. He was a bit stockier than Victor, which could mean he was hired muscle. Victor didn't want to get close enough to find out.

He and Mary made their way across the street and through the park, moving at a brisk pace. They veered around a wagon parked along the sidewalk and wormed their way into the crowd of shoppers.

Victor looked over his shoulder. Their tail was out of sight, blocked by the tall delivery wagon. Grasping Mary's hand, Victor raced down the block, dodging pedestrians and mumbling rushed apologies.

They darted past an elderly woman with a small dog, only to be nearly decapitated by a young man carelessly swinging his umbrella.

"Sorry!" Mary squeaked, though Victor wasn't sure whether she was speaking to the woman, the man, or herself.

He risked another look back. When he didn't spy their pursuer, he tugged Mary toward the nearest shop entrance. "In here."

The shop—a milliner's to be precise—was small, but smartly laid out, and lit with warm electric lights. Hats of all sorts for ladies and gentlemen alike covered shelves on the walls and hung on racks.

"Good afternoon," the shopkeeper greeted them. "I'm

Osmund, owner of Osmund Hats and Headwear. Come to purchase a new hat for your lovely wife?"

"Er, uh, yes," Victor stammered. "For Valentine's Day." He knew Mary would play along, but he would be doing some serious apologizing for his presumptuousness when they were out of this mess.

"Of course, of course! We've just put out an assortment of new styles. Everything you'll need for the upcoming spring. Fancy an Easter bonnet? Something floral for a spring tea?"

Victor seized a random hat and plopped it on his head. He turned the mirror sitting on the shop counter so he could watch out the front window as he pretended to examine the merchandise.

"And, naturally, we have many hats for the discerning gentleman as well," Osmund added. "That one suits you very well, though the size appears to be incorrect. Shall I take a measurement?"

Victor's gaze flicked to his reflection, before returning to watch the street for the man chasing them. The hat didn't suit him at all. It was one of those big, western-style hats he'd seen in photographs of cowboys and Texas Rangers. Victor could neither shoot a gun nor ride a horse, and he'd never aspired to the Wild West fashion. The hat did, however, nicely conceal his features from anyone who might peer into the shop.

He turned toward Mary. Her gaze was focused on the front of the shop, her expression wary. Watching, like he was.

Victor made a quick scan of nearby ladies' hats. Good Lord, but they were awful. Heaped with fake flowers, feathers jutting out at all angles. He seized one of the worst offenders, which had an entire bird on one side, plus more feathers draping down from it which clearly had never belonged to the poor stuffed creature whose perch they shared.

"This one is perfect." He snatched Mary's fuzzy cap from her head and replaced it with the avian monstrosity. Between the wide brim and the dangling feathers, she nearly disappeared.

"Oh, but you can't see her lovely face," Osmund protested. "Perhaps—"

"And it's quite warm in here," Victor interrupted, shrugging out of his overcoat and tossing it aside. He couldn't swap clothes entirely, but even a small change in appearance might serve to conceal his identity. "It won't do to get overheated, will it, Mary?"

Behind the feathers, her eyes widened in understanding. She cast aside her own coat.

"I don't think that hat is quite right for you, dear," she murmured, reaching for a rack of men's hats. "Try this one." She selected a low, wide-brimmed boater and swapped it with the cowboy hat, all the while watching the shop entrance behind him.

Osmund came out from behind the counter, a smaller hat with a smaller bird in his hand. Aesthetically speaking, it was no improvement on its larger counterpart.

"Perhaps this might suit Madame better? It will not hide her pretty features."

Victor glanced out the window. A woman strolled past, but there was no sign of the man who'd chased them. Yet.

"No, no," Victor told the shopkeeper. "She needs something to keep the sun off her face. Can't abide freckles, you know." He took hold of one of the free-standing hat racks and dragged it away from the wall, putting it between himself and the shop entrance. "Here, darling, try this one."

Mary joined him, bringing along another gentleman's

hat. This one was a tan, four-indent planter hat. Appalling. He handed Mary a black straw sailor hat with a full-face veil. Her lips puckered in a grimace, but she accepted it. She positioned it on her head, and for the first time ever, she actually looked the widow she was.

Victor's chest tightened. He hated that she was expected to mourn a man who'd been nothing but horrible to her. Her life shouldn't be one of black clothing and melancholy. She deserved freedom and joy and fun. Victor wanted to see her smile and hear her laughter. To watch her face light up in scientific discovery. To hear her sigh in delight and scream in ecstasy. If he had the power, he would give her a life of pure happiness.

"Victor!"

Her low cry and her hand gripping his arm snapped him out of his brooding. His gaze flew to the window. The burly man with the tilted top hat ambled slowly by.

Osmund stepped in front of the hat rack, cutting off Victor's view. "That hat is much too somber for such a charming young lady. Perhaps Madame would like to try one of our new fedora hats. Very popular. Sarah Bernhardt herself is known to wear the style."

Victor shifted to see around the milliner. Top Hat Man was gone. Dammit. Had he seen them? Which way had he gone? Or was he hovering in wait outside?

Mary's fingers dug into his arm. "We'll have to wait," she whispered. "Keep watching. Give him time to move on."

"What was that?" Osmund asked.

"I think you're right about this hat," she said, louder. "It's not for me. Let me try the fedora."

Osmund knew his craft. The soft felt hat, in dark gray and sporting a narrow black ribbon, suited Mary to perfec-tion. With it sitting at a jaunty angle atop her blond curls, she was nothing short of adorable. Had they not been in public, Victor would have kissed her for hours.

"Ah." The milliner chuckled. "I see you like that one."

Victor reined in his over-enthusiastic smile. "Yes. But we should consider all the possibilities." He caught Mary's eye. "All of them."

For the next quarter hour, they considered nearly every hat in the shop. One of them watched the window at all times, but as the minutes ticked by, their stalling technique turned into something of a game. They suggested the worst of the worst for one another, snickering at each extravagant chapeau.

Victor even tried on a ridiculous smoking hat, which clung tightly to his skull and sported a draping gold tassel. It made him look like a shifty museum curator who snatched up anything he deemed "exotic," without even bothering to learn about the culture he'd stolen it from. Ugh. Victor disliked museums and didn't smoke. He moved on to an alpine hat with enormous duck feathers.

"Poor birds," Mary whispered. "Sacrificed for silly hats." She discarded the feathery confection she wore.

Don't buy her things with feathers, Victor noted.

He picked up the fedora from where it rested on the counter. "I think this one does suit you best, after all."

"And I think you should try the gentleman's fedora," Mary replied, pointing to one of the few hats he had yet to put on.

Victor placed the hat on his head and for once actually studied himself in the mirror. The fedora looked good. Stylish. Gentlemanly, with a touch of rakishness.

"Perfect!" Osmund declared. "Matching hats for a charming couple."

They weren't exactly a couple. And matching hats

probably belonged in the same category as formal courtship and meeting her parents. Mary was smiling, though, so Victor paid for both hats, then set about putting the shop back to rights. Osmund objected, but Victor had made the mess. The least he could do was tidy it up. And leave a generous tip.

The sun was sinking in the west when they finally stepped out the door, attired in their new headgear. Victor made a slow perusal of the area, but found no sign of Top Hat Man. He and Mary linked arms. Ten minutes and they'd be home.

They walked quickly and quietly, still wary, but this time no one appeared to be following them. Victor's stomach rumbled. Dinnertime was approaching, and all he wanted was a nice meal and an evening alone with the woman he loved. Maybe they would make love again. Maybe he could begin to confess his feelings to her. Explain that he would always be her friend, eagerly be her lover, and—if she desired—be all the things Clay ought to have been to her. Protector. Partner. Husband.

Franklin Castle loomed ahead of them, lights aglow in its windows. He wanted to walk her in the front door, as if this were her home, too, and they belonged here together. Discretion was still advised, however, so he made for the side of the house and the path to the back entrance.

He had barely set one foot on the sidewalk, when a masked figure leapt out of the bushes and came barreling at him. Victor sprang back in alarm, but the man swerved at the last second, going after Mary instead.

She cried out as the villain's arm wrapped around her, but the blackguard swiftly muffled her shout with a gloved hand over her mouth. Victor dove at them, but the man was too fast, and he had allies. An autocab zipped up next to them and the driver flung the door open. The man shoved Mary inside and scrambled in after her, leaving Victor grasping at thin air.

The cab door slammed closed, and the vehicle tore off down the street.

"No!"

"Victor! What's happened?" called a familiar voice.

Victor spun to find Hal and Callie riding up on bicycles.

"Your mother invited us for dinner," Hal began.

Victor couldn't wait around to discuss the problem. Hal had barely set a foot on the ground when Victor yanked the bicycle right out from under him.

"They took Mary! I need your bike!" Victor put his feet to the pedals and pumped with every ounce of strength he had.

Chapter 30
Free Ride

Mary huddled against the door of the cab, as far as she could get from the bushy-bearded bruiser who had kidnapped her. She'd already tried opening the door, but it had been welded shut. So much for the hope that this was an ordinary cab.

She wrapped her cloak snuggly around her, hugging her arms across her chest. The position kept her trembling to a minimum, as well as keeping her warm. Hiding her fear was pointless. These men meant her harm, and fighting them was not an option for a woman of her size and abilities. Let them believe she'd given up.

They hadn't killed her outright, which gave her hope. If they meant to kill her later, they'd likely take her to a remote location to do the deed. Whoever was in charge would want the murder carried out and arranged in a specific way, as they'd done with Clay.

Somehow she had to escape. Not only for herself, but for Victor, who would surely come after her. Away from populated areas, they could both be killed, and their bodies placed in such a way as to look like an accident. Or perhaps a murder-suicide.

The cab driver glanced back at her. "Still got nothing to say, Missy?" Already he'd asked her about half a dozen pointless questions. She'd answered none of them, but she was glad he'd made the attempt. She recognized his voice as that of one of the smugglers. Now she made note of his face: round, with narrow, light-colored eyebrows, a snub nose, and pointy chin. Clean shaven.

"Shut up and drive," Bushy Beard grumbled. He, too, was one of the smugglers, Mary believed, though she wasn't as certain as she was about the other man.

Thick black beard with hints of gray. Pale skin. Light eyes. Scar across left eyebrow.

If she'd had a notebook, she would have scribbled notes beneath her cloak. As it was, she would have to rely on her memory. Outside, the industrial part of town rolled by. They were headed west, the same direction the smugglers' truck had taken that night. Would they go to the soap factory again?

Mary kept her new hat tilted down and her body curled into as small a space as possible, but her eyes roved everywhere. The autocab was a typical closed-compartment steam car, with a boiler in the rear, a bench seat for up to three passengers, and seats up front for the driver and one additional passenger. A coin-operated meter sat in the center so riders in the front or the back could easily pay their fare. The machine sat silent. Too bad this driver wouldn't be kicking her out for not paying.

Her gaze lingered on the meter. The cast iron shell bore the logo of the Riverside Cab Company. Another direction for her investigations. Assuming she ever got out of here.

Their path turned northward for several blocks, then slanted west once more, past the Michigan Central railyard. Train cars undergoing repairs or under construction were large, blocky shadows in the fading twilight. A faint chugging sounded in the distance as a train passed through on its way to the passenger station downtown.

The hard metal of the door poked into Mary's back. If only she could get out of this vehicle. The railyard would be a perfect place to hide. With the rapidly darkening skies, she'd disappear easily among the buildings and cars. Even better, the railyard would have telephones and telegraphs, and be staffed 'round-the-clock. She could get help.

The cab pressed onward, past the smokestacks of the railyard shops, then veered off onto an unpaved road. A short time later, the vehicle began to slow. A shiver ran down Mary's spine. This area was too isolated and gathering clouds turned the purple skies to black. If the men killed her now, no one would ever know. She kneaded her skirts, gathering up her courage. She would fight, scream, do whatever she could to get away.

"This'll do." The driver brought the cab to a full stop with a quick tug of the brake. He pushed open his door and swung a leg out.

Mary scanned the instrument panel. She knew steam cars. If she could get into the front seat, she could drive off and leave the men behind.

The driver stepped out and closed the door behind him. Bushy Beard opened his door, but didn't climb out.

"Let's go," he snarled at her.

Mary's pulse pounded. If only he'd leave. She was fast enough to get into the front seat while she had the element of surprise. But if he was still in the cab, she couldn't drive away. He'd grab her and hurt her to prevent any escape.

"Now," the brute snapped.

Mary shied away from him, pressing against the locked door behind her and calculating angles. She only had one chance.

Bushy Beard lunged at her, and she leapt, diving over the meter into the front seat. Her hands fumbled for the instruments as he cursed and grabbed at her. Driving away would be impossible. Her fingers flew to the controls to flush the system.

"Help me, you oaf!" Bushy Beard shouted at his companion.

The driver yanked open the door, but Mary was quicker. She flicked the switch to kill the pilot light. Already she could hear the trickle of water and hiss of steam from the valves she'd opened. Even warm from the drive, the engine would take time to reconfigure and start up again. They'd be unable to drive after her, and she'd have a head start.

As the driver reached into the car to pull her out, Mary scrambled for the passenger-side door.

Please, God, let it be unlocked.

If it had been fused shut like the back door, her plan would be for nothing. Her hand found the handle and yanked. When the door swung open she almost shouted in relief. She sprang from the cab and tore off toward the main road, her legs pumping as hard as they ever had. If she could only make it back to the railyard.

"You stupid bitch!" Cab Driver shouted.

Mary didn't look back. She had to get to the railyard. She had to. No matter what.

"Mary!"

Victor!

She almost stumbled. Victor materialized out of the darkness, speeding toward her at a faster clip than she would have thought possible for a man on a bike.

"Get them!" Bushy Beard roared.

The distance between Mary and Victor closed rapidly. If she could hop on the bicycle, they could get away. Even with two people, the bike would be faster than a man on foot. She could do it. They would escape.

The crack of a gunshot split the air. Mary tripped, scrambling to keep her balance. Ahead of her, Victor's bike swerved wildly. He cried out in pain as the bicycle clattered to the ground.

"No!"

Oh, no. Oh, no.

Terror clawed at her chest. She couldn't lose him. She couldn't leave him bleeding on the ground to die.

Another bicycle appeared, one that appeared slightly too small for its rider.

"Mary!" Dr. Finch's voice rang out. "Quick! Hop on!"

She'd nearly reached Victor, who had begun to struggle to his feet. "Go!" he shouted. "Get out of here!"

Another gunshot cracked and Mary screamed.

"Hal, get her out of here!"

Despite the awkward size of his bicycle, Dr. Finch deftly pulled the vehicle into a tight arc, spinning it a full hundred and eighty degrees and stopping barely a foot from Mary's side. Victor was still scrambling to right himself and the bicycle. In the darkness, she couldn't see how badly he was hurt.

"No, I won't leave you!"

Dr. Finch grabbed her around the waist and swung her up onto his handlebars. Mary grabbed at her hat to keep it from flying off.

"Go, goddammit, go!" Victor shouted.

A click sounded from somewhere beneath her, followed by the electric buzz of a motor. Before Mary could even attempt to say anything else or jump off, the motorbike shot off down the road.

She screamed Victor's name as he vanished into the darkness behind her.

Chapter 31
What Friends Are For

Thank God it was dark. Poor visibility was probably the only thing saving Victor from a bullet to the brain. Chunks of dirt splattered his leg as another round slammed into the ground. Shit. That made two near misses. Too close for comfort.

Victor flipped the switch on the handlebars and the electric motor whirred to life. The bicycle lurched into motion. Pain shot up his arm. He'd definitely bruised something in his crash, but he couldn't spare the time to dwell on it.

Keeping a tight grip on the handles, he maneuvered the bike across the treacherous dirt and gravel terrain, praying he wouldn't slip again. Much to his relief, he could no longer see Hal and Mary ahead of him. Given Hal's skill with a bicycle, she'd be safely at home in no time.

The gun barked again. Victor ducked low over the handlebars to make himself the smallest target possible. He could do this. The main road stretched out ahead of him. He made a sharp turn onto it, then cranked up the motor as fast as it would go.

No more shots sounded.

Victor let out a long breath and gave the motorbike a pat. "Thank you, Calliope Finch."

If it weren't for Callie, the bicycle would never have been

fitted with a motor, and he would've had to pedal the entire way. He'd never have made it. Hal hated machines, but he loved his wife more. The motor on Callie's bike had been installed for her ease of travel, and Hal had done the same to his bicycle so they could ride together. Victor was going to hug them both for an improperly long time.

The ride back was uneventful, though Victor kept his hands tight on the handlebars and his eyes and ears alert for any signs of trouble. Once he reached the well-lit streets of downtown, he caught sight of Hal and Mary in the distance ahead of him.

"Thank God," he breathed. He truly didn't know what he might have done if anything had happened to her. Only that it wouldn't have been good.

The moment Victor pulled up in front of his house, Mary came running toward him. Her cloak and hat were both askew, but still on, and her ease of movement suggested she'd suffered no physical harm. She barreled straight into Victor, throwing her arms around him.

"I thought I'd lost you," she gasped, the words a breath away from a sob.

Victor gathered her close. "No chance of that. I'm not leaving you for anything."

Mary began to pat his arms and his chest. "Are you hurt? Do you need a doctor?"

"Fine." He rubbed her back to soothe her. "No blood. Just some dirty clothing. Perfectly well."

Hal cleared his throat loudly. "Perhaps you two might consider moving this reunion indoors?" He picked up the bicycle Victor had let fall to the ground. "I'll take the bikes around back and then join you."

Victor reluctantly released Mary. Hal was right. Outdoors was potentially dangerous and left them vulnerable to more scandalous gossip. Mary was safe and needed to remain so. Anything else could wait.

He walked her to the front door, pausing only to retrieve his own hat, which had blown off when he'd first leapt onto Hal's bicycle.

"We still match," he said brightly.

Mary smiled up at him. "I'm glad."

Before he could do anything foolish, like kiss her right on the doorstep, he pulled the bell to announce their arrival. Much to his surprise, instead of Sakai or one of the footmen answering the door, his mother opened it, then seized both their arms and dragged them into the foyer.

"Oh, Victor, I was so worried!" she exclaimed. "You two are not to go out again, anywhere. You're to stay in the bunker until the police have captured these criminals!"

"Mother, we—"

"Don't argue with your mother, Victor," his father said sternly. "The situation has gotten out of hand. You need to stay where it's safe."

Victor hung his hat on a peg and began to remove his overcoat. "We are both responsible adults. Of course we aren't planning on waltzing out into danger." Which didn't mean he necessarily intended to remain in the bunker forever. Only until he'd come up with a good idea for how to protect Mary.

"Good. Your friends are waiting for you in the parlor. There's food and drink available if you need it."

"I definitely need a drink," Victor replied.

He helped Mary out of her cloak, then escorted her to the front parlor. Nemo and Callie sat in side-by-side armchairs, talking in low voices. They paused when Victor and Mary entered and looked up.

"Oh, you're safe!" Callie hopped up from her seat and

rushed over. A crinkle of worry creased her brow. "Is Hal with you?"

"Right here," her husband answered, striding into the room still dressed in his outerwear. He gave Callie a quick kiss, then tossed his hat and coat on a sofa.

"We've been beside ourselves with worry," Callie said. "Of course I called the police, but I had so little to tell them other than what direction you'd gone."

"I was able to get out of the cab," Mary explained. "Then Victor and Hal came riding up on the motorbikes, allowing us to get away." She'd regained her usual calm. Damn, but the woman was resilient. Victor intended to give her a thorough kiss, praise her courage to the skies, and do his utmost to ensure that she never found herself in such a situation again.

He faced the Finches. "I owe you both big, awkward hugs for those motorbikes."

Callie didn't hesitate to drag Hal right over to Victor for a three-person hug that was, indeed, quite awkward, in part due to Callie's round belly and in part due to Hal's inability to find an appropriate place to put his hands. Eventually he settled for giving Victor a stilted pat on the back, then retreated to a safe distance.

"An extra person makes that rather complicated," he said, then coughed. "Er, but you're welcome. We're always here for you."

"I love you both," Victor stated adamantly. "I hope you know that. And you, too," he added, looking at Nemo, who remained in the chair sipping a drink. "I don't doubt you also rushed to come to our aid."

"Had a chat with the chief of police," Nemo replied.

Victor walked to the sideboard where drinks and snacks

had been laid out. He poured himself a large glass of brandy and piled a plate with slices of bread and cheese.

"I hope he found the information about the soap helpful."

Nemo's brows knit together. "What soap?"

Mary turned from gathering up her own food. "Did he not tell you? Perhaps he thought it needed to be kept confidential? We dropped off some bars of soap at police headquarters this afternoon. From Simpson Fine Soaps and Lotions. We believe they're tainted with Sobridyne."

"Aw, fuck," Hal muttered. "Not that again."

Nemo hopped up and strode toward Mary and Victor. "You visited headquarters *today*?"

Victor took a big swig of the brandy before replying. "We were there mere hours ago. It's how we ended up in this whole mess. Someone followed us from the station. We thought we'd shaken him off, but he changed tactics and decided to lie in wait for us here, instead."

Nemo bit out a Bengali curse word. "There's no record of you visiting headquarters. I was specifically told to ask you to go in for an interview. Or to give you a number to call if you feared danger and preferred someone come to you instead."

"Damn right we fear danger," Victor retorted. Especially after this evening's events. Whoever was responsible for this wanted them too terrified to breathe another word of what they'd discovered. And that was the best case scenario. No one was more silent than a dead man.

Mary nibbled on a bit of cheese, her brow creased in thought. "We spoke to Detective Daide, answered questions relating to Clay's death, and handed over the soaps. Is there a chance the report hadn't made it to the chief's desk when you spoke?"

"Daide." Nemo tapped one booted foot against the floor. "Don't know him. Did you sign in at the desk?"

"No," Mary answered. "He came out to get us."

Victor gulped more brandy. "That's bad, isn't it?"

"Absolutely against protocol," Nemo replied.

"We are *not* going back there. Not if it's going to lead to kidnappers chasing us and detectives hiding information from their superiors. If anyone wants to talk, they need to come here. And they can't show up unannounced. We need a specific, pre-arranged time or we're not talking to anyone." He glanced at Mary. "Right?"

"Yes. That's a sound idea."

"I'll report this," Nemo assured them. "If Daide is corrupt, maybe he has secrets he'll swap for a reduced sentence. Do you have any more of those soaps?"

"No, but my mother might," Victor replied.

"I'll speak with her before I leave. But I should go now. I'll send you a note if I learn anything new."

Victor clasped Nemo's hand. "Thank you."

"What are friends for?" Nemo pulled him into a hug, gave him a firm pat on the back, then strode from the room.

Victor sank into a chair. He polished off the rest of the brandy before digging into his food. Part of him wanted to get so drunk he'd forget about everything. But he didn't dare be anything but sober so long as Mary was in danger.

Hiding out until the situation was resolved sounded good in theory. Unfortunately, Victor wasn't a sit and do nothing sort of person. Mary even less so. She'd never agree to wait idly by and let other people solve her problems. Which meant finding some way to protect her whenever she ventured out. She needed a bodyguard.

"The baby needs some food," Callie declared, standing and heading for the sideboard. "And the rest of you look like you need a distraction. So, tell us, Mary, how are you enjoying living in sin with a handsome and charming man?"

Mary turned bright red and had to cough to avoid choking on her food.

"Ooh, is it that good?" Callie grinned. "Excellent. You both deserve happiness."

"How about the metal man?" Hal asked. "How's he coming along?"

"Great," Mary said, appearing relieved to change the subject.

Rehashing their latest work with Mecha-Man kept Victor occupied long enough to fill his belly with food and drink, but unfortunately, even a chat with good friends couldn't push the worries from his mind. The terrifying image of that ruffian grabbing Mary replayed in his head. He'd almost lost her.

Good God, he'd almost lost her.

His distraction made his goodbyes perfunctory, though he did hug Callie and Hal again—separately this time—as he showed them out. He also bade goodnight to his parents, promising to remain in the bunker. Though he didn't say for how long.

It wasn't until the bunker door closed behind him that he realized how tight his muscles had become. He needed a long, hot shower. Or a long, hot fuck with his lady love. Or maybe both, given how on edge he was.

"We're safe here." Mary laid a hand on his arm. "We can rest for tonight."

Victor reached for her, grasping her about the waist and drawing her closer. "I should be the one comforting you. You were the one kidnapped."

"You were almost shot!" she argued. A touch of moisture sparkled at the corners of her eyes. "Oh, Victor!" She threw her arms around him and hugged him tight. Pain blossomed where her arm pressed against his bruised one, but he didn't care. Pain was immaterial when he had her close.

Mary pulled away and frowned up at him. "You're wincing. What's wrong?"

He shrugged with the uninjured arm. "Nothing. It just smarts a bit from my crash."

"Are you certain you weren't shot? Could anything be broken?"

"I'm quite confident neither of those things are true," he assured her.

"I need to see." She took hold of his hand and tugged him toward the trolley. "Come. We need to get you to the bedroom so I can check you for injuries."

"Does this involve taking off my clothes? Will you kiss any injuries to make me feel better?"

She fixed him with a stern look. "Checking first. Then kissing."

Victor hopped into the trolley. "Yes, ma'am."

Chapter 32
First Time's the Charm

Mary carefully stripped away the layers of Victor's clothes. He'd definitely done an injury to his right arm, though he continued to act unconcerned. He grimaced every time she touched it. The skin was unmarked, however, and she'd found no blood or bullet holes. His arm had full range of motion, thankfully, and the bone felt solid. Only a bruise, though she suspected it would become quite a colorful one over the next few days.

"I don't think you need a doctor," she declared.

His lips twitched. "Not unless that doctor is you and you intend to check in my trousers, too."

Mary met his teasing gaze with a serious one. "I intend to check you everywhere." Victor was always trying to protect her and care for her. It was time he let someone take care of him. "I told you the plan. Checking before kissing."

His eyes sparkled in the lamplight. "I love your plans."

Mary's heart thumped. It wasn't an "I love you," but it felt like one. She longed to wrap her arms around him and hold him forever. To kiss him every day and fall asleep beside him every night. She'd nearly lost him today, and now that she had him back, all she could think about was how much she wanted him. All of him. Always.

She stripped off his trousers and his stockings, because

she needed to be certain he wasn't hiding some other, more grievous injury. The fact that it allowed her to run her hands all over his body was a pleasant bonus. One he was enjoying thoroughly, judging by his jutting erection.

Tonight, she was going to feel him inside her. Her secrets didn't matter anymore. Victor wouldn't fault her, mock her, or shame her. He'd always accepted her as she was. So if she had to explain her embarrassing lack of experience, she would.

"You might want to double check that area," he said, apparently having noticed where her gaze was lingering. "Make absolutely certain it's all in perfect health."

Mary looked up and he gave her a smirk and a wink.

"You appear to be mostly undamaged," she declared. Without another word, she clambered atop his body and kissed him.

The stroke of his tongue was heavenly. The firmness of his body beneath hers a delight. He was alive and well, and she wanted to drink him in, hold him tight, and revel in the knowledge that he was safe and he was hers.

Victor nipped gently at her lower lip. "You are a teasing minx."

"Me?" Mary raised up on her elbows. No one had ever said anything remotely similar to her in her life. No one called her coy or flirtatious. No one found her seductive or enticing. No one until Victor.

"Yes, you, my beguiling beauty. Here I am, naked as the day I was born, while you are completely covered in one of those simple, modest dresses that drive me utterly out of my head."

She sat up. "My dresses drive you out of your head?"

"Yes. They're so *you.* So unassuming and sensible. But I know you're full of passion underneath. I can't help wanting to pull aside the sensible layers and see what I find. Maybe you'll be wearing more of those wool undergarments and you'll be adorable in your practicality. Or maybe someday I'll discover that you've put on frilly and nearly transparent drawers in the hopes that I'll catch a glimpse on a windy day and ravish you on the spot."

"They're the same wool style as you've seen before," Mary admitted.

"See? Adorable. We'll save the open-air ravishment for a warmer day."

Mary slid off the bed and began to undress, her body heating under Victor's ardent gaze. "You would never do such a thing in public. You're much too decent."

"Not in public," he chuckled. "Perhaps a secluded garden, where I could lay you on the grass and admire the way the sunlight plays across your naked body."

Her fingers slipped from the button she'd been undoing. Why did she need so many blasted layers?

"Want some help?" Victor asked.

"Yes, please."

Between the two of them, they stripped her to the skin in record time. Fully naked, she fell into Victor's arms, and they kissed and groped their way to the bed.

"One moment." she said, when he tried to pull her down onto the sheets. She scampered into the bathroom and drank a dose of her contraceptive tonic. She was doing this. She was going to let him have her body the way no man ever had.

Victor lay sprawled on the bed, lean and lovely and delicious. Mary scrambled up next to him, and he pulled her atop him.

"Everything all right?" he asked.

"Yes. I wanted to take my contraceptive tonic."

His answering smile ran ear-to-ear. "I've been taking one every morning since the day you first kissed me."

Mary laughed. "How very optimistic of you."

"I was hoping for 'prescient.' And I wanted to be prepared. I don't particularly want children. I'd be a wretched father. I intend to spoil Hal and Callie's children instead and then hand them back when they become troublesome. So you see? I can plan sometimes, too."

"It's an excellent plan. I don't desire children, either."

Her heart beat wildly. Were they discussing *the future*? Hopes and wants and family arrangements? The foundation of a life together?

For so many years she'd been making the best of a bad situation. She hardly dared believe she might have the chance at the life she'd once imagined. A marriage with a man who admired her as she was and wanted the same things from life as she did.

Stop.

She was getting far ahead of herself. Victor had made no proposals or declarations of love, nor should she assume he would. He was being responsible, that was all. Tonight she would focus on the now. On seizing all she could of the moment. She lowered herself back down and claimed Victor's mouth.

Hands flew everywhere, his and hers, stroking bare skin, teasing nipples, sliding down between them to caress intimate flesh. Mary gave herself over to passion, making no attempt to hold back the gasps and sighs of pleasure Victor's touch pulled from her throat.

"Mary." His hoarse groan burrowed beneath her skin while his lips traversed the slope of her breast. Lord, how she wanted him. Longed for him. Loved him.

"Victor," she answered breathlessly.

"God, Mary, you are exquisite." He moved to the other breast, licking and suckling her skin. An odd hope swelled in her that his ministrations would leave a love mark. A mark no one would ever see but the two of them. "I swear I'm going to make this good for you. So good."

He was already making it good, but the only way to tell him that was with her body. Forming words was becoming increasingly difficult, and when he moved down between her legs, she lost all speech capabilities. Her fingers tangled in his hair, her hips bucking to get more of his lips, more of his mouth.

Yes, yes, oh, God, yes.

The pleasure climbed up and up, tightening her muscles, filling every tiny cell of her body. He would make her shatter into infinite pieces, and she wanted it. Wanted it more than anything.

Mary let herself scream when the orgasm took her, rejoicing in the freedom to surrender to the ecstasy. Delighting in the knowledge that he liked it when she did. Victor drew gently away, and she drifted down to earth, a feather softly falling in the breeze.

Victor climbed back atop her, kissing her with lips that tasted of sex and sin. In his arms, a good girl could be wicked and not be ashamed.

Perfect. He was perfect. They were perfect together. Her flaws and fears didn't matter here. Here, she too, could be perfect.

He settled his hips between her thighs, and Mary adjusted herself until she felt the crown of his shaft nudging at her entrance.

"Do you still want this?" His warm breath tickled her ear as he spoke the soft words. "Because we can stop any time."

Mary put her arms around him and dragged her hands down his back and over his buttocks. "Yes. Yes, I want you." She shifted as a nervous tremor ran through her. "U-unless it bothers you that I'm… well… inexperienced."

He chuckled. "Love, I'd been celibate for years until we started this. I assure you, you can't disappoint me. I've been aching to be inside you."

She nodded. "Good. Go ahead, then."

Victor nuzzled her neck. "You cannot disappoint me," he repeated, the words low, husky, and resolute. "You are everything I ever wanted."

Mary's mouth opened in an O of wonder. Once again, that sensation that they were stepping into the future overtook her. She clung to it, the way her hands clung to his body as he pushed inside her.

Her muscles began to tighten. The stretching sensation between her legs was odd and uncomfortable. She understood that she would become accustomed to it, but when? How?

Victor froze above her. Oh, no. She'd done something wrong. He'd been wrong about enjoying this. Now what? Should she move? Talk? Apologize?

"Christ Almighty," Victor groaned.

Mary gasped at his blasphemy. He sounded almost in pain. She loosened her grip on him and checked that she wasn't putting any pressure on his injured arm.

"Mary, God, you feel good," he continued. "I think I might die if I start to move."

Oh.

She was bringing him pleasure, not pain. The tension began to leech from her body.

"And I think I'll definitely die if I don't move," he finished.

For a second, Mary was stunned by this ridiculous declaration. Then she laughed. Happiness burbled inside her, spreading outward from her chest, relaxing her limbs. As her body unclenched, the discomfort where they were joined began to ebb.

Victor slid part way out, then back in, releasing a hiss of tortured pleasure. Mary shifted slightly, and the next stroke felt better. The third, better still. Victor reached between them, finding her clitoris and rubbing his finger in delicate circles.

The noise she made might have been an "Eep!" Some odd sound between a breath and a squeak. The sort of sound that might have embarrassed her in another context. Here, it was only the prelude to a whole string of noises that seemed to spur Victor into moving harder and faster inside her.

Mary dug her fingers into his shoulders and canted her hips, rocking her body to meet each thrust. She couldn't make her tongue speak his name, but it ran through her mind nonetheless.

Victor. My Victor.

She had found perfection twice in one night, and this time she would take him with her. They would soar together.

The climax hovered over her, creeping ever nearer as their bodies moved as one. She pulled him closer, longing to feel as much of him as possible when she finally broke.

"Mary. Mary." Victor rasped her name over and over, each syllable a new pulse in her body and her heart.

Yes, love, yes. Hold me. Be with me. Love me.

Her head tipped back and her mouth opened but no sound came out. She was lost to him. Lost *with* him. She squeezed her eyes tightly shut and held on, fingers and toes curling. The orgasm rolled through her, flooding her with pleasure until her lungs at last found breath and she cried his name to the heavens.

Victor sank into her in a final frantic thrust. Shuddering and coming inside her, he let out a shout almost as loud as her own. A moment later, he collapsed atop her.

"Christ," he swore again. He rolled over, snuggling up against her and wrapping his uninjured arm around her. "That was a damned fine bit of business. See? I told you you couldn't possibly disappoint. I hope *I* didn't disappoint *you*?"

"Not at all." Mary twisted so she could kiss him. "Thank you for making my first time so beautiful."

He flinched. "What do you mean, 'first time'?"

"I told you. I was inexperienced. Didn't you... feel my maidenhead or..." She waved a hand. "However it works?"

"N-no... but..." He rubbed his temple. "But you were married!"

Mary let out a heavy breath. "Clay didn't want me. After the wedding, he didn't speak to me, and once we arrived at our new home, he took himself off to do work." Her cheeks began to flame with mortification, but she pressed on. She had to tell someone, and Victor would never judge her. "I was confused, but I thought maybe he was nervous, as I was. When he didn't come to my bedchamber in the evening, I made a plan."

Victor hugged her closer and planted a kiss in her hair. "Of course you did."

"I... I stripped down to nothing, then put on a thin dressing gown from my trousseau. I thought he would like it. I went to him in his study. When he didn't respond right away, I opened the dressing gown so he could see me and told him I was ready."

"Jesus," Victor muttered. "And the fool didn't grab you

in his arms and pleasure you until you were delirious and tell you you were the most perfect woman he'd ever beheld?"

She shook her head, tears gathering in her eyes. "He c-called me a hussy. A b-boring hussy."

Victor's embrace tightened even more. "Oh, my love, I'm so sorry. You know neither of those things are true, right? They are one hundred percent not true." He lifted a hand to her face, swiping his thumb across her cheek to wipe away a tear.

Mary wanted to bury her face against his chest and simply let him hold her, but she needed to finish her story.

"He told me kissing me had been a chore, and that..." She took a deep breath. "I remember this perfectly. He said bedding me would be 'like bedding a wooden shop mannequin.' I ran away crying. From then on, he was cold and cruel whenever he spoke to me. Calling me more names and belittling me. When he left town, I was glad to avoid him."

Again, Victor kissed her. First her hair, then her forehead, and finally her lips. "Shall we dig up his corpse and reanimate it? I'd happily kill him again for you."

Mary ran a hand down his chest. "Sweet of you, but no."

"I know I can't undo the pain he caused. But I'm going to keep telling you how wrong he was. He didn't deserve you. He didn't deserve to walk the same earth as you. You are brilliant and beautiful and all that is good. I want you to hear that one million times more often than you heard a nasty word from him."

"Thank you. For listening and for caring."

Victor stroked her hair. "Anytime, love. Anytime."

Mary closed her eyes, content to fall asleep in his arms, where she was safe and loved.

Love. He'd said that word so many times tonight. Maybe

this was a step toward the future. Maybe he loved her the way she loved him. Tomorrow she would have to face the world with its dangers and troubles. But tonight, she had hope.

Chapter 33
The Best Defense

Victor gave up on any attempt to sleep properly at some ungodly hour of the morning. He'd dozed a bit, but only briefly. Maybe it was Mary's confession of Clay's mistreatment. Maybe it was the danger still lurking somewhere outside the safety of their bunker. Whatever the cause, his body wouldn't stop buzzing with the need to watch over her. Protect her. Give her all the love and support she'd been lacking.

He could have stayed in bed cuddled up beside her, but he'd had an idea and he needed to act on it.

Victor hopped out of bed and threw on a pair of trousers and a shirt. Mary's dress from yesterday lay on the floor where they'd discarded it before love-making. He snagged the skirt and the shirtwaist and headed out into the main room of the bunker. Using a barrel of wine and a few smaller boxes, he managed to construct a small tower. When covered with the pieces of Mary's dress, it made a reasonable approximation of a woman.

"All right, Mech, here's what we're going to do." He directed the automaton to stand facing Mary's stand-in. "I'm going to teach you how to protect this lady. Now watch."

Mecha-Man couldn't understand the words, of course, but Victor found his task easier when he explained it. He began by demonstrating protective positions. Legs spread wide for balance, he showed the automaton how to guard the woman from both the front and from the side, with either his arms spread wide or his fists raised.

Mecha-Man took to the positions easily, but showing him when they were needed was a much trickier matter. After a bit of trial and error, Victor set Mech to walking at different speeds and from different angles. Whenever his movements could be interpreted as threatening, Victor jumped in front of his faux lady, adopting a defensive posture.

Dozens of demonstrations later, they finally switched places. It was slow going, but the idea was working. If they kept at it, Mech would be able to defend Mary when—not if—she decided to venture out again.

"What on earth are you doing?"

Victor froze in mid rush when he heard Mary's voice behind him. Mecha-Man remained vigilantly beside the dummy, ready to leap in Victor's path should he attempt to get too close too fast. Victor spun around.

Mary stood at the entrance to the room, her bare feet peeping out from beneath her voluminous dressing gown. No. Not hers. His. Apparently she'd found his large, fuzzy robe in the closet and wrapped it around her probably otherwise naked body.

Victor's skin tingled. Maybe Mecha-Man could wait. Maybe they ought to go right back to bed.

No getting distracted. You have to do this. She needs to have protection before she goes out again.

"That's my dress!" Mary strode toward Mech and the false lady. "What are you teaching him?"

"He's learning to defend."

"Defend? Defend what?"

"You. I'm training him to be your bodyguard."

Her eyebrows shot up. "Me? He can't defend me. If he's

fighting and throwing punches it will only fuel the rumors that Clay was killed by an automaton!"

"No. Defense only." Victor rushed toward Mary before she could decide to snatch her dress away and he lost his dummy.

With two swift strides, Mecha-Man cut Victor off, blocking him from reaching Mary. Victor retreated a step, then tried again, this time keeping his pace moderate.

"You see?" he explained. "Mech doesn't attack anyone. All he does is prevent anyone threatening from approaching you. If anyone runs or jumps at you, he'll get in the way, and he's big enough to be a hindrance and certainly solid enough to withstand a punch or other attack."

Mary crossed her arms. "I don't know. I'm still worried people might get the wrong impression."

"Here, let me demonstrate. I'll show you everything he's learned, and then you can judge for yourself."

A soft sigh escaped her kissable lips. "Very well. Show me."

Victor walked Mecha-Man through his paces, demonstrating all the ways he would maneuver to block someone who ran or jumped from various angles. The automaton acquitted himself well, keeping Victor away, but never punching or lashing out. Mary watched the entire process with a pinched frown and a studious gaze.

"That's not bad," she admitted at last. "I'm still not certain it's a wise idea, but I'm confident he won't attack anyone by accident. Hmm." One bare foot tapped against the floor as she thought. Victor wanted to catch that foot, rub it between his hands, then work his way up over her calves and thighs.

"Mech will be a good bodyguard," he said confidently. Quashing his lustful thoughts was impossible. But if he could convince Mary that his plan was sound, perhaps they could return to the bedroom.

He executed one final test, springing at the dummy from behind, only to crash into Mecha-Man, who moved even faster than expected. Victor lost his footing and ended up in a heap on the floor.

"Fine," Mary agreed at last. "He can be the bodyguard. But only if he's fully dressed, including a high collar and large hat, to make him appear as human as possible. And I want to teach him how to protect you as well."

Victor blinked up at her. "Me?"

"Yes. You're in danger too. I can't accept him protecting me at your expense. He needs to defend us both. Those are my conditions."

Part of Victor wanted to protest that she was all that mattered, but he also found himself grinning. She was so lovely in her concern for him. The way she'd checked him over for injuries last night had nearly undone him, not only physically, but deep down in his heart. He loved her so much he could hardly contain himself from shouting it to all the world. The only thing preventing him from doing so was the desire to let her determine the pace of the relationship. She'd been hurt before, and he wanted her to feel absolutely safe with him.

"I accept." He got to his feet. "Let's teach him to protect me too."

Teaching Mech went much faster with both of them participating, and before long the automaton had expanded his defensive abilities. Mary seemed pleased, but Victor fretted. He couldn't allow Mech to protect him too much or Mary could be left exposed. If an attack happened, she needed to be the first priority. Which meant running Mech through situations where he was guarding the both of them.

Victor constructed a second dummy beside the first, dressing it in one of his coats. A hat atop the stack of boxes made it look the part of a helpless gentleman.

"Let's see what he does when he has two of us—" Victor stopped mid sentence. A clacking sound came from the tunnel. Food delivery? They still had plenty remaining from the last drop-off. He looked at Mary. "Do you hear—"

"Victor!" his father's voice boomed. "Good morning!" A thunk announced the arrival of the trolley, and a moment later Edward Franklin appeared at the bunker entrance, a picnic hamper in his hands. "Your mother decided you should have a hot breakfast."

"Oh. I, uh…" Victor's brain couldn't form words. His body wouldn't move. He stood frozen in horror as his father took in the scene before him. Most notably, their state of undress.

"What is going on here?" he demanded.

Victor's mother walked in behind him, carrying a pot of coffee. "Edward, what is the matter?" Her gaze fell on Mary. "Oh! Well."

Mary clutched the dressing gown. "P-please excuse me. I wasn't expecting company." She scurried off into the bedroom.

Victor clenched his jaw to prevent the countless expletives running through his mind from spilling out. Why hadn't he had the sense to insist that they both dress properly before working with Mecha-Man?

Because you like seeing her in your robe and you didn't expect anyone to barge in.

He ought to have expected it, though. His father had gone to all the trouble of building this place. Naturally, he'd be checking up on anyone who was using it. Especially when that person was alone with a lady he wasn't married to.

Victor decided to play it cool, despite the fact that he was attired in nothing but an untucked shirt and a wrinkled pair of trousers and Mary had dashed away in embarrassment. They were adults, after all. They could make their own decisions.

"Just working on the automaton," he said, making a brisk wave at the stand-in pedestrians. "Teaching him what to do when he's near people."

"You know full well that is not what I meant," Victor's father replied. "I told you you were to behave like a gentleman."

Victor had been a perfect gentleman. He'd respected the lady's wishes, let her make the decisions, given her everything she wanted, and arranged to provide protection for her. How much more gentlemanly could one be?

He narrowly avoided opening his mouth and making exactly such an impertinent remark. Not because he thought better of it, but because his father continued talking.

"The young lady is newly bereaved. You ought to be particularly sensitive to her welfare. Instead, I find you taking advantage of her."

"She's not bereaved. She's free of an intolerable man. And I haven't taken advantage of her."

"Then why did we find the two of you in here together, completely undressed?"

"We were both fully covered."

Victor's mother stepped between the two men. "Why don't we go into the sitting room and have a nice cup of coffee? I'm sure we can sort this all out."

"There is nothing to sort out," his father growled. "Victor has behaved inappropriately and now he needs to rectify the situation." He wagged a finger. "You will do the right thing by that young woman, do you understand?"

Victor jerked back in alarm. "Whoa. No, wait." He stepped toward his father until the two of them were nearly nose-to-nose and spoke in a low voice. "You can't do that. I won't let you. Nothing you say can compel me to force her into marriage, and don't you dare try to pressure her into it."

"I don't care that she's a widow, Victor. She is an innocent young woman and she should be under your protection, not in your bed."

The words stabbed. She'd been more innocent than his father realized. But giving that up had been her choice, and marriage had to be her choice as well. Victor would not allow it to be any other way.

"I will defend her honor to my dying day," he vowed. "But I will never make her do anything against her will." Her last experience with marriage had been traumatic. Forcing her to put herself in that vulnerable position again would be the worst kind of betrayal. "*Never.*"

"There's no forcing, Victor. I'm sure she'll see reason, and she seems genuinely fond of you."

"It's not your decision. Our relationship is none of your business. This conversation is over. Please leave."

Victor's father opened his mouth to say something more, but stopped when his wife touched his arm.

"Let's discuss this another time, when everyone has had time to relax," she said. "It's no good to argue when you're both so startled. Here, Victor, have some coffee." She thrust the pot at him.

"Um." Victor took hold of the pot, since the alternative was letting it crash to the ground. He didn't need that on top of everything else. "Thank you."

"Leave the basket, Edward, and come along." Victor's mother tugged on her husband's arm and he reluctantly set down the basket of breakfast foods.

"We will discuss this later."

"There is nothing to discuss," Victor insisted.

"Let's leave the youngsters to talk things over," his mother cooed. "I'm sure that will make everyone happy in the end."

Victor's father harrumphed, but turned to depart. "The nerve of that boy," he muttered.

"I knew this would happen," his mother replied, sounding oddly cheerful. "They're so sweet together, don't you think?"

Whatever else they said was mercifully too quiet to hear. Victor shut off Mech, then took the breakfast into the sitting room and arranged the table so they could eat. Might as well at least get some food in his stomach. Maybe then it wouldn't ache so much.

"I will not let them force me to marry her," he muttered. "Not now, not ever."

The door to the bedroom opened and Mary stepped out, attired now in a pale green shirtwaist and darker green skirt. Her cheeks were still red. Victor hated that she'd been embarrassed and hated even more that he'd been partly to blame.

"Breakfast?" he offered. "It smells excellent."

"Thank you." She crossed the room and sat primly in the chair opposite him. "This is lovely. We ought to eat well, because we have a lot of work still to do."

"More testing of Mech's defenses," Victor agreed, scooping up a bite of food.

"Yes. And then I intend to go out. We have investigating to do."

Victor nodded around a mouthful of egg. He wanted to argue, to insist they let the police handle everything. They were safe here. They could conduct experiments and make love and everything would be fine.

But he understood her all too well. So much of her life had been out of her control. She'd seen a glimpse of a new life, and she wouldn't stop until she'd claimed it. Victor could never fault her for trusting no one but herself to do what needed to be done.

I will not pressure her. I will not tell her what to do.

Damn, damn, damn. He didn't know which was worse, dealing with his father or knowingly going back out into danger. Either way, he had one and only one priority: keep Mary from getting hurt.

Chapter 34

Field Test

"Mrs. Clay. I'm glad to hear from you," the lawyer's voice sounded through the telephone. "I have some new information to share with you. Are you able to come into the office?"

"I will stop by this afternoon, if that is acceptable?" Mary replied.

"Half past three?"

"Yes. That will be just fine. And I have a request for you, if it's possible. I know of two companies that Mr. Clay may have had questionable dealings with. Simpson Fine Soaps and Lotions and Riverside Cab Company. If there's anything you could tell me about those companies and whether they have any connection—legal or otherwise—to Clay, I would greatly appreciate it."

"I will see what I can do. Good day, Mrs. Clay."

"Until later, Mr. Biggs."

Mary hung the telephone mouthpiece back on its hook and turned to see how Victor was progressing.

Mecha-Man stood near the two fake pedestrians, guarding them from any peril. Victor circled the small group like a cat stalking a mouse, seeking an opening of attack. He sprang at them from Box Lady's unprotected side. Mecha-Man flung an arm out, saving her from destruction at his creator's hands. Victor smacked into Mecha-Man's arm and staggered backward.

"Blazes, you're fast! Nice work, Mech," Victor applauded.

"That was impressive," Mary agreed.

Victor began to pace again, eyeing the automaton. "I know we were still working on limiting his strength, but for now I'd like to leave him as he is. I don't want to risk diminishing any of that speed while he's acting as your bodyguard."

"*Our* bodyguard," Mary corrected.

"Of course. Shall we test him against multiple opponents now?"

"Yes. I'd like to be able to take him out this afternoon. Mr. Biggs has information for me."

Victor nodded, his jaw tight. "Then I'll make damned sure Mech is ready."

Mary took up a position a few yards away from Victor. Within minutes, they'd settled into their usual easy working routine.

She and Victor had always worked well together. Since she'd moved into his laboratory, however, their association had evolved into a true partnership. They knew one another well enough now that much of their communication was unspoken. Working side-by-side had become the norm rather than the exception. It would be all too easy to hole up in this little sanctuary and pretend the outside world didn't exist. Pretend she would never have to face the future.

Mary walked briskly toward Mecha-Man while Victor moved in slowly from the opposite direction. The automaton's peripheral vision was so good it was difficult to catch him unaware from anywhere but behind. He would be ready to protect them come three-thirty this afternoon.

Because as tempting as it was to ignore the future, she

couldn't. Not taking charge of her life had proven disastrous once. She wouldn't allow it to happen again. No one would keep her here, hiding in a bunker. She deserved better. Hadn't Victor told her that himself, with his words and his body? Hadn't Callie and Nisha encouraged her dreams?

She would not let them down. She would not let herself down. Miss Mary Amesbury would make herself known—not as a widow, a suspected murderess, or a troublesome snoop who had learned too much about some nasty criminals—but as a scientist. No one would stop her. She would make her future her own.

The memory of Victor's face that morning popped into her mind. His eyes hard. His mouth turned downwards as he muttered to himself. She hadn't heard exactly what he'd said, but it had been something about not being forced to marry her. Their thoughts were in accord there. He wouldn't allow anyone else to dictate his life, either.

The knowledge ought to have made her happy. She wanted freedom to choose her own path, and wished the same for Victor. They were adults who deserved to be left to make their own decisions.

Why, then, had she spent all morning with a pang of distress in her chest? Why did she fear that when she'd tracked down her criminal everything would end between them?

That was nonsense. Victor obviously cared for her, or he wouldn't be working so hard to keep her safe. He'd been an adoring, generous lover. He'd spoken as if their relationship meant something to him.

Maybe you misinterpreted his words. Maybe he wasn't anticipating a future together. Maybe he doesn't want any attachments, ever. Or worse, maybe he simply can't imagine marrying you.

Mary slapped the thought away. How ridiculous. She didn't even know if she was willing to risk another marriage. She was only now coming to understand her feelings for Victor. What reason did she have to fret over any of this?

"Ha-ha! Way to go, Mech!" Victor cheered, as the automaton stopped yet another attempt. The excited, boyish grin on his face made Mary's heart skip a beat.

That was her reason. This wild yearning for him. The aching desire for him to return her feelings.

He does. You know he does.

But no matter what she told herself, the doubt and fear lingered. Maybe something was wrong with her. Maybe she was too dull, too quiet, too peculiar.

"Mary?"

She turned her attention back to the matter at hand and tried to smile. "I think he's ready."

"So do I. Shall we dress him up all fancy so he's prepared to go out?"

Her smile came a bit easier this time. "Yes. Let's."

* * *

The lawyer's eyebrows arched in surprise when Mecha-Man stepped into the office behind Mary.

"What's this?" Mr. Biggs gasped. "The mechanical man is real?"

"Indeed," Mary replied. "He's harmless. But considering my circumstances, having another man at my side—even an artificial one—gives me a greater sense of safety."

"O-of course. Your well-being is of tantamount importance. Please, sit down."

Mary and Victor took their seats, leaving Mecha-Man standing behind them. Biggs cast suspicious looks at the automaton, but said nothing further.

Mary rubbed a bit of her skirt between her fingers. Her old doubts came creeping back. Perhaps bringing Mecha-Man along hadn't been a good idea. If even the people who knew her feared him, what would the average person on the street think? Nothing good.

"You had something important to tell me?" she asked.

Biggs's gaze fell on her. "Yes." He shuffled some papers. "As next-of-kin to Mr. Clay, all his assets now belong to you."

Mary started. "He had no other family?"

"None that I could locate. You are his sole heir. Clay Shipping now belongs to you. I've conducted a preliminary review of the company, and while we will want to make an in-depth investigation before finalizing anything, my initial findings suggest that your best course of action will be to sell the company."

"I certainly don't want it for myself," Mary answered. If this turned out to be just one more problem Clay had brought into her life, she might reconsider Victor's request to reanimate him. She had a few choice words she wouldn't mind saying to him. "Is the company ailing?"

"It appears so," Biggs said. "Clay had long been losing money. Then, in late December, he sold a large interest in the company to an organization called SD Imports. He appears to have been living off the proceeds of that sale since."

"What's SD Imports?" Victor asked.

"As far as I could see, they are nothing more than a company that buys into other companies," Biggs replied.

Victor sniffed. "Some kind of money-making scheme, then."

"Perhaps. After your phone call this morning, Mrs. Clay, I discovered something else interesting."

Mary leaned in. "Oh?"

"The two companies you inquired about, Simpson Fine Soaps and Lotions and Riverside Cab Company are among other recent purchases by SD Imports. SD Imports owns neither one outright, but does have a significant interest in both."

Victor whispered something that might have been a curse. He and Mary exchanged a long look.

"Who owns SD Imports?" Mary asked.

"I don't know," Biggs replied. "I found very little information about the company. They are based in Windsor, so there may be quirks of Canadian law that will affect any dealings with them. But I will continue to look into it. They will obviously be interested in any sale of Clay Shipping."

"Canadian?" Victor blurted. He spun in his chair to face Mary. "The cars on the ice. Want to wager that this SD Imports is the source of the Sobridyne? It's still legal to make in Canada. All they have to do is smuggle it across the river."

A worried furrow appeared in Biggs's forehead. "I must advise you against making any such accusations outside these walls. If you know of suspicious activities, that is a matter for the police, and you should tell them so they may handle it appropriately. I can arrange to accompany you to an interview."

"Thank you," Mary replied. Sadly, she didn't trust the police. If that Detective Daide was corrupt or incompetent, who was to say that others in the department were not similarly suspect? She trusted no one but Chief Majhi, and him only because he was Nisha's father.

Mr. Biggs repeated his caution twice as he escorted them to the door. All Mary could do was nod. Her investigations must continue. Today's information helped. She could return to the bunker knowing she'd made progress.

"I don't like this," Victor murmured, once outside. "The more we know, the worse I think these bastards are. If they're really the same people who caused all the trouble for Hal last year, they don't hesitate to play with hundreds of thousands of lives for their own gain. They killed Becher when he caused too much trouble. They killed Clay, probably because his behavior was too suspicious. We know too much. They won't hesitate to kill us, Mary." He gave her a swift hug. "Please, please stay close to Mech."

Mary looked him straight in the eye. "I will. But you must promise, too."

"I promise. But I do still need to lead him. It's too bad he isn't programmed for directions as complicated as 'walk home' yet."

She nodded her understanding. The sidewalk was too narrow to walk three-abreast, so it was the best they could do. They started off in a tight cluster, Victor first, with Mary and Mecha-Man never more than a step behind.

A cold drizzle had begun, so their little group kept close to the buildings to shelter from the rain. Several blocks from the attorney's office, they paused beneath the wide awning of a corner store, waiting for traffic to clear before they crossed the intersection. In the middle of the street, a pair of horse-drawn carriages going opposite directions stood at an impasse. Both drivers shouted and gesticulated, insisting the other move over and make more space.

A gust of wind caught the awning, and it creaked overheard. Mary glanced up automatically, wincing at the eerie shriek of straining metal. The canvas flapped and the support beams bounced up and down before settling. The rain came harder, beating down on the thick cloth. In the street, the shouts of drivers and honks of autocabs vied for supremacy with the whistling winds.

Mary pressed closer to Victor. Despite the canopy overhead, she felt exposed. "Should we walk around them?" *Before someone leaps out of a building and kidnaps me again? Before a man lying in wait takes a shot at Victor?*

Again, the canopy creaked. A spray of raindrops blew sideways into Mary's face, making her shiver.

"Yes, let's—" A sharp crack, like that of a gunshot, cut Victor off mid-sentence.

Mary screamed. The horses in the street reared up. Mecha-Man shuffled around in confusion. Another crack sounded, followed by a scream of twisting metal directly overhead.

Mary's gaze snapped up in time to see another gust of wind catch the awning, tearing it from the building, beams and all. She screamed again and covered her head as it came crashing down atop her. Something heavy banged into her, knocking her to the ground, and for an instant she was certain she'd be crushed to death. Metal clanged against metal, fabric enveloped her, and then, silence.

"Mary." Victor's urgent voice accompanied the brush of his hand against her arm. "Mary! Are you all right?"

She took a shaky breath. "I-I'm unhurt." Trapped, though. She pushed aside a torn piece of the awning, and the dim, gray daylight seeped in, giving her a view of her surroundings. Mecha-Man was above her, on his hands and knees, blocking the debris from harming her. She crawled out from underneath him. "Our bodyguard protected me."

Mary climbed to her feet and Victor scrambled after her. He also appeared unhurt, though she doubted he would admit to any injuries. Together, they disentangled Mecha-Man from the ruins of the canopy. The automaton limped slightly when he took a step.

Victor gave him a pat. "Attaboy. Let's get you home and then I'll fix you right up."

They hurried off as fast as Mecha-Man's damaged leg would allow, skirting around the snarled traffic and splashing heedlessly through icy puddles. Mary couldn't help glancing back at the wreckage behind them.

"That could have killed me." She shivered. "Or you. I d-don't believe it was an accident."

"Neither do I," Victor gritted out. "I think Clay's killer wants us either dead or too incapacitated to talk. We need to tell the police everything. And not just anyone this time."

"Nisha's father."

"Yes. We'll phone as soon as we get back."

"Thank you. And thank you for thinking to make Mecha-Man a bodyguard. It was a good idea."

Victor gave her a wan smile. "I do have them now and then."

"You have them often," she insisted. "We're going to solve this. We'll prove Mecha-Man innocent, and bring the smugglers to justice. And then we can present Mech to the world as the brilliant creation he is."

Victor took hold of her hand and gave it a squeeze. "I'll do everything I can to make that dream come true."

Chapter 35
Part of the Club

Clang. Clang.

Victor's mouth moved, but Mary couldn't hear him through the earplugs. She popped out one of the small cotton wads.

"I'm sorry?"

"I said I'm relieved Mech was the one dented and not you," Victor replied. He adjusted the piece of metal plating and lifted his hammer again.

"Agreed," Mary replied, quickly replacing her earplug before the hammering began again. In the cavernous main room of the bunker, the sound echoed from every surface and stabbed into her ears. How Victor could stand it, she had no idea.

She turned back to her work on Mecha-Man's damaged leg. The snapped wires had been replaced, and she'd done a thorough inspection to make certain nothing else had lost its structural integrity. His components looked good. As soon as Victor finished hammering out the last of the dents, their automaton friend would be back up and walking.

Ring. Ring. Ring.

Mary jumped. Even muffled by the earplugs, the unexpected noise startled her. She would never be able to feel one hundred percent relaxed again until Clay's murderer was behind bars. And it was only the telephone. Probably Victor's parents checking on them.

Victor answered the call, and Mary again removed her earplugs to hear.

"Uh-huh," he was saying. "Excellent. We'll be up shortly." He hung up the phone and turned to Mary. "Our friends have arrived. Sounds as though they've made arrangements for our police interview. If you give me one more minute to smooth out that plate, we can snap Mech back together and go up to greet them."

"And dress him," Mary added. "I know it seems silly, but even going upstairs I'll feel safer if he's with us."

Victor's warm smile made her heart flutter. "So will I."

A quarter of an hour later, Mecha-Man received his first formal introduction as Victor ushered him into the main parlor of Franklin Castle. The automaton bowed to their friends, who greeted him with smiles and cheerful hellos.

If only the newspapers could see this. If people knew the truth of Mecha-Man, they would never believe those nasty rumors swirling around Clay's death. Someday, she vowed, she would make the world understand.

"Now that we've all met your new friend, let's get down to business," Nisha declared. She crossed the room to hand Mary a bundle of clothing. "Here's your disguise. My father will be waiting for you at the club. We'll all stay here while you two go and visit."

"Men's clothing?" Mary asked. She frowned down at the bundle. "I don't even know how to put these things on."

"The opposite of how you take them off Victor," Callie suggested.

Mary flushed. As usual, Callie's insights were helpful, but embarrassing.

"I like this," Victor declared. "Anyone watching would

have seen you all come into the house. If they see Mary, Mech, and I driving to and from the club, it will appear I'm going with Hal and Nemo for our usual meeting."

Mary couldn't disagree with the logic of the plan. She slipped into the washroom to change. Familiarity with the fastenings from undressing Victor, did, in fact, help her. Within minutes, she donned trousers, shirt, and waistcoat. A long overcoat would further disguise the shape of her body, and a large hat would conceal her hair and face.

The clothing, which must have been Nisha's, fit well enough when Mary tucked the too-long trousers into her boots. She couldn't say she liked the outfit, but neither did she feel as bashful as she'd feared.

"That's quite cute on you," Callie praised when Mary returned to the parlor. "What do you think, Victor?"

Victor's eyes caressed Mary up and down, but the answering heat in her cheeks wasn't from any embarrassment. She'd come to adore that sweeping gaze of his, even more so now that it was bolder and more frequent.

"I think she looks beautiful in anything at all," he replied.

Mary thrilled to the sincerity in his voice. They needed to discuss this passion between them. To clarify what this was and what it meant for their future. Next time they were alone, she would find a way to declare her feelings and ask for his.

Mary accepted Nisha's overcoat and a hat that belonged to Dr. Finch, and then she, Victor, and Mecha-Man headed out the rear exit for a drive to the club.

Mary had never been inside a gentlemen's club. Had never even contemplated entering one. And though she knew this particular club welcomed women, she hesitated when she stepped inside, as if intruding where she didn't belong.

"Welcome, sir, miss," the man at the cloakroom greeted them, entirely unperturbed by Mary's masculine dress. He didn't even seem fazed by Mecha-Man, who doffed his hat and handed it over exactly like Victor did. Then again, with lady engineers like Nisha among the club's membership, the staff here probably saw unconventional dress and unusual machines on a daily basis.

Chief Majhi waited for them in a private room, holding a teacup while a vibrating machine filled it with steaming liquid. The police chief had a jolly, round face, a full head of graying hair, and the same warm, medium-brown skin tone as his daughter.

"Delightful contraption, this autokettle," he said, in a smooth voice with a hint of an East Indian accent. "Please, have a seat. Would you like a cup of tea?"

"Please," Mary replied. The police chief held a second cup up to the autokettle, then passed it to Mary. "Thank you."

"This is the infamous mechanical man?" He nodded at Mecha-Man, who had taken one of the remaining seats. "He seems harmless enough."

"We've been teaching him proper conduct and table manners," Mary explained. "He's learning quickly how to fit in."

"Interesting. Now, tell me what you young people know about this curious case of ours."

Victor and Mary ran through all they'd discovered, from the smuggling trucks to the Sobridyne to the tainted soaps. Mary even added the new information about SD Imports and the ties to Clay's business. Chief Majhi listened attentively, making occasional notes in a pocket-sized journal.

"This all fits neatly with what we've learned," he said, stroking his moustache with a single finger. "And what of

Detective Daide? Could you explain your interaction with him?"

They recounted their visit to police headquarters in detail. Between herself and Victor, they could recall the entire conversation nearly down to the word. Chief Majhi looked grim, but thanked them for their efforts.

Mary sipped at another cup of tea, nicely refilled by the autokettle. Now that she'd been in the club for a time, she'd lost most of her apprehension. Perhaps she'd even ask Victor for a tour before they departed. The trousers, however, pressed oddly against her legs, and didn't offer plentiful folds of material to rub between her restless fingers.

"While I cannot relate details of our investigation," the police chief stated, "I can say that we are progressing toward a resolution in this case, and that neither of you need to fear being accused of a crime. We have already obtained a sample of the soap you mentioned, but there remains the matter of the Sobridyne. You say you have a bottle in your possession?"

"I have the bottle," Victor admitted. "But it's empty. After the apothecary analyzed it, we disposed of the drug so it couldn't harm anyone. I suppose I didn't consider it might be needed as evidence."

"The bottle is glass?" Chief Majhi inquired.

"Yes."

"Good. Don't touch it again. I'll send someone to collect it. Even the smallest remnant may be enough for our purposes. Failing that, we have new technologies that can find fingerprints on glass and various other surfaces. We may be able to identify who else has touched the bottle."

Mary's eyebrow rose. Fingerprint identification? Fascinating.

"I'll make sure it remains safe until then," Victor promised.

"Fitzsimmons handles the fingerprint studies. He will come by in a day or two to collect the bottle. Don't give it to anyone but him." The chief checked his watch. "I should be going. Thank you for your time and the information. This will be of help to the department."

They all rose and shook hands.

"Please take all possible care," Chief Majhi advised. "The closer we come to pinpointing our criminals, the more desperate they will become. And desperate men may act unpredictably."

Mary fought to hide the shiver that ran down her spine. She made an appropriate goodbye to the police chief and took Victor's arm when he offered.

"Would you like a look around?" he asked.

"Please." The distraction would be welcome.

With Mecha-Man trailing quietly behind, they wandered the building from top to bottom, peeking into card rooms, the cozy nook where Victor and his friends liked to gather, and the basement bar serving up a multitude of drinks. While many of the men present were drinking and gambling, plenty of others were reading or engaged in scientific endeavors. The club served much the same function that Callie's library did for Mary and other ladies.

"I see why you like it here," she observed. "It must be relaxing for you."

"It is. If you'd ever like to visit again, I'd be happy to bring you along."

"Perhaps every now and then. In general, I think I prefer the smaller crowds at the library."

Victor covered her hand with his own. "That doesn't

surprise me. I prefer small groups, myself, and you are more solitary than I."

His gentle fingers tickled the back of her hand and she sucked in a breath. "Not entirely solitary, though."

"No." The word was low, husky. "Shall we return home? It's growing late."

"Yes, please. You can bring me for a longer visit another day. When I'm dressed in my own clothes."

Once more, he made a slow perusal of her outfit. "Don't like the trousers?"

"They rub against my legs and are strangely tight across my bottom."

Victor stopped walking and leaned back to take a look at her from behind. "Oh, are they?"

Mary nudged him with her elbow. "You can look all you want when we're alone in the bunker."

His mischievous grin made his eyes shine like candle-light. "Promise?"

She'd sworn to herself she'd clarify their relationship. Getting Victor in bed would be step number one.

"Promise."

She could determine the other steps later.

Chapter 36
Letting Off Steam

The rules of proper etiquette were lacking in many key areas, Victor decided. For instance, there was no polite way to tell your friends, "Please get out so I can go under-petticoating with my lady friend."

Not that Mary had a petticoat to go under at the moment. Which was part of the problem. Those damned trousers. From the way she'd been shivering and rubbing her hands over her thighs when she thought no one was looking, Victor suspected she wasn't wearing much beneath. If anything. His fingers kept twitching with the urge to strip the clothes off her and warm her with his own body.

"The meeting went well?" Nemo asked. From the crumb-covered plates and empty glasses scattered around the parlor, it appeared their friends had enjoyed Victor's parents' hospitality.

"It seemed to," Mary replied. "We passed on all our information and were reassured that we're not about to be arrested."

"That's positive news," Hal said. "Not that we were worried." His wife gave him a skeptical look. "Perhaps I was *a bit* worried."

Mary once again smoothed her hands down her trousers, then quickly clasped them behind her back when she caught herself. "Thank you for the clothes, Nisha. I'll have them washed and then return them to you."

"No hurry." She polished off the last of whatever she was drinking. "I have plenty to wear, and you might have need of a disguise again."

Mary frowned in thought. "True. I will hold on to them, then, until the case is resolved."

Victor rocked from one foot to the other. Was this the opportune moment to tell everyone to leave? He could try, "It's getting late," or, "Would you look at the time?"

Mary beat him to it. "If you will all excuse me, I'd like to change into my own clothing now. Thank you for visiting and helping. I hope to see you all again soon." She nodded politely and started for the door.

"I should put Mecha-Man away," Victor excused himself, motioning for the automaton to follow him. "Can you all see yourselves out, or should I walk you to the door first?"

Hal coughed, hiding a snicker of laughter, most likely. "I think we can manage."

"Have fun!" Callie called, giving Victor a little wave. "See?" Victor heard her murmur to her husband. "Didn't I tell you they'd be perfect together?"

Let them talk. His relationship with Mary wasn't much of a secret anymore, what with the way his parents had walked in on them. As long as no one was making her into a public spectacle, he didn't care who knew.

Although, maybe she did? Blast it all, had he messed up again in his eagerness to be alone with her? He hurried after her, ready to apologize if necessary.

His long stride allowed him to catch up by the time Mary reached the steps to the cellar. She glanced back at him and her mouth ticked up into a seductive smile.

Heat flared across Victor's skin. He hadn't messed up.

Thank God. He trailed her down the stairs into the secret tunnel, pausing to admire her when she climbed up into the trolley.

Those trousers really did stretch tightly across her bottom. If she wanted her own trousers to wear, she'd need something tailored to be looser around her hips and her rear, with the legs hemmed shorter. For tonight, however, Victor would take advantage of the inappropriately snug ensemble. After all, she'd promised him he could look all he wanted.

Mecha-Man walked past Victor, cutting off his view and jarring him back to reality. His brain may have decided that making love to Mary was the number one priority, but that didn't mean the rest of the world agreed.

The automaton climbed easily into the trolley, a feat that not long ago would likely have baffled him. He'd come a long way.

"Look at you, Mech," Victor said proudly. "Doing everything right."

Mecha-Man promptly sat down in the place beside Mary. The place Victor had intended to take. Now he'd be stuck sitting behind her, out of easy reach. Perhaps his praise of his creation had come too soon.

Victor settled in one of the rear chairs, telling himself he was being ridiculous for feeling disappointed. Why was his lust so out of control tonight? A lingering need to reassure himself of her well-being after the incident with the awning? Relief that the police were working to catch their villain? A bit of both, probably, combined with the knowledge that she really did want him.

She wants me.

Even after last night, Victor remained awestruck at the thought. Years of pent-up longing did not resolve easily, it seemed. Now he longed for more. For forever.

The drive through the tunnel at long last came to an end, and Victor hopped out of the trolley. He held out a hand to assist Mary down from the vehicle, though she had no puffy skirts to tangle and was entirely capable of alighting on her own.

Sparks shot through his body the moment her skin met his own. Yes, his lust was running wild tonight. He could only pray she was as eager to slake it as he was.

"You promised me I could look all I wanted at your adorable behind in those trousers," he murmured, keeping hold of her hand and stepping closer. "But I think what I'd really like is to look at you without them."

Mary gave him her bewitching smile again, so he drew her into an embrace, sliding one hand down over her buttocks and the other upward to cup one plump breast.

"As a doctor of science, it is my learned opinion that these clothes are no better than your usual." He bent to press a kiss to her neck. "They still bar me from the perfection of your skin. You should shed them as quickly as possible."

Mary nudged him and he straightened up.

"Something wrong?" he wondered. *Please, God, do not let there be something wrong.*

"You might want to pause before Mecha-Man decides he needs to join this embrace."

"Right." Victor raked a hand through his hair. "I'll, uh, walk him to his room and shut him down."

Mary looped her arm through Victor's. "I'll come with you. And then you can warm me up. I've been chilly without my usual layers of petticoats."

Victor gestured for Mech to walk. "I can remedy that. I'll wrap you in layers of blankets and cuddle with you beneath them."

"Or…"

She paused to think and Victor froze, anticipation making his breath catch. If she proposed something naughty, he was sweeping her up and leaving Mecha-Man here in the middle of the main room, and to hell with everything else.

"We could warm up in the shower. Together," Mary finished.

Victor stared at her, transfixed by the perfection of her suggestion. The mere thought that she had a fantasy similar to his own made his cock stiffen. Hell and damn, how he adored her. Adored how despite her shyness and fears she still dared to tell him what she wanted. Dared to try something new and different.

Her coy smile faded to an uncertain frown. "Unless you don't want to?"

"I want to," Victor blurted. "I very much want to. Mech, go into your room." He gestured to point the way, but the automaton was already walking. Victor cocked his head. Had Mecha-Man responded to his words? Impossible. They hadn't done anything with the hearing sensors yet. He was imagining things. Too distracted by Mary and the shower fantasy.

Victor rushed after Mech—who he didn't want to leave standing in the main room after all—and turned him off for the night.

"Now." He turned to Mary, bending to brush his lips across hers. "Tell me about this grand shower idea."

She didn't so much tell as show him, half-dragging him to the washroom, stripping off pieces of his clothing as she went. In his ravenous desire for her, Victor only dimly registered that they'd left his coat somewhere in the sitting room and his vest on the bedroom floor. By the time she'd shut the washroom door, he was down to his union suit—blue stripes today—and trousers.

Mary's hands flew over the shower's many knobs, spinning them with a well-practiced touch. Water spurted, then hissed, before stabilizing into uniform jets of spray. A cool mist spattered Victor's cheeks.

"Finish undressing now, while the water warms up," Mary instructed. "Then we can get into the shower and warm ourselves."

"You're already warming me."

Victor allowed his gaze to caress her from head to toe, then back. Pink touched her cheeks, but she kept her eyes on him. Aroused, not embarrassed. His chest swelled. Once upon a time, he would have avoided any possibility of looking at her that way. Now, though, he admired her openly. Because when she responded with shimmering eyes and parted lips, his blood boiled and his heart sang.

Mary tore the borrowed clothes from her body, vest and shirt landing in a puddle in the corner, soon followed by her corset and chemise. She kicked off her boots, one by one. Victor fumbled with his own clothes, too focused on her to pay attention to his hands.

Slim, dextrous fingers worked the buttons of her trousers, peeling them slowly down. Victor groaned audibly. Christ, she really wasn't wearing anything underneath. No bawdy burlesque had ever been so erotic. He yanked at his own clothes, needing to free himself from the constricting cloth that kept his nakedness from hers.

Steam curled from the rapidly warming water. Mary extended one hand to test the temperature.

"Mmm," she sighed, the elongated syllable a carnal caress. "Perfect. I love how quickly the shower heats up."

She stepped into the shower, sighing in pleasure. Victor goggled at her. Bathed in nothing but crystalline droplets, she resembled some ethereal water nymph, risen from the lake to tempt him. To lead him to his doom, no doubt. And he'd go willingly.

Her sky-blue eyes moved up and down, taking him in. "That is very enticing," she purred, "the way your most intimate parts are barely concealed."

Victor glanced down at himself. His union suit hung from his hips, barely held up by the last button. It left the v-shaped groove beneath his hip bones and the line of hair running down from his navel fully exposed. The slightest twitch and his cock would spring free, the garment falling to the floor.

Mary licked her lips. Victor twitched.

In a flash, he'd pulled off the union suit and his stockings and joined her in the shower. Hot water streamed over him, but the real warmth came from Mary's hands against his chest. Her thumbs grazed his nipples and a low moan burst from his throat. He reached for her, stroking smooth skin, cupping perfect breasts. Rivulets of water cascaded down her body. Moisture glistened on lustrous lashes.

"I'm dreaming," he gasped. "This is some kind of fantasy world and you are its love goddess."

"No. I'm just a woman. And you're the man who's going to fuck me." Her already pink cheeks went scarlet as she said the vulgar word, but she remained staring brazenly up at him. "Am I a hussy now?"

Her words were teasing, but Victor knew her too well to miss the trace of vulnerability beneath. She craved reassurance that she could be bold with him. And nothing would stop him from giving it to her.

"I don't give a damn whether you are or not," he replied. "I love the things you do. The things you say. Whether you're being brave and brazen or sweet and shy, I love it. I want you to always speak your mind. To always be yourself." He cupped her chin in his hand, tilting her head to stare directly into her eyes. "I want you to shine for the world the way you shine for me. And to the devil with anyone who doesn't like it."

He couldn't tell whether the droplets glistening in her eyes were tears, or merely water from the shower. Her hands snaked up his chest to wind around his neck.

"Kiss me," she begged.

Victor obeyed, clonking his elbow against one of the shower's ribs in the process. The sharp tingle of pain shooting down his arm was nothing to the joy of her lips. The hot, eager stroke of her tongue into his mouth banished all discomfort, leaving only a hunger unlike any he'd known. They teased and tormented one another, hands groping and exploring as they sank deeper into that magnificent, bone-melting kiss.

The shower was plenty large enough for two when they were upright. Bending to kiss and fondle her, however, had Victor repeatedly banging and scraping against the metal pipes and spouts. The awkwardness wouldn't stop him. Not with her body pink from the warmth, her skin slick from the water, and her lips claiming his with a passion that made his mind go blank. Any bump and bruise was worth this price.

He dragged his mouth from hers and bent lower, aiming for the place where her neck met her shoulder, intent on kissing a path down to her taut nipples. The side of his head smacked into the shower. The blow was more startling than painful, but his yelp alarmed Mary, who drew back from him as much as she was able in the confined space.

"This isn't working. I'm too short."

As much as Victor didn't want to admit it—his body screaming *don't stop*—she was right. Perhaps they should pause, dry off, and resume this effort in bed.

"I have an idea," Mary declared. "Pick me up."

"Far be it from me to foil any plan of yours." He grasped her about the waist and lifted her off the floor.

Mary reached up to grip the topmost pipe, holding herself up while she wrapped her legs around his waist. She braced her feet against one of the shower ribs, taking some of the weight from him.

Sweet Lord above. Victor brought his body flush to hers. When his cock slid against her slick sex, she released a moan of pleasure. He adjusted their position so one of the water jets sprayed through the small space between them, grazing her clitoris. Her moan deepened and her back arched.

"Like that, do you?" he murmured, nuzzling her neck.

"Oh, yes," she groaned, her voice hoarse with need.

His cock throbbed against her. Ride her hard and fast? Or make it last all night?

"Do you use the shower like this when you're alone?" he had to ask. "Pleasuring yourself and thinking of me?"

"Y-yes." Her hips bucked. "Please," she begged.

Hard and fast. He wasn't going to make it longer than that, and he didn't think she would, either. He thrust into her, an inarticulate noise of rapture escaping his lips.

"Mary," he rasped. She was brilliant. So utterly brilliant with her thoughts and her plans and this wild shower tryst. He withdrew, then thrust again. And again, reveling in every glorious sound she made when he moved within her.

Victor wanted to sing her praises from the rooftop. To shout it on the streets. To tell everyone, everywhere how irrevocably he loved her. Would always love her.

His mouth couldn't form the words, he was so lost inside her. Mary swung her body back and forth, driving him deeper, urging him faster. He could only cling to her and let her take him along on the ride.

He could sense the orgasm coming, his body tingling and tightening. Even so aware, it hit him hard, the pleasure rippling through him in unending waves. When Mary's vaginal walls clenched around him in her own release, he saw stars. Their mutual cries of delight echoed from the tiled walls, muffled only by the steady stream of water.

Victor lowered Mary to the floor, and they sagged against one another, breathing hard.

"You," he gasped. "You…" He couldn't seem to get more words out.

"Me?"

"Are brilliant," he finished. "So brilliant. My God, Mary." He hugged her close. "I've never wanted anything more than I want you. This. Us. Forever and ever. I love you so damn much. I want to gaze into your beautiful eyes. To hear your voice. To feel you near me when I sleep. Every day of my life."

She made a small gasping sound. Victor loosened his grip immediately.

Oh, shit.

What had he done? He'd sworn no pressure. If she panicked and fled, it would be all his fault.

Mary gazed up at him with a dazed expression. She pressed a hand to his heart. "You are the most wonderful man I've ever known."

I am?

Victor tamped down the bubbly sensation building inside before it caused him to start gushing again. He wasn't so wonderful. He couldn't even keep his mouth shut. And he still couldn't forget the way he'd slighted her during their hydroconductor project. She didn't owe him sweet words or anything at all.

"You make me feel wonderful too," she sighed. The sigh

quickly morphed into a yawn. "Dry me off and take me to bed?" she asked, her shoulders sagging. "It's been…" She yawned again. "A long day."

Yes. A very long day. Maybe he'd gotten lucky. Maybe in the post-orgasmic haze his declaration of love didn't surprise her. In the morning, though, she might recall his words and wonder if he'd truly meant them.

He had. He meant them with every tiny cell in his body, and now that they were out there, he wouldn't take them back. He would own his feelings, reiterate his desire and love for her, but also promise that he had no expectations of her and no claim on her future.

He guided her out of the shower, wrapping her in the biggest, fluffiest towel they had before shutting the shower off.

"We should do that again another day," Mary murmured sleepily. "It was lovely."

Another day. Yes. He'd take all the other days she offered.

"Exceptionally lovely," he agreed. "Like my lovely, genius partner."

For tonight, he would hold her and dream of forever.

Chapter 37

Acting on Impulse

He loves me. He loves me!

Mary bounced around the bedroom as she dressed, her heart lighter than it had been in years. Victor's impassioned declaration last night had wiped away the last of her doubts. She would always carry a shard of uncertainty, she suspected, but not about him.

After that spectacular encounter in the shower, she'd been sleepy and dazzled, so her response had perhaps not been as sensible as she might have liked. No matter. They would find a time today to have a long talk, air their feelings clearly, and discuss the future. Questions remained, many of them in her own mind, but for once she faced life with more excitement than trepidation.

A distant ringing interrupted her morning preparations. Mary scurried out into the main room to answer the telephone, her shirtwaist scandalously unbuttoned. Victor would applaud her daring, if he were awake.

She snagged the mouthpiece mid-ring. "Hello?"

"Miss Amesbury," Victor's father greeted her from the other end. "Good morning. There is a police detective here, asking to see you and Victor. We've left him in the front parlor. We can send him away or inform him that you are here. The choice is yours."

A detective? That was quick. The police chief's warning resounded in her head. *Desperate. Unpredictable.* Her muscles tensed.

Mary steadied herself with a slow breath. She would bring Mecha-Man. They would verify the detective's identity. All would be well.

"We'll speak to him," she replied. "Chief Majhi said he would be sending someone by."

"Excellent. I'll have tea and coffee brought around for you all."

"Thank you. We'll be up shortly. I will have to wake Victor."

A low huff sounded through the phone. "I trust the two of you have reached an understanding by now?"

Mary's mouth quirked. "Victor is the very best of men. You needn't fret for me, and I hope you are proud of him."

Dr. Franklin paused a long time before answering. "I am. Can't say I always understand the boy, but, yes. He does us proud. Good day, Miss Amesbury."

Mary hung up the phone and returned to the bedroom. Victor lay sprawled on his back, having claimed most of the space she had vacated. She gripped his shoulder and gave him a gentle shake.

"Victor, wake up."

"Already?" he grumbled.

"Yes, already. The policeman has arrived to collect the bottle."

"The who?" He rubbed his eyes and blinked, eventually focusing on Mary. "You're nearly dressed. Damn."

She laughed. "Get up. Let's take care of this and get you some coffee to wake you up. You may ravish me later."

Mary finished dressing and pinned her hair while Victor stomped into the closet to find something to wear.

He emerged in a few minutes, mostly presentable, brushing his hair into place with his fingers.

"I hope no one expects me to have donned a coat or shaved at this hour," he declared. "In fact, I think it should become customary not to dress oneself before liberal application of stimulating beverages."

"Your naked tea in bed?" Mary smiled at the memory.

"We should make a habit of it." He waggled his eyebrows.

"I will give it some consideration. For now, get the bottle and let's deliver it to the policeman."

"Yes." Victor ducked back into the closet and emerged with a small bundle that he tucked into his trouser pocket. "I'm ready."

Mary took his arm. "Excellent. Each step closer to resolving this matter brings me a little more peace." She couldn't suppress a tremble. "Let's get Mecha-Man. I'm still nervous."

"Of course."

A short trolley ride later, the three of them entered the house. Victor's father waited for them near the cellar stairs.

"I think I'll accompany you this time, if you don't mind," he said.

Victor shrugged.

Dr. Franklin smiled at Mary. "Good morning, Miss Amesbury. You are looking well this morning. It's so nice to have another sunny presence in the house to counter my son's morning grumpiness. We would be delighted if you made a habit of joining us for breakfast."

The unexpected invitation brought a smile to her face. "Thank you. That sounds very pleasant."

A habit of family breakfasts? A nervous shiver joined her smile. She'd been alone for so long, rarely even seeing her own family since her father's retirement. Company every morning would be too much. But maybe she could alternate family breakfast and naked tea with Victor.

Thoughts of the future still whirring in her head, Mary walked with her companions to the front parlor. Time to remove one more obstacle to that future.

"Good morning," she called. The policeman stood with his back to them, looking out the window. "Thank you for coming to see us, Detective—"

The man turned and Mary froze in horror.

"Daide," he supplied.

"Daide, now I remember," she replied, recovering. *Please, please don't let him have seen me falter.*

Mecha-Man stepped up beside Mary. Victor took a place at her opposite side.

Daide eyed the automaton. "So this is the infamous metal man. Seems harmless enough."

"What can we do for you, Detective?" Victor asked. His voice was calm, but his body tense beside her.

"At our previous meeting you provided me with certain samples of soap," Daide stated coolly. "They are being analyzed, naturally, but we cannot be definitive without a comparison. I will need the bottle you found."

"We don't have it," Mary replied.

"We disposed of it as soon as we knew what it was," Victor added, the partial truth giving him an air of sincerity.

Daide's brows drew together and his jaw tightened. "Disposed of it where?"

Victor shrugged. "Poured it down the drain and tossed it in the trash."

The detective took a step forward. "I need that bottle."

"Sorry." Victor spread his hands. "I wish we could help."

Daide pulled his shoulders back and straightened up to his full height. "Mrs. Clay," he said firmly. "I am certain you understand the urgency of the situation. This is no time to be playing games. Where is the bottle?"

Mary summoned up the stoic demeanor that had gotten her through years as Clay's wife. "It's as Dr. Franklin said. We feared the substance was harmful so we disposed of it."

Beside her, Victor nodded. His father wore a slightly bemused expression, but said nothing.

"Where?" Daide demanded.

"In a trash bin in the laboratory," Mary replied, not wanting to drag the apothecary into the situation. "It will be long gone, I'm afraid."

Daide stalked toward her. "You are one hundred percent certain of this? Because if you are lying to the police…"

Lying to the police? What an unmitigated ass, accusing her of failing to cooperate with the very people he was trying to sabotage.

"I am not," she retorted.

"This is no trifling matter, Mrs. Clay." Daide loomed over her. His hand dropped to the firearm holstered at his side.

Mary staggered back a step.

Victor thrust out an arm to bar Daide from moving any closer. "Do not threaten her," he snarled.

Mary almost reached to pull him back, then stopped herself. Daide couldn't possibly draw his weapon. Not here. Not with so many witnesses.

"Hand over the bottle," Daide ordered.

Victor didn't move. "I don't have it."

The detective glared. "I don't believe you for an instant. Hand it over or I'll have you arrested." Again, he put a hand to his weapon.

Mary grabbed Victor's arm and waved frantically at

Mecha-Man, trying to put the automaton between him and potential danger.

"Now look here," Victor's father cut in, "There's no reason—"

Daide drew the gun. "Call off that monster, or I *will* defend myself."

Victor shoved Mary fully behind him. "Put down the gun, Daide."

"Victor," Mary hissed. She tugged on his shirt, trying to pull him toward the door. "Please."

Victor held his ground, Mecha-Man beside him. "Father, could you phone Chief Majhi? I believe the detective has overstepped his authority."

Dr. Franklin glanced at the door, clearly torn between summoning help and staying to protect his son.

Mary tugged harder on Victor's shirt. They had to run before Daide made good on his threats. Mech was fast, but not fast enough to jump in front of a bullet, and he wouldn't understand the danger of a weapon.

Victor's father spoke up, raising his voice loud enough for anyone in the hall to overhear. "Lower your weapon at once, or I will summon my entire household and report your crimes to the Detroit Police Department, the Pinkerton Agency, the United States Marshals, and fifteen U.S. senators who I happen to know personally!"

Daide gaped, then bolted for the door. "You'll regret this!" he shouted as he tore from the room. "I'll have your heads for this!"

Victor took off running. "Get back here, you bastard!"

Mary whirled around. "Victor, no!" She seized Mecha-Man's arm. "Hurry, Mech, we can't lose them!"

Blast, blast, and damn! What was Victor thinking, to run off alone after an armed villain?

"That foolish, impulsive boy," his father groaned.

"Dr. Franklin, call the police." Mary's words came almost on top of one another. "Insist on speaking with Chief Majhi. Tell him what happened and that Daide knows he's been unmasked. I have to go after Victor."

She tore from the room, the automaton loping along easily beside her. Ahead of them the front door slammed, then slammed again seconds later. Mary gathered her skirts and ran faster, dashing from the house with no hat or coat, her ankles on display for anyone happening by. The chill winter wind stung her cheeks and whipped away the pins she'd used to pull back her hair.

No cold, no bashfulness could stop her. She ran on, heedless of anything but Victor's figure down the street ahead of her.

Daide had headed straight for the heart of town, hoping to lose himself among the traffic and pedestrians, Mary guessed. Crowds wouldn't slow her. Her small stature allowed her to duck through spaces Daide and Victor couldn't fit through. By the time they'd reached Cadillac Square, she'd closed most of the gap between them.

Mecha-Man shot past her. He couldn't dodge the way she could, but in a clear lane he was faster than any human, and without his coat and hat to disguise him, people leapt from his path. In moments he would catch up to Victor. Thank God.

"Stop that man!" Victor shouted. "He's a criminal! Stop him!"

All around them, people had begun to stop and stare. Unintelligible murmurs reached Mary's ears. She was causing a scene. They would think her a hoyden or strumpet.

Let them. Let them say what they wanted. Let them talk about her in the newspaper. Victor wouldn't care what anyone else thought of her. Her friends wouldn't care. Even Victor's parents, with their clear ideas of how things were supposed to be, wouldn't fault her for this. Not when she was protecting their son.

"Help us!" she called to the crowd. "Help us catch him!"

Much of Mary's initial fear had dissipated, now that Mecha-Man had caught up to Victor. Daide couldn't be so foolish as to use his weapon here in public. But he could skip town. If he vanished, the police might lose a vital clue to solving this case. They had to catch him so he could be interrogated.

"Someone help us!" she cried.

The onlookers remained frozen, gawking.

"The metal man is after me!" Daide shouted. "Save me, save me!" He grabbed hold of a fruit cart outside a grocer's shop and shoved it toward Victor.

Victor darted to one side, avoiding a collision, but losing his momentum and stumbling against the shop window. The heavily-loaded wagon kept rolling toward a group of nearby pedestrians. Most of them yelped and ran, except for a small, frightened boy, who stared at the cart barreling toward him in mute horror.

Mary opened her mouth to scream, but in the split second before the crash, Mecha-Man leapt in front of the cart, scooping up the boy and shielding him from the impact. Fruit flew in all directions. Mecha-Man staggered from the blow, but didn't fall.

Mary came to a halt beside them, gasping from the running and an acute sense of relief. She bent over, hands on her knees, trying to catch her breath. "Mech," she panted. "You're a hero."

The boy began to wail. Mecha-Man held him out at arm's length, head cocked to the side in confusion.

"My boy!" a woman shrieked. "The monster has my boy!"

Mary shot up straight. "No! He saved him."

She motioned to tell Mecha-Man to set the child down gently, but her instructions came too late. The woman jerked the child from Mech's hands and battered the automaton with her handbag.

"You vile creature!"

"No, you don't understand," Mary protested.

"Get him!" someone shouted from behind her.

An orange struck Mecha-Man in the side of the head. An apple bounced off his shoulder.

"Get him, get him!" more voices cheered. "Get the monster!"

More fruit sailed through the air. Mecha-Man caught an apple and hurled it back at the young man who had thrown it.

"It's attacking!" the youth screamed. "Kill it! Kill it!"

Mary waved her arms, still calling for the people to stop, but her quiet voice and small body left her all but lost in the clamor.

"Stop!" Victor's powerful baritone cut through the noise and Mary's head swiveled to look at him. He glanced briefly over his shoulder, as if debating whether to continue after Daide, then abandoning the thought. "Leave him alone."

"He attacked me!" the apple thrower insisted.

A large man raced past Mary and tackled Mecha-Man to the ground. The crash of metal against pavement stabbed into her skull. She grabbed at the man's coat, but couldn't pull him off the automaton.

"I've got him!" the man declared. An instant later, Mecha-Man flipped them both over, reversing their positions. The man shrieked. "He's killing me! Help!"

"Stop it!" Victor forced his way toward them, shoving

past riveted bystanders. "Stop fighting him! He doesn't understand. He's like a puppy. He thinks you're playing."

"Get him off me!"

Mary tapped Mecha-Man on the shoulder, gesturing for him to stand. The automaton began to rise and the man scurried away.

"This is all a misunder—" she began.

"I'll get him!" another man's voice sounded behind her.

She spun around to find a man racing down the street, holding aloft a heavy metal snow shovel from the tool shop two doors down.

Her hand went to her throat and she sprang backward with a yelp of alarm. The instinctive movement gave the attacker a clear path to Mecha-Man. Too late, Mary snatched at him, grasping nothing but air as he barreled past.

With a roar of triumph, the man swung his shovel like a battle axe, straight at Mecha-Man's head.

Victor leapt in front of his creation, hands raised to defend him.

All the breath rushed from Mary's lungs.

"No!"

Chapter 38
What Comes Next

A bellow of rage tore from Victor's throat. He caught the shaft of the shovel mid-swing, the force of the blow sending a jolt of pain up both arms. He staggered, but he'd slowed the momentum of the improvised weapon enough. No one was hurt.

"You bastard!" With a single, anger-fueled jerk, Victor ripped the shovel from the other man's hands. He held it in front of him like a quarterstaff, legs spread in a fighting stance. He glanced left, then right, scanning the crowd for enemies.

"All of you," he snarled. "Look at yourselves. Throwing yourselves into senseless abuse and violence." Victor hurled the shovel to the ground. "You disgust me. You would attack a harmless creature with no provocation. If he learns to hurt, it's because of people like you. He knew only good. Only protection and defense and caring. And now, you do this." He jerked a hand at the splattered remnants of fruit on the pavement. "*You* would teach him violence. *You* would teach him hatred. None of you, none of this world, deserves him."

Victor grasped Mech's arm and steered him toward home. Mary took the automaton's other arm. All along the sidewalk, people drew back, leaving them space to pass though. Whether they shied away in fear or in shame, Victor didn't know. Nor did he care, so long as they were out of his way.

No one spoke until they were past Jefferson Avenue, Franklin Castle rising ahead of them along the riverfront.

"I'm sorry Daide escaped," Victor broke the silence.

Mary released Mecha-Man and hurried around to take Victor's other arm. "Oh, Victor, I was so scared. First when you ran after him alone, and again when you jumped in front of Mecha-Man. I thought… I thought I was going to lose you."

He winced. "I apologize. I believe we've established that I don't think before I do things."

Her hand stroked his arm. "You misunderstand. I'm not faulting you for it. I'm merely recovering. You are so very brave and so very good. I don't want to imagine a world without you in it. Yes, you are impulsive, but you aren't selfish or careless. You act out of love. Of course you risked yourself to save Mech. He's your baby."

Victor gazed down into her soft blue eyes, his heart swelling with love. Mary understood him, even if no one else did.

"He is *our* baby," he corrected. "He would never exist without the work you did. He belongs to us both."

Mary laughed. "And here we said we didn't want children."

"Only metal ones, I suppose." A tingle began where her hand rested on his arm, spreading outward. "Perhaps when we arrive home we should talk. About the future."

He barely got the words out. Too much of him still feared her answers. What would he do if she told him her feelings weren't as strong as his?

You'd go back to living how you did before and thank

God you'd shared as much with her as you have, he scolded himself, though inside he still longed for more.

"We should," Mary agreed, her voice soft and solemn. Slowly, her mouth curved into a smile. "Are you making plans, Victor?"

He beamed down at her. "I think maybe I am."

* * *

Making plans was delayed for a time by his mother fussing all over them for running outside without proper clothing. She whisked them into the breakfast room, where they warmed themselves with coffee and hot porridge. Mech joined them, sipping politely from an empty cup. Victor noted the need for a micro-incinerator so the automaton could ingest real food and convert it into power.

"Your father called the police," his mother said, nudging both the teapot and the coffee pot in Victor's direction.

"Good." He waved off the offer of drinks. "I've had plenty, thank you."

"They're sending men after this Daide person," his mother continued. "I'm sure they'll take care of it. Meanwhile, I think the two of you should rest and relax at home. There's been altogether too much dashing off after dangerous people of late."

Mecha-Man picked up a piece of toast and held it in front of his face, studying it. Victor plucked it from the automaton's grasp.

"Don't eat that. You're not ready for real food yet." Maybe he never would be. Not a chance in hell Victor was taking him out in public again any time soon. Not even to play bodyguard, if they could possibly avoid it. "We're not going anywhere," he told his mother.

"I'm glad. And, honestly, Victor, you ought to dress

properly before leaving your rooms. You look as though you rolled straight out of bed."

"That's because he did," Mary replied. "He was sound asleep when Dr. Franklin called down."

Victor's mother smiled across the table at Mary. "I suppose I can't say that is terribly surprising. Victor certainly could benefit from having a good woman as a permanent fixture in his life."

Mary turned pink.

Victor pushed his chair back from the table before his mother's blatant hints could turn into, "So when are you getting married?"

"We ought to be getting back to work," he said. He touched the side of Mecha-Man's head, where the pavement had left long scratches in the metal. "I'll have to buff this out and shine him up again."

Mary rose from her seat, though not as eagerly as Victor would have expected. "Yes, I suppose we have things to do."

Victor fought back a frown. Not long ago, she'd been pleased with his intentions to talk of the future. Had his mother's insinuations of marriage unsettled her?

"If you'd rather remain here…" he began.

"No," Mary reassured him. "It's only that I'm tired of the bunker. The thought of hiding any longer is exhausting. Everyone knows who we are and where we are. The police are on the case. And I don't care about journalists or gawkers anymore. I don't want to be down there, in the dark. I want to look out a window. I want to be in the sunshine."

Victor's worries ebbed, and this time he had to struggle not to grin like a fool. "I have the perfect spot for you to sit in the sunshine." He waved for Mecha-Man to stand. "Come on, Mech. Let's take the lady on a tour."

Victor led the way from the breakfast room to the main

staircase, which curved from the massive foyer up to the second floor.

"Where are we going?" Mary wondered, her eagerness returned.

"My suite."

"That sounds very… intimate."

"It can be, if you want it," he replied, honestly. "But I meant it only as a place where you can enjoy your sunshine while we have our talk."

She stepped closer to him, her arm brushing his. "That's intimate, too."

"Yes, I suppose it is." He unlocked the door to his sitting room and invited her inside. This was the least interesting of his rooms, and one he rarely used. If he had visitors, he entertained them downstairs. Until this moment, he'd never had a single guest enter this space. And yet, it didn't feel wrong. It felt as though he'd been waiting. Waiting for the right time. Waiting for her.

"Victor?"

"Sorry. Lost in my thoughts. Would you like to go straight to the sunshine or have the grand tour?"

He gestured for Mecha-Man to have a seat, then shut the automaton down.

"Grand tour, please."

"All right, then." Instead of offering his arm, Victor held out his hand, and Mary grasped it, twining her fingers with his. "This is the sitting room. Dull. Seldom used." He walked her through the door to the left, into his bedroom. "Bedroom. Mostly taken up by my enormous bed."

Mary eyed the high, canopied bed with open admiration. "Looks comfortable."

"It is. You are welcome to try it out at any time. This first door, here, is my dressing room."

Mary peeked inside. "It's half empty."

"It's extremely large," he agreed. "I couldn't possibly fill the whole thing."

That wasn't quite true. He could easily have bought enough to fill the room. For some reason, he simply… hadn't.

"Then there's my washroom." He didn't enter this room, either, but paused at the door so Mary could look in. "Not as large as the one downstairs, but still adequate. I think I'll have the bathtub replaced with one of those ribcage showers."

Mary's eyebrows twitched. "That sounds like a lovely idea."

"And now, the best part."

As much as he enjoyed having Mary in his bedroom, showing it off to her didn't have the significance that this next room would. Victor only slept in his bedroom. In his library, he *existed*.

He escorted her back into the sitting room, to the carved oak door that shielded his sanctuary from the world beyond.

"This is my favorite room in the house," he told her, then swung the door wide. "And there, my dearest, is your sunshine."

* * *

Mary took two hesitant steps into the library, her head lifting and turning to take in the whole room. No wonder it was Victor's favorite. If she could claim one room in the world as the room of her heart, this would be it.

The coffered ceiling was of a dark, rich wood, matching the side walls with their built-in bookcases. A simple table stood a few feet ahead of her, topped with an elegant reading lamp. Chairs were neatly tucked in on either side. The perfect place for research or writing.

Beyond were more chairs, large and plush, with matching footstools. Pretty, well-used pillows adorned the chairs, and quilts with book and science patterns had been draped over the backs. Mary could curl up in any of those chairs and read for hours.

Except that the sunshine beckoned her. She moved closer.

The far end of the library was a massive bay window, curving out to give a view of the river and the Windsor shoreline beyond. The southern sunlight beamed through the crystalline panes, casting a grid pattern on the floor and bathing the entire end of the library in a cheerful glow. Beneath the window lay a wide, padded window seat, festooned with additional quilts and pillows, and a worn toy elephant.

Mary covered her hand with her mouth, tears springing to her eyes. How many hours had Victor spent here, lost in a book, or staring out the window dreaming impossible innovations?

"Like it?"

Slowly, she turned to face him, letting her hand drop to her side. "It's beautiful. I can't imagine a more perfect place to rest and relax."

"It's been my special place since my father built this house when I was thirteen. I'm honored to be able to share it with you."

She was honored too. He hadn't said as much, but she suspected he didn't bring many people here. The space was too private, with its relics of childhood and books with cracked spines and bent corners.

Mary studied the shelves to her left. Unlike those opposite, these were bare, save for a scattering of old toys and antique scientific equipment.

"Why are half the shelves empty?" she asked.

Victor lifted one shoulder and let it drop. "I don't have enough books to fill them."

"I am *sure* you could have filled them if you wanted. The same goes for the closet. Why didn't you?"

His dark eyes locked on her with an intensity that took her breath away. "I've always wanted extra space, I suppose," he said. "In case I needed it for something."

For some*one*. Mary's heart thumped. Victor was a romantic soul. Always dreaming of beautiful, fantastic things. Why not a beautiful, fantastic love? Because what she saw here proclaimed his world was meant for two. All he needed was someone to join him.

"I love your plans," she whispered.

"My what?"

Mary laughed and strode to his side, lifting her hand to his chest. He was more like his father than he realized, and all the more adorable for it.

"I love this room. It's as perfect as I could imagine. I could see myself living happily in a place like this."

He laid a hand over hers, pinning it to his heart. With his other hand, he gestured to the empty shelves. "I have room. It's yours if you want it."

"I do. I want this. I want us. We're so good together, you and I. I think we make each other better."

Moisture shimmered in his eyes and he blinked rapidly. "I think so, too. Will you have me, Mary? Not just while we're hiding, or while we're collaborating, but for all time? I won't beg or insist, but if you'll choose me, I swear I'll be as good a man as I'm able for you. And if you don't love me the way I love you, I will respect that. You need only tell me."

Her own gaze grew watery. "You're worried I don't love you?" She laughed. "Victor, every day you make it more and more impossible for me to hide all my feelings. Me! Who's been hiding her feelings for years. Maybe forever. But then you say these glorious things and the feelings gush out of me in a way I can't control. I don't know what to do about them, or how to talk about them, so I babble, like this. Or I say nothing and kiss you instead. But I do love you. I love you so much it scares me. Being close to someone scares me. Risking marriage again scares me. But you make me want it anyway."

"We don't ever have to get married," he assured her. "God knows it didn't work for you last time. I promise I won't ever ask you unless you tell me to."

She pillowed her head on his shoulder. "I'd like to know what a real marriage is like. A true love match, like in the storybooks. But I'm not ready now. Maybe tomorrow. Maybe in a month. Maybe never. I don't know."

Victor stroked her hair. "You don't have to know. I've been waiting for you since the moment I met you. What's a bit more waiting?"

"The moment you met me?"

His fingers made gentle caresses against her scalp. "Yes. And every day I've known you, I've loved you more."

Mary sighed and let her eyes slip closed. "I think maybe it's been the same for me. Only I keep it all more tightly inside." She let herself bask in the embrace for a few moments, then opened her eyes again. "Can we snuggle in the sunshine?"

"Absolutely." Victor whisked her across the room to the window seat, where he plumped up some pillows and gathered her in his lap, wrapping a quilt around them to ward off any drafts from the window.

"I could snuggle here for days," she sighed.

Victor planted a kiss on the top of her head. "I'm so glad.

You're welcome to sit here, with or without me, as often and for as long as you like."

Forever. She still feared to say it out loud, but she knew she would someday. Because each day she grew a little bit stronger and a little bit more comfortable claiming what she wanted.

"I love you, Victor," she vowed. "And I promise you that when I'm ready to marry, you'll be the first to know."

His arms tightened around her.

Chapter 39
And Automaton Makes Three

The luxuriant halls of Franklin Castle no longer intimidated her, Mary reflected, as she and Victor walked from the laboratory to his father's study. True, they were more numerous and more ornate than her personal taste, but knowing the family more intimately had brought a sense of homeyness to the mansion.

Nor did she fear speaking to Victor's father any longer. She'd grown fond of the man and his superficial gruffness.

"I think it's time I installed a telephone line for you," he declared, the moment they stepped into the room. "Rather tedious, having the phone ringing here all the time and then needing to summon you. I'll have one phone put in the laboratory and another in your quarters upstairs, if that suits?"

Victor nodded. "I think that's a good idea. I'm rather tired of intruding on you as well. Although, honestly, I'd prefer people stop calling altogether. I never had this problem when I did all my work at night."

He looked toward Mary and their eyes locked for a moment. *But then I wouldn't have you*, his expression seemed to say. She replied with a fond smile.

Victor picked up the telephone. "Victor Franklin, here. Oh. Nemo. Hi." He listened for a moment, his expression darkening. "Dammit." He covered the mouthpiece and whispered, "Daide's dead."

Mary gasped. Of all the things she'd expected from this call—updates on the investigation, possible arrests, the altercation with Mecha-Man the other day—a dead enemy hadn't been among them.

"Not again," Victor moaned. "Are they still there, working? Uh-huh. We'll be right there. I'm bringing Mecha-Man. The experts can compare on the spot, and prove we had nothing to do with it. Uh-huh. Yes. Meet you inside."

The click of the phone hanging up made Mary jump.

"We should leave at once," Victor declared, already striding for the door. "I'll explain on the way."

"Victor!" She jogged after him. "Where are you going? And what's this about Mecha-Man? I thought you wanted to keep him at home, after the… incident."

Victor's long stride carried him toward the laboratory at such a clip that Mary had to run at times to keep pace.

"Daide was found dead. Strangled, in the same way Clay was."

Mary's stomach knotted. "Oh, no!"

"They found him outside the Michigan Central depot. Nemo's there now, observing from inside." Victor yanked open the laboratory door and hurried over to where Mecha-Man sat waiting. He switched the automaton on. "If we go now, while the investigation is still ongoing, we can prove Mech's innocence. And ours, incidentally. The investigators can directly compare Mech's hands with the markings on the body. It's the best way to be done with this nonsense once and for all." He strode toward the door to the outside, snatching an overcoat and hat from the pegs nearby.

Mary hurried to his side, grabbing his arm before he could stuff it into the coat. "Victor."

He looked directly at her for the first time since running from his father's study. "What?"

She put her hands on her hips. "If we're going to be together, you can't go about making all the decisions on your own. These are the sorts of things we need to discuss."

"I..." He blinked. "Sorry. I was acting on instinct. Again."

"I know." Mary reached for her cloak. "And I understand that acting swiftly is a part of your nature. But I do want to be consulted."

Victor nodded. "I will endeavor to improve."

"Thank you. That's all I ask."

His brow furrowed. "Do you think this is a bad idea?"

She considered it. "No. I think it's logical. With friends nearby and Chief Majhi's men on the scene, we should be safe. Let's get going."

The railroad depot was less than a mile away, and within minutes they were walking through the main entrance, merely a few more people in the crowd of comers and goers. With Mecha-Man concealed beneath a large floppy hat, no one paid them any special attention. They wove their way through the depot, dodging luggage carts and tired passengers.

A train had recently arrived, slowing their progress through the station, as the predominant traffic moved in the opposite direction. Mary hung close to her companions, her eyes scanning the crowd and her ears perked for a greeting.

Steam hissed and a train whistle blew. "All aboard!" a conductor called.

The platform beside the departing train was much clearer, thank goodness. As they approached, Mary dared to put a bit more space between herself and Victor and breathe easier.

There! Up ahead she at last spied a friendly face. She lifted a hand to wave.

"Nemo," Victor hailed their friend. "There you are. I— Oof. Sorry."

Mary's head swiveled toward him. Victor staggered back a step from the man he'd bumped into. An all-too-familiar man, with a bushy black beard and a scar across his left eyebrow. She opened her mouth to scream, but too late. The smuggler seized hold of Victor's arm, while his snub-nosed companion darted in to grab him from the other side.

Startled, Victor had no chance to fight. The men hauled him onto the chugging train just as it began to move.

"No!"

Mary leapt after them, clutching the handrail and scrambling up the steps while the locomotive picked up speed. Mecha-Man, with his superhuman quickness, easily vaulted onto the train behind her. Mary pushed through the door into the carriage with only a single thought in her head: save Victor from whatever lay within.

The train car could only be a private carriage. Gilt paint adorned the ceiling, and a plush carpet cushioned her feet. Green and gold curtains framed every window and both doors, tied neatly back with tasseled cords. Electric lights in frosted sconces brightened the space, casting every detail into sharp relief.

The space was more open than a standard train carriage, furnished with chairs scattered here and there instead of the wide built-in seats. A single table stood in the center of the car, against the lefthand wall, draped with a decorative tapestry. A heavy-bottomed vase sat atop it, wilting flowers drooping over the rim.

Mary gestured for Mecha-Man to remain still.

"Nice of you to join us," Snub-Nose sneered. "Figured

you meddling kids wouldn't be able to stop yourselves from running to the scene of another murder." Victor squirmed in his grasp, but with two men holding him, he was unable to break free.

Mary pressed back against the curtain, her fingers curling around one of the tassels of the decorative tie. She tugged and felt it move. Another tug and it came loose, falling to dangle behind her skirts.

"Release him," she declared, feigning more bravado than she felt. The two men could be armed or trained fighters. She and Victor were only scientists. They would have to rely on their wits to save them.

Bushy-Beard snorted. "Sorry, Missy. You and your boyfriend are about to be found dead, murdered by your own monster. Should've listened to your husband."

Snub-Nose chortled. "Only thing Clay ever did right was screaming about that metal man. Gave us the perfect sap to take the fall when we eliminated him. And now we'll do the same with you blabbermouths."

Mecha-Man took a step forward, his head swiveling as he looked between Mary and Victor. He raised one hand, then dropped it.

Mary reached for her anger to steady her. Poor, confused Mech couldn't even understand what was happening, much less attack anyone. But he made a good story for the papers, and that was all the enemy needed. *Monster kills people* would smother any news of riverfront smugglers.

"The police will realize what you've done," she countered. "I'm sure they'll stop the train."

"And there are two of us and two of you." Victor attempted to stomp on Bushy-Beard's foot, but the larger man moved with the swiftness of an athlete, twisting Victor's arm until he cried out in pain.

The door at the far end of the carriage swung open and two more men strode in. The taller of the men wore a pair of metal gauntlets covering his hands. Mary's stomach lurched.

Snub-Nose laughed. "Two of you. Four of us. Johnson, grab the girl and hold her still so Blair can take care of her."

"No!" Victor thrashed in his captors' arms. His rage gave him strength. If Mary could provide help, he could free himself.

Her hand clenched on the rope. It was now or never.

Mary darted forward, swinging the rope at Bushy-Beard with all the force her small body could muster. The tasseled end slapped him across the face. He yelped and staggered.

It was enough. Victor broke free of his grip and turned his full attention to Snub-Nose, tackling him to the ground and pummeling him with fists and elbows. Mecha-Man staggered back and forth in bewilderment, throwing his arms wide in a useless parody of the defensive moves they'd taught him. Mary darted behind a nearby chair for protection, her improvised weapon clutched tight.

"You bitch!" Bushy-Beard stalked toward her, dodging her rope as she whipped it around to keep him at bay.

The two newcomers rushed forward. Mary swatted at Bushy-Beard, her heart hammering and her hand growing sweaty against the rope. Across from her, Snub-Nose grunted in pain as Victor wrestled him into the wall. If they didn't incapacitate their opponents soon, they'd lose their chance at escape.

Bushy-Beard continued to dodge her rope, growling in annoyance. She'd never do him real harm with such a weapon. Victor could likely throw or swing a chair, but she wasn't strong enough. She crouched low and flicked the rope at her attacker's legs, thinking to trip him or throw him off balance.

His hand shot downward, catching the end of the cord and jerking it from her hands. "I'm onto your tricks, Missy," he sneered. He cast the rope aside, grabbed the chair, and flung it away.

Mary ran. Bushy-Beard swiped a hand toward her, but she ducked under it, offering up a prayer of thanks for her small stature.

"Grab her!" Blair, the man with the gauntlets, shouted. His partner Johnson ran at her, seizing hold of her cloak as she raced by. Mary flicked the clasp open and the garment fell away from her.

Blair stalked toward Victor.

"Victor, look out!" Mary cried. She waved a hand frantically at Mecha-Man. If he could stall even one of the men, it might save Victor's life. The thought of those metal gauntlets around his neck, squeezing the air from his body, choking off his life, his light, his love...

Mary almost couldn't breathe. She dove beneath the table, the only shelter available to her, and pressed herself up against the wall. Through the gap between the dangling tablecloth and the wall, she saw Snub-Nose's head slam into the wall. He fell still and Victor scrambled to his feet. Mecha-Man ran toward him, then paused and turned in a full circle. Looking for her?

"Mech, please," she whispered, even knowing that his programming had never accounted for anything like this melee. "Help him."

She grabbed the tablecloth and pulled it aside for a better view. Her pull was met with a slight resistance. The vase up top had some weight. If she could drag it down into her hands, perhaps she could do something.

A hand groped beneath the table, and she slammed her fist down hard on the exposed fingers. Whatever happened, she couldn't let the men haul her out into the open until she had that weapon. She curled as far into the corner as she could, her hand tight on the tablecloth and her eyes glued on Victor.

"You never should have tried to cross us, boy," Blair taunted. He swung a metal-gloved fist at Victor, but the punch was slow and Victor effortlessly avoided it. "It'll be such a shame when the cops discover that your homicidal metal man attacked you and your lady friend."

Victor dodged another swing. "I will strangle you with your own damned gauntlets before I let you touch a hair on her head!"

Johnson sprang at Victor from behind, pinning his arms. "Get him, Blair."

No!

Mary pulled harder on the tablecloth, but it stuck fast.

No, no, no!

She tugged and tugged, but the cloth had snagged on some corner or nail and wouldn't budge. Bushy-Beard's grasping hands clawed at her beneath the table, trying to find purchase on her skirts. Mary kicked at him, her boot colliding with something soft, causing him to yelp.

Blair flexed his metal hands as Victor fought to disentangle himself from Johnson's grip. The villain's bone-chilling laugh reverberated through the air as he reached for Victor's throat.

"Mech, help!" Mary cried. She clung to the tablecloth, pulling with all her might. She was too late. Too late. All she could do now was launch herself at Blair's legs and hope she might be strong enough to knock him off balance.

Before she could move, an inhuman howl shook the air. Metal hands clamped down on Johnson, ripping him away from Victor and flinging him aside. Victor staggered backward and Blair's gauntlets closed around empty air.

Once more, Mary yanked on the tablecloth, and this time it tore free. The cloth slithered to the ground, and the vase tumbled into her outstretched hands. She darted from beneath the table to see Blair lunging for Victor once more, murder blazing in his eyes. She hefted her weapon and slammed it into the back of the killer's head.

Blair staggered. Mary brought the sturdy vessel crashing down on him a second time and he crumpled.

The world seemed to slow. Her chest heaved with great gasping breaths of relief. Victor was alive. Thank the Lord.

A hand clamped down on her shoulder.

Mary screamed, trying to spin and swing her vase at the man who had caught her from behind.

Mecha-Man roared again, a strange tinny yowl from the primitive voice-box they had never calibrated. He charged at Bushy-Beard, who leapt away from Mary, throwing up his hands in surrender.

"Don't kill me!" he pleaded.

Mecha-Man pushed him back against the wall and stood in front of him, barring any path to freedom. Again he let out the metallic howling noise.

Victor and Mary lunged together for the nearest window, grabbing for the curtain ties. For an instant they froze, looking at one another. A hint of a smile touched Victor's lips.

"Great minds think alike," he said.

They tied Bushy-Beard to a chair, then bound his injured companions. Snub-Nose and Johnson had begun to groan, but Blair remained unconscious. Whenever one of the men made noise, Mech rounded on him, hands raised to fend off any attack.

Victor patted the automaton on the shoulder. "Relax, buddy. We're safe. You did good." He reached for Mary and pulled her into an embrace. "You and my brave, remarkable heroine." He kissed her cheek. "I love you."

"I love you t—"

Her words were choked off when Mecha-Man wrapped his arms around them both, crushing them in a slightly too-tight hug.

"Yes," she chuckled. "And you too."

Chapter 40
Case Closed

"Very good, very good," the police inspector muttered, jotting a few more notes.

Victor shifted closer to Mary. The shock of their latest ordeal hadn't entirely worn off, and even a slight distance between them made him antsy. If they weren't standing on a public train platform, he would have his arms wrapped around her.

Some yards off, a cluster of police officers surrounded the smugglers, escorting them toward the exit and the patrol cars that would carry them off to jail. Thank God.

"I think that does it," the police inspector declared. He hefted one of the metal gauntlets he'd taken from the man named Blair. "We'll confirm that these are a match for the marks on Daide's body, of course. But I'm quite certain these are the murder weapon." He glanced at Mary. "Begging the lady's pardon for speaking of such things."

Mary's eyebrows rose slightly. She'd hardly finished giving testimony about a kidnapping and attempted murder, and already the inspector was fearing for her nerves? Men always underestimated her. Victor vowed to try his best never to do so.

"As long as the man is put securely behind bars, I have no qualms about speaking of such things," she answered in her usual calm style. "Better to be absolutely clear about the facts."

"Right you are, ma'am," the inspector replied. He tucked his notebook away and tipped his hat. "Ah. Looks like the chief has arrived. He'll be wanting to speak with you."

Victor and Mary turned to follow the inspector's gaze. Chief Majhi was indeed striding toward them, but ahead of him came Nemo, barreling down the platform to catch the both of them up in a double hug.

Victor made a gesture reminding Mecha-Man to stay still, lest they find themselves in another mechanical embrace. He had his doubts whether the automaton would obey. Mech was clearly a creature with a mind of his own now, and it would take some experimenting to figure out what he had learned beyond their direct teaching and how it had affected him. Victor looked forward to the challenge. The outside world might never understand or accept Mech, but Victor would always look upon him with love and pride.

"I was so worried," Nemo blurted. "I was absolutely cursing myself when those bastards grabbed you. I ought to have considered that it might be a trap."

"I don't know how any of us would have guessed they would have their own private train car," Mary argued. "Thank you for alerting the authorities. Even though we had the men trussed up, it was a relief to see the police waiting when we reached the next station."

"It was the least I could do." Nemo's brows arched slyly. "I want to examine the engines of the new patrol cars they're using. Those things are fast!"

"You're welcome to do so once we're back downtown," Chief Majhi spoke. He looked at Victor and Mary as their little cluster separated. "Thank you, you two, for apprehending those men. I am heartily sorry you found yourselves in danger. If you'd like, I'll appoint a guard to escort you out and about for the next few days. But with these men behind bars, I expect you'll be safe. They're highly likely to inform on one another, and even if they don't, we now have enough proof to see that justice is done." The chief eyed Mecha-Man. "Your metal man assisted you?"

"He incapacitated two of the villains," Mary replied, beaming at the automaton.

"And yet, here he stands, entirely polite and harmless."

"His heart may be metal, but it's kind," Victor said. "He's quiet and gentle, but he'll fight to protect us."

"Like any good friend," Nemo declared.

Victor grinned. "Exactly."

"Well," Chief Majhi murmured. "I suppose that's that, then. We have a patrol car waiting to escort you home. Get some rest, and don't hesitate to call us with any concerns you have."

Victor shook the man's hand. "Thank you. We will do that."

Going home to rest sounded just the thing. In fact, Victor wanted nothing more than to snuggle with Mary in his library—*their* library. They would cuddle, light a warm fire, read some books, and make love. Quiet domesticity. With their enemies in the hands of the police, he looked forward to a long and uninteresting life together.

Mecha-Man let out a metallic screech, and everyone in the vicinity winced.

Victor chuckled to himself. Maybe not an *entirely* uninteresting life.

He took Mary's hand. "I think Mech is telling us it's time to go."

"I think he is." She nodded at Chief Majhi. "Thank you

for the ride home, sir. And good luck with wrapping up the case neatly."

"Thank you," he replied. "I'm sure my daughter will keep you apprised of all developments."

"Of course I will," Nemo declared. She grinned as Victor, Mary, and Mech started off down the platform. "See you all later!"

"Goodbye, Nisha," Mary replied, and they strode off for home.

Chapter 41
Reevaluation

The cobra's tongue darted in and out, sampling the air as the hand brushed lightly over its scales.

"Disappointing, is it not, my pet?" the low voice rumbled. "Another group of minions lost. Long may they languish in prison. You see now why I never trusted them with my identity?"

The snake hissed softly.

"Yes, you understand," the voice murmured. "You, like I, are a successful predator. So many in this world are but our prey, waiting to be devoured."

A knock sounded at the door.

"Enter," the voice boomed.

"Sir." The minion bowed. "Production at the soap factory has been halted, and arrangements have been made to sell our interest in the company."

A hand trailed over the cobra's coiled body. "Excellent. Mark the experiment down as successful."

"Yes, sir." The minion bowed again and departed.

"The plan moves on, despite certain failures on the part of underlings." A long silence fell. "But these adversaries we have faced," the voice spoke at last. "They are no mere subordinates. These are the smartest, the strongest among humans. Rather impressive, for such seemingly inconse-quential youths. I do wonder…"

The snake lifted its head, surveyed the room, then slithered into a new position.

"Perhaps," the voice mused, "it is time for a new strategy."

Chapter 42
All's Well

Three weeks of quiet domesticity. More or less. They'd experienced a few bumps since moving all of Mary's things up into Victor's suite. Such as the first day they'd started working on Mech's voicebox, when the automaton had decided a constant stream of noise was great fun. Or the meals with Victor's parents, where he'd had to deflect their not-so-subtle "when's the wedding" hints. Overall, though, life had been blissful. No disturbances. No danger. No nosy reporters.

A knock sounded at the door that led from the laboratory to the outside. Victor cocked his head, frowning. No one ever used that door except himself and Mary.

"I'll get it." Mary, who was nearer, hopped up from her seat and walked to the door. Victor scrambled to follow, in case his thoughts about their quiet, happy life had invited bad luck.

A man with round glasses and a flat black hat stood outside the door. He clutched a pad of paper and pencil in one hand, and wore an expression of eager curiosity. A reporter. Damn.

"Can I help you?" Mary asked.

The reporter tipped his hat. "Mrs. Mary Clay and Dr. Victor Franklin? My name is Mr. Pepperidge, and I was hoping you might have a few minutes to answer some questions for—"

"We're not giving any interviews," Victor cut in. "All questions relating to recent matters should be directed to police headquarters."

Pepperidge blinked. "Oh! You misunderstand me. I'm with American Science Monthly. We hoped to do a feature on your mechanical man."

A gust of wind blew through the door and Mary shivered. "Please come in, Mr. Pepperidge. It's chilly out."

"Yes, thank you." The reporter entered the laboratory and stamped the slush from his boots. "What a beautiful laboratory you have here." His eyes grew round behind his spectacles as he gazed around the space. "Quite beautiful. It must be a joy to work here."

Victor knew that look. That reverent voice. Genuine scientific admiration. A giddy happiness pushed aside any doubts about Pepperidge. This was it! His chance to present Mech to the world, not as a strange and scary thing, but as the technological marvel he was. All Victor had to do was answer the man's questions, then sit back and wait to read the story in print.

He jolted.

No. No, he couldn't do that. That was what he'd done to Mary before. Shut her out. She was the one who deserved her name in the magazines. She deserved the credit.

"Miss Amesbury here can tell you everything," Victor told Pepperidge. "She's absolutely brilliant, and this project owes everything to her dedicated work. I'll leave you two to talk." He nodded and started for the door to the house.

"Wait!" Mary dashed after him, taking hold of his arm to stop him. "Please excuse us a moment, Mr. Pepperidge." She tugged Victor's arm.

Victor allowed her to drag him to the corner of the laboratory, where they could have a semblance of a private conversation.

"I owe you," he said, before she could speak. "Take the opportunity. This is your chance to shine. To get the recognition you deserve for your work. I took it from you once, and I won't do it again."

Mary folded her arms across her chest, shaking her head. "No."

He blinked at her.

"You don't 'owe me.' Yes, you messed up. But you apologized. You learned from the mistake. Victor, you have proven again and again that I can rely on you. You are my truest friend and staunchest ally. You will probably make mistakes again in the future. We both will. But what matters is what's in your heart. You're a good man, and I know you'll always be willing to step up and make things right. It's who you are. It's why I love you."

Mary uncrossed her arms and reached up to lay a hand on his cheek. "We are partners, you and I. That's the future I want. We work together. We prop one another up. And we give credit where credit is due. Mech isn't yours, remember? He's not mine, either. He's *ours*."

Victor stared at her a long moment, moisture gathering in the corners of his eyes. Slowly, he nodded. "Partners. But may I at least make the gentlemanly gesture of allowing the lady to begin the interview first?"

Her smile was sweet and loving, and his heart melted for her all over again. As it always would.

"Yes," she replied. "Thank you."

They returned to Mr. Pepperidge and situated themselves around the large worktable to begin the conversation.

"Miss Amesbury has agreed to go first," Victor told the reporter.

Pepperidge tapped his pencil against his notebook, his nose wrinkling. "Amesbury, is it?" He turned his puzzled gaze on Mary. "I'd been told your name was Mrs. Mary Clay. Is that not the name you wish to use for the article?"

Mary hesitated a moment, then asked, "When do you expect the article to be published?"

"Oh, not until the end of April, I expect. It takes some time to get everything written up, and then to prepare the issue for printing. Why?"

Mary caught Victor's eye. She reached out to cover his hand with hers. "Because by that time, I believe I will be Mrs. Mary Franklin."

Victor's heart did a somersault. "Truly?" he whispered.

She nodded. "We intend to be married soon," she said, in a no-nonsense tone, returning her focus to Pepperidge. "I don't much like being a widow."

The reporter scribbled a note. "Mrs. Franklin it is. Now, let's talk about this remarkable mechanical man of yours."

If the article mentioned Victor at all, it was probably going to say that he wore a perpetually foolish grin and he had difficulty focusing on the questions. His mind was, admittedly, elsewhere. He had a wedding to prepare for.

Mary always had the best plans.

Epilogue

June, 1892

Mary gently poked at the internals of her latest project, securing and adjusting any parts that weren't tight enough or had been knocked out of alignment during the construction.

"Could I have the small screwdriver, please?" she asked.

Mech strode over to her and held out the tool.

She smiled at the automaton. "Thank you."

"You. Are. Welcome," he replied in his halting, metallic voice.

Her eyebrows lifted in surprise. "Very good!"

"That was a whole sentence!" Victor applauded. "And in the correct circumstances, too."

Mech's voice box had required months of work in order to enable him to pronounce intelligible words. Since then, he'd gone through a long period of speaking single words, often entirely out of context. Today marked the first time he had put together a complete sentence.

"Thank. You," Mech said.

"That's my boy." Victor patted him on the back, then handed him a wrench. "Come over here. I need to tighten a few bolts, and you can work on some fine motor skills."

The laboratory door creaked open.

"Knock, knock!" Victor's mother swished into the room,

arrayed in her usual finery, a wide smile on her face. "I do hope I'm not interrupting?"

"Good afternoon, Mrs. Franklin," Mary replied. "How can we help you?"

"I was hoping I might borrow Mech for a time. The ladies have come for tea and I've been promising I would introduce him."

Mary glanced at Victor. She had no qualms about Mecha-Man visiting Mrs. Franklin's friends, but Victor was more protective. The article in American Science Monthly had received great acclaim among the scientific community, but average people continued to harbor suspicions about walking, talking machines. Even after the sensational trial of Mr. Blair and his metal gauntlets had been written up in all the papers.

"He can go for a visit," Victor replied. "Although I would feel better if we accompanied him. His experience with groups of strangers is still quite limited."

"Of course you can come along, dear. I'm sure the ladies will have questions for you."

A "maybe I spoke too soon" expression flashed across Victor's face, but he gave a little head shake and set down his tools.

His mother wafted over to Mecha-Man and placed a hand on his arm. "Come along, dear. My friends are so eager to meet you!"

"Thank. You," Mech answered.

"Oh, and you're talking so nicely! How exciting."

"Thank. You," the automaton repeated.

Victor offered Mary a hand up from her seat, then drew her in close to his side. "I'm somewhat concerned about this new spate of talking," he whispered. "You know my own language in the laboratory is not always Society Lady friendly. If anyone drops a spoon Mech might blurt out a 'goddammit!'"

Mary attempted to quash a giggle, which only led to an undignified snort. "I'm sorry, that's the funniest image!" she whispered back. "Picturing your mother's friends…" She turned her face into Victor's chest to smother her laughter.

Victor's mother led the way to the parlor for her get-together, chattering as she walked. Mech made occasional replies, most of them only a word or two, and all of them perfectly polite.

"Mech, you are such a darling," she exclaimed, the moment she stepped through the doorway. "Everyone will love you, I'm sure." She looked over her shoulder at Victor and Mary. "Victor, dear, when are you going to build me another metal grandbaby? Mech needs a companion. Maybe a lady automaton."

Mary's cheeks heated. Life as part of an attentive family was an ongoing adjustment, and sometimes relatives said the most embarrassing things. Still, Mrs. Franklin had been accepting of their disinterest in human children, so Mary couldn't be too bothered by this particular request. She took a seat on an open sofa beside her husband and watched Mech charm the ladies.

"It might not be the worst idea in the world," Victor murmured. "Making him a companion, I mean."

"Perhaps."

Mech demonstrated his ability to drink tea, and the ladies *oohed* and *aahed*. A small wet patch appeared on the back of his shirt.

"Although we may want to patch that leak first." Mary made a discreet gesture.

Victor grimaced. "Real eating and drinking is harder than I anticipated."

Mary grinned at him. "That's one of my favorite things about science. You never know exactly what to expect. There's always something new and interesting to learn."

"I agree. And any pitfalls are always easier to overcome when I have a brilliant woman working as my partner." He took hold of her hand, lifted it to his lips, and pressed a kiss to her knuckles. "Remind me again what I did to deserve such a wife?"

Mary edged closer to him, pressing their hips together. "You loved me. You saw me when others didn't. Shy, bookish, awkward me."

"Quiet, but brave and exceptional, you."

Because they were in public, he didn't make any further advances, but the warmth of his body and the love in his eyes heated Mary's blood all the same. Later, she might suggest they go upstairs and make love in the library near the fireplace. For now, she would simply enjoy his presence.

Across the room, the ladies peppered Mech with questions, most of which he couldn't answer. He remained polite, however, and didn't spout any rude words, even when he squeezed too hard picking up a biscuit and it crumbled in his hand.

Victor surveyed the scene with his head cocked to one side, wearing his thoughtful frown.

"What's going on in that brain of yours?" Mary asked.

"I'm wondering." He lowered his voice. "If we do build him a friend, will they learn to mate?"

"Well, I'm certainly not demonstrating for them," Mary whispered back. "And I think it's not the best idea to make them anatomically correct."

"Hmm. You may be right. But it does give me an idea for something else we can build."

Mary would've had to possess very little imagination

not to have some idea what her husband was thinking. She turned toward him, brushing her lips over his cheek directly below his ear.

"Make it waterproof."

The End

About the Author

Award-winning author Catherine Stein believes that everyone deserves love and that Happily Ever After has the power to help, to heal, and to comfort. She writes sassy, sexy romance set during the Victorian and Edwardian eras. Her stories are full of action, adventure, magic, and fantastic technologies.

Catherine lives in Michigan with her husband and three rambunctious kids. She loves steampunk and Oxford commas, and can often be found dressed in Renaissance festival clothing, drinking copious amounts of tea.

Visit Catherine online at
www.catsteinbooks.com
Join her VIP mailing list for a free short story.

Instagram
@catsteinbooks

Facebook
@catsteinbooks

Also by
CATHERINE STEIN

Potions and Passions

The Earl on the Train - Book 0.5

How to Seduce a Spy - Book 1

Mishaps & Mistletoe -
A Holiday Novella -Book 1.5

Not a Mourning Person - Book 2

Once a Rake, Always a Rogue - Book 3

Love at Second Sight - Book 4

Sass and Steam

Love is in the Airship - Book 0.5

A Shot to the Heart - Book 0.75

Eden's Voice - Book 1

What Are You Doing New Year's Eve? -
A Holiday Novella - Book 1.5

Priceless - Book 2

Sass and Steam (cont.)

Dead Dukes Tell No Tales - Book 3

Beyond Repair - Book 4

Luck Be a Lady Pirate - Book 5

Arcane Tales

The Scoundrel's New Con - Book 1

The Spinster's Swindle - Book 2

Mad Scientists Society

The Courtesan and Mr. Hyde - Book 1

Other Books

Mating Habits - Book 1

Idle Nature - Book 2

My Heiress, 'Tis of Thee

Available at your favorite online retailer.
www.catsteinbooks.com

Thank you so much for reading!

If you enjoyed the book and are so inclined,
I would love for you to leave a review.
Happy readers make an author's day!

I love hearing from readers, so feel free
to contact me on social media, or email:

catherine@catsteinbooks.com

www.ingramcontent.com/pod-product-compliance
Lightning Source LLC
Chambersburg PA
CBHW031313210726
48287CB00005B/1528